THE BLACK BOOK

WITHDRAWN

by Lawrence Durrell

THE
BLACK
BOOK

by
LAWRENCE DURRELL

Introduction by
GERALD SYKES

A Dutton **dep** *Paperback*

NEW YORK
E. P. DUTTON & CO., INC.

"Mos gus yod na
Khyl so od tung."
(Tibetan Proverb.)

"Where there is veneration,
Even a dog's tooth emits light."

LAWRENCE DURRELL, a British citizen of Irish parentage, was born in the Himalaya region of India. His first ten years were spent in India. After schooling in England, he decided to become a writer. Throughout the 1930's Mr. Durrell devoted most of his talents to his poetry which has won much acclaim. His first novel, *The Black Book*, was published in Paris in 1938, and was cited by T. S. Eliot as being one of the great hopes for modern English fiction. *The Black Book* was published in the United States for the first time in 1960.

World War II temporarily interrupted Mr. Durrell's literary career. During the war years and for some time thereafter, he served Great Britain in various official and diplomatic capacities in Athens, Cairo, Rhodes and Belgrade.

The publication of *Justine* in 1957, and the subsequent appearance of *Balthazar* (1958), *Mountolive* (1959), and *Clea* (1960) as parts of the same magnificent series called "The Alexandria Quartet" devoted to an examination of the various aspects of love, immediately caused Mr. Durrell to be recognized as one of the greatest and most important writers of modern times.

INTRODUCTION

BY GERALD SYKES

Most readers will turn to *The Black Book* only after some acquaintance with Lawrence Durrell's *Alexandria Quartet,* the four novels called *Justine, Balthazar, Mountolive* and *Clea* which made him famous. It will be like examining a master's palette after seeing an exhibition of his best paintings in a museum. *The Black Book* was started in 1936, when he was twenty-four years old, the first book which he signed with his own name. All of his favorite colors are already spread out on the palette; they are merely waiting to be put to a mature use. What is more, *The Black Book* tells essentially the same story as the *Quartet* tells two decades later. It is the story of the education of a poet—in an earlier phase of his career. In Alexandria he has to cope with a man-sized portion of the modern world, dazzlingly international; in London (the principal setting of *The Black Book,* though it is written on the Greek island of Corfu) he has to extricate himself first from what he calls "the English death."

Readers of *Clea* will recall that the *Quartet* ends with a fortissimo huzza for the poet Darley, who has survived his whiff of grapeshot and ovaries, and is now ready to become a writer. This event is treated as one of more than personal interest, as symbolic of a victory that we all desire in our deepest being for ourselves. In *Clea* we find the significant line, "let us define 'man' as a poet perpetually conspiring against himself." In other words, as *The Black Book* also choruses, let us not take the usual "English" view of ourselves, that we are mere members of the most disciplined nation in the world (with the mildest policemen and the purest hotels) and therefore must submit to poetic castration for the

7

good of the race. Let us, on the contrary, hold on to our poetic virility at all costs, even if it means we must get the hell out of England and live by our wits in the Levant.

Some readers may at this point be inclined to identify Mr. Durrell with Britain's Angry Young Men, though he came along sooner, and it is true that there are some superficial cross-generation similarities. But Mr. Durrell is notably inferior to John Osborne and Kingsley Amis in one important respect: he is *not* an outsider who is also a spoilt child; he does *not* know how to squeeze the most applause out of each of his temper tantrums because he has shrewdly realized that an economy of post-war abundance has produced a great many other spoilt children who will pay well for any chance to score off the Bastards Who Run the Show. The protagonist of this distinctly un-evil *Black Book*, who quaintly calls himself Lawrence Lucifer, has none of the new tricks that enable Jimmy Porter in *Look Back in Anger* to get under the theatrical skin with what is a clinically demonstrable case of self-indulgent paranoia. He also lacks Lucky Jim's pathological gift for collecting injustices where none exist and for triumphing perfectly over every enemy in sight.

By comparison with these slick contrivances he is as innocent as Rimbaud; he doesn't even seem to know that the mass media exist and can be worked even by outlaws, if they are cute enough, for large amounts of money and mass approval. His attitude is different: "I know now, for the first time, where I stand. We are nothing if we cannot convert the dross of temporal death: if we cannot present our cheque at the bank, and receive for our daily death, a fee in good clean sovereigns—images, heat, water, the statues in the park, snow on the hills. The terrific action of the senses. The dead bullion of dying cashed in clean coin day by day, and every morsel of broken tissue redeemed for us; by this love, perhaps, this winter comet, a poem . . ." Twice he uses images of money, and both times they turn out to be, not real money but just images, mere progress in his costly education.

His book is about the private consolations he will always find

8

in his precarious craft. The four-letter words that have made it a scandal-collector's item are nothing but a tribute to the magnitude and subtlety of the forces of respectability that encircled him. If British proprieties had not been omnipresent, he would not have had to use so many obsenities. Now they are a weakness, because they have been handled somewhat woodenly, as opposed to the joy that creeps spontaneously into gentler passages. They do not communicate the zest we get from Rabelais or Joyce or Henry Miller, whose bawdily hilarious *Tropic of Cancer* had a welcome liberating effect on Durrell. For that matter, they do not equal the polished indecency, indicated in easily deciphered asterisks, that now and then enlivens the *Quartet*. At twenty-four Durrell was still too young to be naughty with style.

He could, however, write. His book is a poet's prose, in the sense that it makes the reader come to it, rather than the other way round, but it immediately sets going so many sparklers, pinwheels, Roman candles, skyrockets and Chinese Dragons, and from so many different directions, that there is a willing "suspension of disbelief" in a fascinated desire to know what is going on. This man was born to put words on paper.

"I am sitting here with my eyes shut, watching the language cross my imagination, each syllable a color. [He is listening to an African girl read English verse in a London school.] . . . Dazzling, in the flash of this last moment's reason, I question myself eagerly. Is this amusia, aphasia, agraphia, alexia, aboulia? It is life."

It is also an autodidact's attempt to match the Oxford coruscations of Aldous Huxley, which were in vogue in those days. (Durrell avoided a university education, in his flight from "the English death.") Soon he switches more feelingly to a domestic scene with his wife in Corfu: "What am I doing with this noisy machine and these sheets of linen paper? It is a kind of trap from which I cannot escape . . . When I think this I am too afraid to continue writing . . . It is then that I get up in panic and go to where you are sitting, working, and knitting, and put my hands on your hands. Then in a moment or two my courage is restored and I return to the pages, turning them over, reading them slowly."

It did not take him long to give up the pursuit of Huxley. His beautifully tender book about Corfu, *Prospero's Cell*, composed of a journal he kept at the time, makes that clear. He turned away from verbalization for its own sake and moved instead toward feeling. His palette was bright, but he obliged his colors to justify themselves. Then war came and ripped him away from his Greek paradise. To escape the Germans, he steered himself and his wife and baby by sailboat to Alexandria. There he was caught up in the bewildering life that finally took form in the *Quartet*.

In this early volume he is still trying to escape from peacetime hazards that he feared more intensely than he ever feared the Germans. And since those hazards are still prevalent today, and in America as well as in England, and perhaps more insidious than ever, *The Black Book* can be recommended both as indispensable to an understanding of Durrell and as a heartening specific against alienation from oneself.

CONTENTS

*\
**

*\
**

PREFACE

This novel—after twenty-odd years—still has a special importance for me and may yet leave its mark upon the reader who can recognize it for what it is: a two-fisted attack on literature by an angry young man of the thirties. . . . With all its imperfections lying heavy on its head, I can't help being attached to it because in the writing of it I first heard the sound of my own voice, lame and halting perhaps, but nevertheless my very own. This is an experience no artist ever forgets—the birth cry of a newly born baby of letters, the genuine article. The Black Book was truly an agon for me, a savage battle conducted in the interests of self-discovery. It built itself out of a long period of despair and frustration during which I knew that my work, though well-contrived, was really derivative. It seemed to me that I would never discover myself, my private voice and vision. At the age of twenty-four things usually look black to one!

The very quality of this despair drove me to try and break the mummy wrappings—the cultural swaddling clothes which I symbolized here as "the English Death"; simply in order to see whether there was anything inside me worth expressing. I wanted to break free, to try my hand at a free book. . . .

I wrestled with the manuscript for over a year, until I was quite exhausted; like the youths of my time, I was able to take courage from my elders. Molly Bloom and Lady Chatterley had

13

already opened a way toward self-explorations of a depth and honesty inconceivable to the writer of Hardy's age or Shaw's; Henry Miller's Tropics had just come over the horizon. The reader will discern the influence of Tropic of Cancer *in many passages of* The Black Book.

I had no thought of publication; in fact I sent the only typescript of the novel to Henry Miller, asking for his opinion on it, and telling him to pitch the text into the Seine when he had read it. This he would not do, and it was due to his encouragement that the book was later printed in Paris in a private edition. To my great astonishment and delight I found that others beside myself had heard the sound of my real voice. It was a turning point in my life as a writer to receive the praise of artists who at that time seemed so remote and out of reach—Eliot and Miller and Cyril Connolly. I had not hoped for such encouragement when I embarked on the adventure of writing.

Of course, the book is only a savage charcoal sketch of spiritual and sexual etiolation, but it is not lacking in a certain authority of its own despite the violence of its execution. Underneath the phantasmagoria real values are discussed, real problems of the anglo-saxon psyche articulated and canvassed. All this has nothing to do, of course, with purely literary merit, which is not for me to discuss. But The Black Book *staked a slender claim for me and encouraged me to believe that I was perhaps a real writer, and not just a word spinner of skill.*

I realized that the crudity and savagery of the book in many places would make its publication in England difficult. I did not wish for notoriety, and was content simply to have heard my own voice. I knew that a sensitive reader would find that the very excesses of the writing were an organic part of the experience described; and indeed a friendly critic of the book once wrote to me: "Yes, I admit that I was shocked and disgusted here and there, but I read it without prejudice and in the light of the central intention. The crudities match and belong. I have never understood why writers should not be regarded by the reader as

14

enjoying much the same rights as doctors. You do not suspect indecency in a doctor who asks you to strip in order to examine you. Why shouldn't you give the writer the same benefit of the doubt? As for your novel—you can't have a birth without a good deal of mess and blood. The labor pains, the groans, sounded quite genuine to me; I suppose because I regard art as a serious business, and spiritual birth as something like the analogy of physical. No, you are not pretending! Hence the impact of the book, I think."

LAWRENCE DURRELL

THE BLACK BOOK

BOOK ONE

The agon, then. It begins. Today there is a gale blowing up from the Levant. The morning came like a yellow fog along a roll of developing film. From Bivarie, across the foaming channel I can see from the window, the river god has sent us his offering: mud, in a solid tawny line across the bay. The wind has scooped out the very bowels of the potamus across the way, like a mammoth evacuation, and bowled it across at us. The fishermen complain that they cannot see the fish any more to spear them. Well, the rufus sea scorpion and the octopus are safe from their carbide and tridents. Deep-water life utterly shut off, momentously obscure behind the membrane of mud. The winter Ionian has lapsed back into its original secrecy.

The slither of rain along the roof. It bubbles in along the chinks of the windows. It boils among the rock pools. Today, at dawn (for we could not sleep because of the thunder), the girl put on the gramophone in the gloom, and the competition of Bach strings, resinous and cordial as only gut and wood can be, climbed out along the murky panes. While the sea pushed up its shafts and coils under the house, we lay there in bed, dark as any dungeon, and mourned the loss of the Mediterranean. Lost, all lost; the fruiting of green figs, apricots. Lost the grapes, black, yellow, and dusky. Even the ones like pale nipples, delicately freckled and melodious, are forgotten in this morning, where our one reality is the Levantine wind, musty with the smell of Arabia,

21

stirring the bay into a muddy broth. This is the winter of our discontent.

The air is full of the fine dust of the desert tombs—the Arabic idiom of death—and the panic world is quite done for, quite used up and lost. The cypresses are made of coal: their forms stipple the landscape, like heavy black brush strokes on a water color whose vitality has been rinsed from it. Yes. Winter, winter everywhere in these nude, enervate symbols.

This is the day I have chosen to begin this writing, because today we are dead among the dead; and this is an agon for the dead, a chronicle for the living. There is no other way to put it. There is a correspondence between the present, this numbness, inertia, and that past reality of a death, whose meaning is symbolic, mythical, but real also in its symptom. As if, lying here, in this mimic death at morning, we were re-creating a bit from the past: a crumb of the death we have escaped. Yes, even though the wild ducks fall in a tangle of wings among the marshes of Bivarie, and all the elements are out of gear, out of control; even though the sea flogs the tough black button of rock on which this, our house, is built. The correspondence of deadness with deadness is complete.

I could not have begun this act in the summer, for example, because in the summer we sit along under the wall on our haunches, and listen to the figs bursting. The sun dries up what is fluid of agony in us, laps us in a carapace of heat, so that all we know is nothing, sunblack, Egyptian nothing. The membrane gathers over our eyes as they close, and only the black bubbles of torpor cross and recross the consciousness, as if born from lava. The milk of sentiment curdles in the veins; an astringency withers humanity; hair freezes along the scalp, or withers to soft gold shavings along the thighs. The very nipples turn hard and black on the breasts of women, while the figs roast. Teats like dark plugs of wood for the fishermen's sons.

Well, one cannot help thinking this in such a dawn, when the

wind is filling the room with the evocative smells of the dust, and
the nascent fust of the tombs: the stale explosions of ancient life
breathed coldly on us like leper's breath. You are so pale and
done for in the morning. Pale, the face on the pillow, as ancestral
as effigies, while the rotten smell of the crusades blows damply
in on us.

This is where I saw the girl get up from bed and brave the cold
for a moment. Caryatid. A dance step among the sinews of the
music. A miming gigue. For a moment the summer almost burst
into bloom again: asphodel, with the brave white brush, pavane
of the merry peacock. Or wild geese hanging across the moon,
and the invisible archer somewhere watching, hand on his empty
quiver. Ah! but here we have only the dregs of yellow smeared
across the windowpanes, and the unclean sea, and the flesh that
quails at the icy contact of bone. Then I knew all at once that
we share that correspondence of death with the season, and with
all those other seasons which oppress me when I begin to write
of them. No mummies, chunks of tissue latched to bone; no
pillars of salt, no cadavers, have ever been half so dead as we
are today.

**

It is today at breakfast, while the yachts hound across the
water, tear-stained and anxious, toward port, that I am dying
again the little death which broods forever in the Regina Hotel:
along the moldering corridors, the geological strata of potted
ferns, the mouse-chawed wainscoting which the deathwatch ticks.
Do not ask me how. Do not ask me why, at this time, on a remote
Greek headland in a storm, I should choose, for my first real
book, a theater which is not Mediterranean. It is part of us here,
in the four damp walls of a damp house, under an enormous wind,
under the sabers of rain. From this nervous music rise those others,
no less specters, who are my mimes. I mean Tarquin, walking
along the iced suburban streets, his scarf drawn across his face,

the disease growing in his womb; I mean Lobo, clambering his suburban girls like a powder monkey; I mean Perez, Chamberlain, Gregory, Grace, Peters, Hilda. Above all I mean this logic of personalities which this paper should exhibit, in all its beautiful mutilations.

Tarquin, for example, six-foot, frost-bound, jackknifed, yellow with jaundice; Tarquin pinned to a slab of rufus cork, etherized, like a diseased butterfly; Tarquin in the bloodless dream of this Ionian morning, among the foam and uproar, extending his lax hand in greeting. Here we are, sitting in the hallowed fug of the lounge, wrapped in rugs, among the declining plants and statues. He is as ancient and exclusive as leprosy. I am afraid to shake hands with him, for fear that the skin will slip the bony structure of the hand and come away. It would take so little to produce the skeleton from this debile bundle of meat.

When I am in the Regina I am dead again. Not with the complete mystery and passivity of the dead organism, but dead in the sense of the little death. With me I carry this little toy ark, with its little toy animals, Lobo, Miss Venable, etc. We are lit up in the signs of a new chaos. We are like patches of tissue, kept warm in sealed flasks, fed, washed, and commanded to multiply under the watchful supervision of a scientist. Our world is a world of strict boundaries, outside which we dare not wander, not even in our imagination; whose seasons come and go without any sense of change. It is medieval in its blindness, this existence. Only in winter, when the snow falls, there is a strange dark light thrown on the walls of our hired rooms. The shadows in corners melt, flow, dissolve, and dwindle to black. This is the season we all hate so much. This carol of snow, when the red robin sits importantly on the rose bushes which line the deserted gardens, and the letter rack is crammed with tradesmen's Xmas cards. *A very merry Yuletide to you and yours!* (Sweep on, ye fat and greasy citizens.)

The gardens have many mirrors, shining up on the drawn blinds, in a chaotic, withering flare of imbecility. In his little cubicle Lobo lies in bed, curled up like a fetus, and rings for his breakfast. The unearthly light of the snow sprawls on the green canvas blind. It is still snowing. It will doubtless continue snowing forever. One begins to disregard these things, such is the spiritual disease of this world. The ambience in which we pin decorations up, inflate balloons, or blacken the snow with our best friend's funeral.

Winter morning. An elegy in swan's-down, ferroconcrete, postmen, Lobo, fetus, halfpenny stamps. Four flights up, Tarquin is brooding on the immaculate conception, while the kettle snores on the hob. In the musical armchair, I smoke and watch Lobo's vague movements in the gloom. It is pleasant to lie like this, somnolent, not daring to touch the cold parts of the bed with his toes. The mirror is arranged so that, by lifting himself on one elbow, he can take a good look at his own swart face, and decide whether the night's sleep has refreshed his majesty, or whether the debauchery is gaining on him. There is also the question of his penis. He is catapulting it meditatively against his belly as he studies his features. We do not speak, for this is a solemn moment. He is checking up on his appearance. His face is a sort of diary on which every triviality of the daily life is written. He is convinced of this. "Every line here or there, dear boy, the nose or the mouth, *has* to mean something; when you do something there is a line; a woman taught me the lines but I don't remember much now, except the virgin line: so." It is impossible to do this without a phonetic system, his argot is so queer. The gloom is swelling with cigarette smoke. Next door Miss Venable is powdering her harelip. The gas fire is playing its mute jazz. The snow is falling. The elegiac morning is opening on the frozen rivers, ponds, eyeballs, wells, fingers, teeth. Not one of us is Canute enough to put his head out of the window and order it to stop. Dactyl, dactyl, the ducks are going to market. The vermilion postman fights his way through drifts of snow to bring me a letter from the white lady, yclept Pat. Lobo is catapulting, catapulting, with a kind of heavy Peruvian rhythm, and thinking over his conquests. The furnaces are being loaded. Chamberlain is letting out the dogs for their yellow morning piddle in the snow. The gorilla is grinning at himself in the mirror, putting on a gaudy tie. There is a seven-inch icicle in his urethra, put there by Jack Frost or Santa Claus. Someone will be made to suffer among the trampled bunting, the gin, the cigar smoke, and the petrified greeting cards on the mantelpiece. Winter morning, with the bacon thawing slowly, as Tarquin's face on the pillow congeals back into sleeping fat. It is a profound moment, set aside for thinking over yesterday's sins and preparing today's. Lobo is cogitating heavily the eternal subject of woman. Particularly the tweed Englishwomen who wear padlocks between their legs. With a groan he is out of bed groping for his can of tepid water outside the door. From the chair one deduces the little ritual toilet he makes: his hairbrushing, tooth scouring, tie pulling. He is very fastidious, very dapper in his Continental-cut clothes. His dressing table is a mass of implements of various kinds, stocked up against the leather-framed exiles, his family. From time to time, when he can drag himself away from his face in the mirror, he pauses massively over the picture of his mother. Ah! that vague Latin sentiment. His mother! But he says nothing. When he is dressed he tidies up and gives a final glance round. The wireless is dusted. His red dressing gown hangs at the door. His tiny shoes lie along the rack in a sentimental Latin ballet. His trousers are pressed in the little wooden rack. Everything is neat and orderly. One glance outside the blind shows him the state of affairs in the outer world. So he turns to the wireless and switches it on.

"Last night she didn't come again."

"Bad luck."

"What to do, dear boy? What to *do*?"

He lifts the flap of his coat pocket and lets his hand lie firmly along the rim, fingers hidden. He bends his right leg, and places his toe outside his left foot. This is a sort of symbolic pose with which he is waiting for Christmas, and the rewards of a whole season's erotic maneuvering. He begins to describe the vigil on the damp common last night. He has caught a cold, he thinks. And all because of that little strumpet. "Think of me, dear boy, with my heart full of lorve, waitin' and waitin'." It is impossible not to. The winter night falling downstairs among a million busted pillows, and Lobo sitting on a tombstone, frozen stiff, but drawn back like a trigger with lorve, starting at every sound on the frosty roads. Lobo, sitting there with his heart full of lorve, and his pockets full of French letters. It is something to be put on a greeting card for a Peruvian Christmas, under a gothic script and a bloody robin. Tarquin must be told. (But I am not paying attention.)

"Think of me, dear boy," and so on.

Whenever possible he likes to put a big tinge of pity into his conversation because it gives his beautiful black eyes a chance to look their best: soft, molten, wobbling in tears, betrayed. Originally this must have been one of his seduction motives, this expressive sentimentality; but his repertoire of expressions is so vast, and changes so continually, that one finds a few castoff leftovers among his ordinary mannerisms. This soft, invocative pity is one of them, left over from erotic exploits long since forgotten, except for the lines of his face, of course. That serious chart which he examines so earnestly every day, to reassure himself that his left-half profile is *really* his best side. With English-women, of course, one needs a touch of healthy manliness, in order to get their pity. This he has discovered. So he wears his hat a bit more rakishly for the nonce, and tries to walk with a flat-footed rugger stride. Later, when his protective coloring is better—then his knockout exploits will begin in earnest.

His breakfast arrives in the arms of the newest chambermaid, who looks healthy, raw, and adequate. He presents his half-profile to her until she leaves. One of these mornings she will be spread-eagled on his bed while the coffee gets cold. This, one recognizes fatally, is one of the conditions of life. The wireless will be on the whole time. Fiat voluntas, with the family looking owlish and the little shoes in their static ballet.

He takes the tray on his knee and begins to eat fastidiously, like a cat, pushing the spoon between his broad ripe lips.

"I think," he says at last, "I will go into a monastery. Will you come with me? Eh? We forget all these bitches, dear boy, and be holy holy holy. In black."

(Draw back the blind and let the soft translucent light into the room. She is lying there in bed among the apple trees and the frozen lakes, long and cool as a dormitory. The immense gothic monastery between her legs, etc.)

Snow like a great chain from pole to pole. The enumeration of our sins, the forgiving of our sins, the postmen, the buses, the letter with the halfpenny stamp in the rack. The gutters are clotted with filth. The buses scatter. Monologue of the white road stretching down past the Catholic Church, the Municipal School, the Lock Hospital, the exchange, the postbox. Tarquin lying like Gulliver in Lilliput while the buses roam up and down him, over his hips and thighs. Tarquin like the island of England in its winter chains, and the hills like many blanched nipples.

"I am a Catholic," says Lobo cleverly, with the air of having done a trick.

His watch strikes the hour in his waistcoat pocket, and he springs to attention. He will miss the lecture on ferroconcrete, and that would be evil, in the moral sense. His dear father is paying his fees. Moral: honor thy father and thy mother in their frames, and learn to build more Catholic churches in ferro-concrete.

He gathers up his manuscript, his instruments, his textbooks, and switches off the wireless. "Well," he says with finality, locking the door carefully behind him.

Half-past ten of a Yuletide season. Lobo has vanished in a sweeping draft through the stone pillars into the main road. His scarf dangles over his shoulders. The streets are sharp with frost, the shops with decorations. The lamb is born, or will soon be born. I present the telephone at my temple gingerly, like a suicide. Marney pipes and blows down the other end. I can feel the hairs stiffening on his hump. No work today. I have a bad cold. He is angry, to be left in charge of the school like this, and deserted by all but a few good-natured oafs. The miserable children are crowding into the form rooms, piping and farting to keep warm, huddling round the tin stoves. The hunchback usher resents my illness. The sounds are all mangled with cold, indeterminate anger, pique, dignity, despair. "I thought we could count on you at least," he says. I am tempted to reply, "Sorry, but I am a Catholic." Instead I ring off and consult the lounge clock. It is too late to go to Communion: the only gesture in this life that contains the full quota of irony. It is too early to go to bed. It is always too late or too early to do anything at all. However, when in doubt, consult the lounge clock. I consult it. New paragraph.

In his little underground Hades overlooking the garden Peters will be lying, pondering on his own genius—or masturbating. The great problem for him is whom to be like, if he is going to be a genius. Leonardo liked port and crabapples, for example, whereas Dowson preferred a cigar. It is difficult. Swinburne took it straight from the bottle, and Wagner wore nothing but silk next to the skin. Beethoven's syphilis, was she contracted or hereditary? If the latter, then it is too much to ask. Frankly, all this is a little boring.

Let us take a novelist-in-the-cupboard peep at Tarquin. He has already managed to crawl out of his tepid bed and lift the window sash. The sight of the snow disgusts him. By instinct he hops back and draws the covers up to his chin, trying to hurl himself back into dream with skinny ferocity. No good. Then he remembers the dream he was having and broods pleasantly upon it. A girl on a riverbank. Or boy? It would be better as a boy on a verdant bank, a Cretan saffron gatherer now, that was the theme. Thou still unravished bride of quietness. Very little in Tarquin's dreams remains unravished. I know because he tells me about them; we discuss them together, examine textbooks to see what caused them, and generally psychologize. For his benefit, not mine. Forty years of pious introspection have given him a nose like a bloodhound for his own weaknesses. In this case it is Clare, who lives in the box room at the end of the landing. I say "in this case," in order to pretend that he does not always dream about Clare. But this is untrue. He seldom dreams of anyone so often or so moistly, as he does of this tall black dancing master with the sparrow's knowingness and the cockney twist of the tongue. Therefore the mornings are pleasantly spent in analyzing his unhappy passion and entering the findings in that long-nosed diary of his. If the dream was wet he gives himself full marks (sublimated); if dry, arid, and intellectual then he gets worried (repressed). There is a grave alarm in the air for the healthiness of his "life sexual" (such a dainty pre-Raphaelite arrangement of those clinical terms, don't you know). Over breakfast we rearrange the clinical scheme, and bolster up his courage for him. It is an endless game of chess with his psyche. Tarquin's effective working life is spent lying on his back, and catechizing himself. His spirit divides itself into two essences, pictured by the words Question and Answer; and he swears to be quite honest with himself, though he does not quite know what he means by this. Honesty and clear thinking are the general idea, however, followed by largeness, scope, and a fine bold spiritual design.

But Clare, on a morning like this? He is painfully dressed, cracking a new packet of candles and filling the sconces. The kettle is boiling. Clare is that unhappy crying for a boy's body at some hour of the evening, or a few scrappy, ill-considered phrases in that remote diary, in which *everything* must be entered before he dies. Clare? The dirty little brute with the bitten fingernails. Clare is this fatal world which you can see if you stand at the window. The long concrete road, its pure white nap now gouged and muddied by the rubber lips of the buses, the carts, the feet of the ants. Clare is this morning, advancing stage by stage, grimly, painfully, like a paralytic; the crisp morning sounds; the eggs frying; the loaded trays moving about; the geysers running in little spurts and gallops, and the steam leaking into the landings; or the figure of Lobo in diminishing perspective on the roads. Actually Clare is nothing of the sort. When Tarquin thinks about him his face is the face of a broken-down actuary.

But I am not here to interpret him, nor even to make him grow. I simply put him to bed on paper among a few random syllables of English. In an atmosphere so homely one can only help oneself and hope for the best. But Clare?

Tarquin raps on his door primly with the air of the Raven. His dressing gown flows over him in exotic folds. Or else he barks "Clare" once, like a siren, and enters. It is always the same. There is no answer. Once the door is open there is nothing to do but to stare in on the customary wreckage of the box room. The usual foul litter of shirts and pants decorates the bare linoleum. The window is open and the snow has been blowing onto the bed, the floor, the table. The gigolo is hidden.

Tarquin calls, "Clare." No answer or movement. The bed might be nestling a corpse. The wall is a solid mass of photographs: dance steps torn from trade journals which moves slowly in the wind—the whole wall, I mean, as if it were about to collapse on him. Tarquin begins walking around, examining the pictures, pretending he is interested in them. From the open door he looks like a maiden aunt visiting the zoo, or the Academy. He hates himself, it is obvious. Why does he worry Clare always like this? Why can't he leave him alone? The dirty little beast! After all, *dirty:* because somehow the sight of Clare's room with its snow and littered underpants is a raw awakening from the idyl, the Marlowesque dream of the riverbank, and the delicate copulation of Narcissi. As usual he does not damn literature, but damns Clare, who cannot live up to the literary reputation which has been invented for him. All this is interesting to the silent partner, the confidant. I am not called upon to remark, or to suggest, or even to admit my own presence. Merely to exist. I am the umpire whose judgment is never even asked for. It is understood that I suffer for Tarquin in his terrible affliction.

He takes a few turns around the room, in such precise don's paces that he almost trips in the snowy bits. On the washstand a comb, thick with dirt and grease from Hylas' sable locks; on the pisspot holder a thriller, face down; the book he had lent the boy on the first day of his campaign for higher thinking and purer love is deep in dust. The bed lamp is on. Hylas is afraid to sleep in the dark. On the shelf is a broken enema syringe and carton of crab ointment. Tarquin explores these things with disgust.

"Clare," he says, "get up."

He has always promised that he would begin to take a strong line with the gigolo one of these days. So "Get up." The truncated body raises itself grimly from the bed: born again on the third day. Clare's soft black curls hang on end with a blue-black electric life of their own. His pillow is greasy. The yellow goat's eyes stare out of the window, not seeing Tarquin. He is not properly awake. At the sight of my beauty sitting up there in his dirty sheets Tarquin is angry. He would like to take a stick and beat some decency into him. He comes and stands behind me, snapping, "Get up, and don't be such a lazy fellow." He is hoping that Clare will imagine the words came from me. Clare sighs, sitting there, as yellow as a potentate in the snowy quilt. Lifts his soiled feet clear of the bed, and lays them down beside him, contemplating the dirty soles.

Tarquin agitates the doorknob and rehearses exits. He is angry but nervous with lorve. "Next thing I'll know," says Clare, "I'll wake up and find you in bed with me." This produces a sort of insanity. Tarquin begins to whistle. "In bed," continues Hylas, "right here in the bloody bed wiv me." In all this I do not exist. Custom merely has demanded my presence.

Tarquin bounds down the passage to his room. As always when he walks, the energy seems drawn to his head, like a top, pulling him up on his toes. He locks the door loudly, insultingly. Without speaking he begins to make tea. He is quivering with rage. His great bald cranium shines. I can see that he will not be able to keep away after all. However, tea, sugar, and a drop of stale milk. Custom has rather staled this eternal psychic crisis, so that I am not surprised when he flings down his cup, and reaches for the door again. In God is my hope, though the Devil will have scope. Tarquin whizzes down the passage to the box room like a prima donna, his robe purling after him. He bursts open the door and stands still, staring in full on the yellow eyes. His resolution to insult, to injure, to ravage, dissolves inside him. His very guts are liquefied by rage and contrition. He is so humble now, so plaintive, so full of expression, so docile, so in love. It is astounding, this change. Then, like a blow in the solar plexus, Clare's yellow voice, "Go away." Boisterously he yells, "Get to fucking hell out of here and lemme be, will yer?"

The world is laid out before the fire like a chessboard on which we plan the most exciting moves. It is only a game. Tarquin is running barefooted on the scorched Cretan rocks, while the dark-eyed shepherd is allowing himself to be overtaken, to be gathered up, covered in kisses. Instead of his gaunt stringy body he should really have a fine lithe trunk. And a sheepskin. Not to mention a flute. "You will not mock me," he says seriously, "because I can see in your face that you believe in love. In dying for love." He holds a spatulate finger between us, which we contemplate, as if expecting it to die there, visibly, in the air. "Now Gregory could never see my point of view at all. It was too strong and positive for him, I think." In silence we are gulping the cold snow, the hot tea, the hotel, the geysers, the stricken pines, the statues, the yellow goat's eyes. And I am pondering on Gregory and Grace and the curious design he made of them both in the little green handwriting. Gregory as a sort of chessman, a little green bishop, entangled in his pawn, and writing with the quiet venom of a player who has forgotten the rules. The book which is my secret, in the cupboard downstairs.

"The presence of oneself!" That is how he begins. "The eternal

consciousness of oneself in substance and in psyche. The eternal
consciousness of that shadow which hangs behind my shoulder,
watching me flourish my ink on this nude paper. What a recipe
for immortality! The one self and the other, like twin generals
divided in policy, bungling a war. The eternal, abhorrent presence of oneself." Small green writing, like lacework on the tough
pages of the blank dummy. Who Gregory *was* I have not properly
discovered yet. This tiny basement room was evidently his. At
some epoch in history he vanished, leaving behind him a few
gross of torn papers, Latin classics, gramophone records, teacups.
On the title page of this book, undated, is the inscription: *Death
Gregory, Esq. To his most esteemed and best beloved self, dat
dedicatque.* Oblivion has swallowed up this chance eviction, and
there remains only the queer speckled personality of this tome,
so durable and recent in age (for Tarquin and Clare and Lobo
exist here) that it suggests recent visitations. I cannot be older
than a thousand years. "I am not speaking of my isolation as yet,
which is six by three. The isolation of a coffin. The isolation of
a gargoyle hung over a sleeping city."

The isolation of the snow, he would have added, if he were
turning the pages today. The isolation in which the hotel broods,
like a baroque incubus.

*
**

Here begins an extract from Gregory's diary:

The question with which I trouble myself is the question of
the ego, the little me. The I, sitting here in this fuggy room, like
a little red-haired, skullcapped Pope, insulting myself in green
ink. The red dwarf, the lutin, the troll—the droll and abhorrent self!

Sweets to the sweet. To Lobo sensual lust. And for the jour-
nalist inevitably, a journal. A journal! What a delicious excursion
it sounds! The path lies ready, the fruit grows on the hedgesides.

But the stupendous arrogance of such a record! What should it contain, then? A pedestrian reckoning by the sun, or aphoristic flights, or a momentous study of my excretions covering years? A digest of all three, perhaps. One can hardly tell. No matter. Let us begin with Lobo. To insects sensual lust. And to Lobo a victory over the female, because that is what he wants. I say victory but I mean a rout: a real beating up of his natural enemy, who degrades him by the fact that she carries the puissant, the all-conquering talisman of the vagina about with her. If it were possible to invent a detached vagina, which has an effective life of its own, then Lobo would be a profound misogynist, I am sure.

But consider him, as he sits there, working over the enormous parchment chart of South London. Consider the lily. Every week after a certain lecture, he takes it down from the wall, and gets busy on it with his tools: compasses, protractors, dividers, his India ink which hardens in shining lines along the thoroughfares; his pencil box full of rubbers, tapes, stamps. On the black wood is a garish cockatoo. This reminds him of Peru, though why, he cannot think. In his childhood there were boxes of oranges with this bird painted on them. Perhaps that is the reason. But it reminds him of Lima, sitting out there on the map, a beautiful gray husk of life. Lima, with the parrots and the oranges, and the almond-eyed whores, and the cathedrals, delicate, delicate. I invent this, because though he is incapable of saying it to me, yet he feels it. Dust, the eternal dust along the highroad, and the hucksters, and fine swish motorcars, and lerv. The facile, hot Latin lerv, with its newt's eyes fixed on anyone ready to ease you of a thimbleful of sperm. Sunlight along the lips of the shutters, or the guitars wombing over the Rimac, hot and seasoned. And the sour booming of many steeples, Santo Domingo, San Augustin, La Merced. He imitates their hollow noises, raising his hand and keeping himself in time with his memories.

Fascinating to watch him sitting there, this little brown man, penning his map; his thin girl's fingers with their unpressed cuticles carefully unstopping bottles, cleaning nibs, clutching a penholder as they move forward to letter or draw. Lobo is as much of an enigma to me as this fantastic locality of blind houses and smoke which he is drawing must be to him.

Perhaps the remark about the insect was a little strong, for it is not my business to raise my own standards to the height of an impartial canon. But it seems to me accurate. The female is a catalyst, unrelated to life, to anything but this motor necessity which grows greater day by day. Lobo! Perhaps this all has something to do with his homesickness, his Latin tears and glooms. What I am concerned with is the enigma, not these erotic maneuvers, all carried out on the plane of nervy, febrile social welfare; the kind of thing Laclos did so vividly. "My God," he says sometimes, "I think *never* to go with womans any more, never. Why is the mystery? Afterwards what? You are dead, you are disgust. *Smell!* It is impossible. I go along the road, pure as a Catholic, then I see a woman look to me and . . ." His heavy head bends lower over the chart; the compressions gather in the cheeks under his bossy Inca nose; he is silent, and it is a little difficult to find anything to say in reply.

Lobo has the fascination of an ancient stamp for me. I can't get past the thought of this little Latin fellow sitting in his room night after night, working like Lucifer for his degree; and all the while his mind riddled with thoughts of home, like a pincushion. He admits it. "It is my home makes me blue, dear friend. I think in bed of Peru many night and I cannot sleep. I put the wireless till twelve. Then I go mad almost. That bitch nex' door. I can kill her when I am alone. Listen. Last night I made a little deceit for her. Truly. I weeped in the night. It was quiet. I weeped a little louder. Nothing. I weeped like hell. Really I was lonely, it was true, but not real the tears. I could not make the real tears. Listen, I heard her put the light and sit in the bed looking. I went on with the tears. Then she speaks: *Who is it?* I was not knowing how to speak. I had no words. Soon she put off the light and lay. No good. I ran to the door and knock it very quietly. I say, *It's only me, Miss Venable*. Nothing. I tap

tap tap but nothing. I was angry. I sniff like hell, but nothing. No good. The dirty bitch. After that I went to bed and really weep, I wet the pillow all through, I am so angry I could kill." His eyes dilate earnestly under the sooty lashes. At such memories he becomes pure emotional idealism. Like the Virgin Mary. He will cut himself one of these days for lerv, he says. I confess I did not know what this phrase meant until the night of the festival, when we returned at three to drink a final nightcap in his room. He was pretty drunk.

"Know what I do when a man make me angry?" he asked. He explored the washstand drawer and appeared before me with a knife in his right hand. He was so gentle and friendly that for a second I was afraid. "See this," he said, and handed it to me as simply as a girl. It was an enormous folding knife, sharpened to great keenness.

"I cut him," said Lobo unsteadily.

Taking it from me he divided the air which separated us neatly into four portions, grinned beatifically, and replaced the weapon in its secret hiding place. When he talks like this, then, it is an enraged hara-kiri that he plans—or a murder.

But confidence for confidence Lobo finds me a very unsatisfactory person. My humility devastates him. Particularly my complete ignorance on the subject of women. He says in tones of gravity and wonder: "You? A man of forty, an Englishman?" Really, to be frank, if one must be frank, I have had few and unsatisfactory experiences in this direction. Literary affairs with aging Bohemians, in which my ability to compare the style of Huxley to that of Flaubert was considered more important, even in bed, than physical gifts; a stockbroker's widow; an experimental affair with an experimental painter, in which, again, our mutual respect for the volumetric proportions of Cézanne's canvases was almost our only bond. Affinities, you might say. I suppose in this direction I must be rather a dead battery until I meet Grace. Lobo is bored. An Englishman of forty? Well it must have been forty years in the wilderness for all the adventures I can recount.

Never mind. I comfort myself with Pascal's remark about the thinking reed.

Chamberlain is not less scathing. This canary-haired zealot, living in one of the flats nearby with a young wife and three dogs, spends his moments happily lecturing us on such esoteric subjects. "Sex, sex, sex," he exclaims roundly, his manner closely modeled on the style of Lawrence's letters. "When will we get the bastards to realize?" Fraternizing in the barroom among the blue spittoons. He is powerful and convincing, standing over his bitter, and appealing to his wife for support. "Glory be to hip, buttock, loin, *more ferarum, bestiarum,* uterine toboggan, and the whole gamut of physical fun. Don't you think? What about more bowels of compassion, tenderness, and the real warmth of the guts, eh?"

Really I am scalded by this curious Salvation Army line of talk. Bad taste. Bad taste. Tarquin winces and bleats whenever Chamberlain gets started.

"Let us invent a new order of marriage to revive the dead. Have another beer. Let us start a new theory of connubial copulation which will get the world properly fucked for a change. Tarquin, you're not listening to me, damn you."

Tarquin bleats: "Oh, do stop forcing these silly ideas on one, Chamberlain. You simply won't admit other people's temperamental differences. Shut up."

He is mopping the froth off his beer with a discolored tongue. Chamberlain turns to his wife, who is standing, breathing quietly, like a big retriever: "What do you think? Tell me." She prefers to smile and ponder rather than think. "There," says Chamberlain in triumph, "she agrees."

"All this damned sexual theorizing," moans Tarquin. "Don't you think, Gregory? I mean damn it!"

"Don't you agree with him," says Chamberlain. "Now, Gregory, you're quite a good little fellow on your own."

"Young man," I say weakly.

"Oh, I know you're a patriarch in years, but that's mere chronology. You need to grow a bit."

"Oh, do stop," says Tarquin, acutely miserable.

"The trouble with you, my dear," says Chamberlain, "is that you're still fighting through the dead mastoid. Now what you need . . ."

And so on. One revolts from transcribing any more of his chat, because it becomes infectious after a time. His personality is attractive enough to make any dogma plausible and compelling to the imagination. As for Lobo, they spend hours quarreling about themes domestic and erotic. This always ends in trouble. "Listen, Baudelaire," says Chamberlain, "you've got yourself up a tree. Climb down and take a look round you." When he really wants to frighten the Spaniard he suggests calling his wife in and putting these problems before her. This is hideous. Lobo's sense of chivalry squirms at the idea. Tearfully, under his sentimental eyelashes he says, after Chamberlain has gone: "A beast? Eh? He is beastly. Doesn't he have the finer feelings? His poor wife, like a prostitute in his home. It is terrible, terrible. He only understands the prostitute, not the *real* woman. He is terrible." And a string of Spanish oaths.

Fog over the gardens. Fog, marching down among the pines, making dim stone those parcels of Greek statuary. In the distance trains burrowing their tunnels of smoke and discord. Lights shine out wanly against the buildings. The red-nosed commercials will be lining up in the bar for their drinks. I can see the whisky running into their red mouths, under the tabby whiskers, like urine. I sit here, in the shadow of the parchment chart, smoking, and eating the soft skin on the sides of my cheeks. The customary madness of the suburban evening comes down over us in many enormous yawns. Ennui. "We do not exist," says Tarquin. "We do not exist; we are fictions." And frankly this idea is not as outrageous as it sounds. Toward evening, when I walk down the row of suburban houses, watching the blinds lowered to salute the day's death, with no companion but that municipal donkey the

39

postman, I find myself in a world of illusion whose furniture *can* only be ghosts. In the lounge the veterans sit like Stonehenge under the diffuse light of the lamps. Old women stuck like clumps of cactus in their chairs. The *Times* is spread out over the dead, like washing hung out on bushes to dry. Footsteps and voices alike trodden out in the dusty carpets; and the faint aeolian sofas appealing to the statues. Night. The clock whirrs inside its green-house of glass, and the Japanese fans breathe a soft vegetable decay into the room. There is nothing to do, nothing to be done.

In the flat that my body inhabits, the silence is sometimes so heavy that one has the sensation of wading through it. Looking up from the book to hear the soft spondees of the gas fire sounding across nothingness, I am suddenly aware of the lives potential in me which are wasting themselves. It is a fancy of mine that each of us contains many lives, potential lives. They are laid up inside us, shall we say, like so many rows of shining metals—railway lines. Riding along one set toward the terminus, we can be aware of those other lines, alongside us, on which we might have traveled—on which we might yet travel if only we had the strength to change. You yawn? This is simply my way of saying I am lonely. It is in these movements, looking up to find the whole night gathered at my elbow, that I question the life I am leading, and find it a little lacking. The quiet statement of a woman's laugh, breaking from the servants' rooms across the silence, afflicts me. I consider myself gravely in mirrors these days. I wear my skullcap a trifle grimly, as if in affirmation of the life I have chosen. Yet at night sometimes I am aware, as of an impending toothache, of the gregarious fiber of me. Dear me. This is becoming fine writing in the manner of the Sitwells. But let me discuss myself a little in green ink, since no one takes the trouble to do so in words of more than one syllable. In the first place, my name is not *Death*, as it ought to be, but *Herbert*. The disgusting, cheesy, Pepysian sort of name which I would pay to change if I were rich enough. Death is part of the little charade I construct around myself to make my days tolerable. *Death Gregory!* How livid the name shines on the title page of this tome. Borrowed plumes, I am forced to admit in this little fit of furious sincerity. Borrowed from Tourneur or Marston. No matter. The show must go on.

My estate, to descend to the level of Pepys, is in a neat and satisfying condition. A lifelong sympathy with Communism has never prevented me from investing safely, hoarding thriftily, and living as finely economic as possible. This means my tastes are sybaritic. On bread I have never wasted a penny, but an occasional wine of quality finds its way into the trap-doored basement I call my cellar. The books I own are impeccable—the fine bindings lie along the wall in the firelight, snoozing softly in richness. Unlike most men, I read what I buy. The table I keep is frugal but choice. The board does not groan, but then neither does the guest, ha ha. Taste and style in all things, I say to myself with rapture, taste and style! Neat but not gaudy, fine but unadorned! All of which makes these nostalgic moods so incomprehensible, so damned unreasonable; for have I not chosen the life of reason and moderation as my proper field?

Chamberlain is in the habit of saying: "Of course, my dear, your system is bound to break down sooner or later. Or else the system will stand and *you* will break down inside it. I'm all for tightrope acts, and fakirs, and trolleys full of pins, provided they entertain. You do not. You are walking a tightrope with no safety net under it, and it bores. Gregory Stylites, come down from your perch and have a slice of ham." All this, however imprecise, is vaguely disquieting, sitting here over the fire, with a calf-bound Pascal and a glass of dry ochrous sherry on the table. Such a comforting system after all! So safe, so cast-iron in construction! Such a clever device, when all's said and done. But then, if one does not fit a system? That is the question. I am reminded of the little formula which he tacks on the end of his customary good night, whenever he calls: "Well, good night," he says insolently. "Grand show you put on." There is a quality in all this which ruins my façade; I am less sure of myself: I wince in a quaint

schoolboy nervousness. Not that I show the least sign of it, I
flatter myself. No. My control is perfect, my poise almost geological
in its fixity. I "carry" my skullcap with distinction none the less,
for I am as proud as Lucifer. But it is a little boorish of him to
pretend that my modish charms do not touch him at all. I like his
wife better. True, she takes her cue from him and tries to find me
amusing, but she can scent that little Prussian core of pride in me.
She is a little awed, in spite of herself, at those qualities which
my skullcap is intended to suggest. Shall I bore you with a dis-
cursion on the intuition of women? It is a subject I know nothing
whatsoever about. But that should not disqualify me from writing
about it. Here is paper, seven pages covered, here is ink, and here
is that isolation which breeds many fantastic notions in my pen. If
you are afflicted by my tediousness, take heart. This might have
been a novel instead of anything so pleasantly anonymous as a
diary.

Talking of loneliness, since we must talk tonight, or suffer the
silence to become unbearable: Tarquin is also a sufferer from
this malady, this geometrical insanity of day followed by night
followed by day, etc. But his study of himself is so strenuous that
he is in a much worse condition. Tarquin is already behind the
screens, attended by the one fatal nurse of the ego. His researches
have been rapidly making a wreck of him. Complex, inhibition,
fetish, trauma—the whole merde-ridden terminology of the new
psychology hangs from his lower lip, like a cigarette in the mouth
of a chain smoker. "One must explore oneself, don't you think?
One must try and reduce one's life to some sort of order, don't
you think? What do you think of Catholicism, Gregory? Sometimes I get such a feeling of devotion—it's like being in love, sort
of raped by contemplation. Does Lobo know anything? I must ask
him. I used to faint at one time, and have dreams or visions, what
would you call them? Trauma, it seems like according to the
books. Real fits, like epilepsy, what do you say? Eh?" And so on.
The terminologies of theology and psychology running neck and

neck, each outdoing the other in vagueness. Duns Scotus and Freud. Adler and Augustine.

"I suppose one really ought to read the best books," he says hopelessly. "One must cultivate one's garden like who was it said? One's taste and all that. But that damned Iliad, Gregory, honestly I can't get on with it. And pictures, too. Christ, I *look* at them, but it doesn't mean more than what's there. I don't *feel* them."

Every now and then he has a syphilis scare, and off he trots to the hospital to have a blood test. The vagueness of the Wassermann torments him. One can never be certain, can one? Standing naked beside his bed he whacks away at his reflexes with a rubber truncheon; closes his eyes and finds that, standing with his feet together, he does not fall. Or he will pace up and down the floor, pausing to examine the microphotographs of spirochetes which hang over his cottage piano. Why is his chest spotty? Why is he always so run down? Is it lack of calcium or what?

Everything is plausible here, because nothing is real. Forgive me. The barriers of the explored world, the divisions, the corridors, the memories—they sweep down on us in a catharsis of misery, riving us. I am like a child left alone in these corridors, these avenues of sleeping doors among the statuary, with no friends but an audience of yawning boots. I am being honest with you for once, I, Death Gregory, the monkey on the stick. If I were to prick out my history for you, as Lobo his plans on the mature parchment, would you be able to comprehend for an instant the significance of the act? I doubt it. In the field of history we all share the irrelevance of painted things. I have only this portion of time in which to suffer.

The realms of history, then! The fact magical, the fancy wonderful, the fact treasonable. All filtered, limited, through the wretched instruments of the self. The seventy million I's whose focus embraces these phenomena and records them on the plate of the mind. The singularity of the world would be inspiriting if one did not feel there was a catch in it. When I was nine the haggard female guardian in whose care I had been left exclaimed:

"Horses sweat, Herbert. *Gentlemen* perspire. Don't say that nasty word any more." I shall never forget the phrase; it will remain with me until I die—along with that other useless and ineradicable lumber—the proverbs, practices, and precepts of a dead life in a dead land. It is, after all, the one permanent thing, the one unchanging milestone on the climb. It is I who change; constant, like a landmark of the locality, the lumber remains. Like a lake seen from different altitudes during a journey, its position never varying: only its aspect altering in relation to my own place on the landscape. I think that what we are to be is decided for us in the first few years of life; what we gain afterward in the way of reason, adjustment, etc., is superficial: a veneer, which only aggravates our disorders. Perish the wise, the seekers after reason. I am that I am. The treasonable self remains. I am not more astonished now by the knowledge that gentlemen can, if they want, have wings, than I was by that pithy social formula; or, for example, that red blood runs in fishes. I shall never be more amazed.

Not even the phenomenon of Grace disturbed my life as much as that glimpse of the social mysteries. Horses sweat, but Grace perspires; very delicately on the smooth flesh, on the thin flanks, under the tiny undernourished breasts. The blue-veined phthisic fingers are moist and languorous. But why the present tense? For Grace is no more; no more the street girl who sat, hugging her knees, and staring at the empty wallpaper. Shall we write of her in the gnomic aorist? Shall we invest her with an epitaph? She would not understand it. She understood nothing. She seemed not to hear. You could speak to her, sing to her, dance before her, and the distances she contemplated were not diminished by one inch.

"Come, Grace, you bitch," one said. "Show a sign of life. Come now, give us a smile."

Like an elaborate circus performer a smile wandered into the oval, disconsolate face. A great feat of concentration required to move the muscles of the face correctly in smiling. Her teeth were

44

small and pure, with little gaps between them—an arrangement that suggested congenital syphilis. Her creator reserved red blood for fishes and journalists. In Grace's veins flowed mercury, the purest distillation of icy metals.

Her skin was transparent almost, and pale. One felt that if one took a piece between finger and thumb, and ripped downward, say from knee to ankle, the whole epidermis would come away wetly, effortlessly, like sodden brown paper, cleaving the flesh and bone open. On her back as she sat on our inadequate bed, I have traced many a curious forefinger among the soft grooves and lucent vertebrae—colorless nuts—protruding under their transparent covering. The white blood never warms (tense again!), never filled her with delicious shudders and ticklings. She might have been dead flesh, dead meat to the world of the male. Passion only interested her in its most ardent conclusions, and then such an incandescence shone in her face, such veins moved in concentration on her temples, such a leaping tropic flame drove her fingernails to a billet in her accomplice's flesh, that one was reassured. She was alive, after all, deep down: at the temperature which melts metals; the boiling point at the earth's center where the beds of ore clang together, and the hot magma liquefies iron and rock. She was alive behind this elaborate mien of detachment.

Gracie was bought, without any bargaining, for the promise of a cup of coffee. I remember it was a night when the snow was driving up past the big Catholic Church so thickly that it blinded one. The road was buried. She was shivering inside the thin clothes, the inadequate covering of baubles and lipstick which decorated her small person. The snow hung in a glittering collar to the astrakhan lining of her coat. Wisps of black hair froze to her cheek. From her nose hung a drop of snot which she sniffed back whenever she could remember to do so. She had no handkerchief.

Inside the hall door she stood passive, like an animal, while I wiped her face, her coat collar, her grubby clothes. Then I drove her, passive and dull, downstairs to my room, guiding her with taps from my cane. In the harsh electric light she stood again, graven, and stared feebly at this row of books, this littered desk. Then, speaking of her own accord for the first time, she said, "In 'ere, mister?" A small, hard voice, running along the outer edges of sanity. I switched on the fire and commanded her to approach it. Slowly she did so.

Regarding her in silence, I was alarmed by the color her face had taken. It was that of a three-day corpse. Under the skin a faint bluish tinge which reminded me of the shadows in snow.

"What's your name?"

She had a habit of regarding one for an age before answering, as if determining whether the truth would or would not be a suitable weapon for the occasion. Her eyes dilated and she gave a sigh, remote, remote, concerning nothing but her private problems.

"Gracie."

Snow dripped from the brim of her shabby coat. The tentacle of hair on her cheek had thawed and hung down beside her nose. She was wet through, and dirty.

"You'd better take off those wet things at once. There's a dressing gown in there. I'll get you some coffee."

When I returned she was sitting naked before the electric fire, with her knees drawn up to her chin. Her flesh was puckered with cold. "Some brandy first," one said with heartiness, becoming the medical man all at once, handing her a goblet. Pondering, she drank the draught at a gulp, and then turned, her eyes dilating warmly, a sudden blush covering her forehead. For a second she seemed about to speak, and then some interior preoccupation drew a single line of worry across her forehead. With little unemotional starts she began to cough up patches of her lung, quite dumbly, like some sort of animal. One got her a clean handkerchief from the drawer and stood looking down at the averted head, a little astonished and disgusted by the perfect repose of the face even in sickness.

46

"Well, this is a business. You've t.b."

She played the trick of staring up with the expressionless black circles in her eyes, like a blind cat. Then she looked away, numb and patient.

"And Grace, you're filthy. You must have a bath."

Her feet were dirty, her fingernails, her ears. Passively she allowed herself to be scraped and scrubbed with the loofah: dried, curried, chafed, and sprinkled with nice astringent eau de Cologne. She took no notice, but practiced this peculiar evasion, which one found so exciting. Afterward in my parrot dressing gown she cocked her little finger at me over the coffee cup. In that tinny voice she gave me a few particulars about herself. She was eighteen and lived at home. Out of work. She was interested in Gary Cooper. But all this was a kind of elaboration of her inner evasion. By giving her a dressing gown and a cup of coffee one had merely brought upon oneself the few social tricks she knew how to perform. She was not interested, merely polite. For services rendered she returned the payment of this lifted little finger and a vague awakening over a cup of surburban coffee. One was afraid that at any moment she would become urbanely ladylike, and revive the Nelson touch which one finds so painful in the ladies of Anerly and Penge. (Preserve us from the ostrich.)

"Tell me," one said, by a fluke, "about your family. Where they live and how and everything."

This interested her. It almost made her face wake up; her gestures became alive and instinctive. Only her eyes could not wholly achieve the change—narrowing, widening, the rim of the blackness. Really, to look at her was as senseless as looking into the shutter of a camera.

Her family, she said, lived in a villa in Croydon. Father had a job at the gasworks. He was a card. Her four brothers were all working. They were cards, too. Her two sisters were on the telephone exchange. They were real cards. Mother was a little queer in the head, and she, Gracie, was the youngest. Mother was a treat, the things she said! Laugh? They fairly killed themselves at her in the parlor. You see, she didn't know what she was saying, like. A bit soppy in the top story. Made them yell, the things she came out with, specially when she was a little squiffy. Laugh? They howled. If you could only write them in a book, it would be wonderful.

One tried to imagine her in the bosom of this roaring family—this animal waif with the voice running along the thin edge of sanity—but failed. There was nothing Elizabethan about her, to suggest that she would fit in with this pack of yelling cards—Pa with his watch chain and clay pipe, Mother with her bottle of Wincarnis. The parlor overflowing with brothers and sisters, and the port overflowing in mother's brain cells.

Her father was a bad man when he was in drink, she said at last. Always having tiffs with Albert. Always mucking about with her and Edith the eldest one. Only on Saturday nights when he wasn't himself, however, and Ted the eldest brother was the same. They knew it wasn't right but what could you do if it was your own father? She coughed a little.

"Do you live at home?"

"When I'm there I'm there," she said patiently. "When I don't go back they don't worry. Glad to be free of me. Not earning me keep any more, see?" I saw.

She finished her drink and put the cup down. Then she strolled over to the bookcase and quizzed the titles. Sniffed, turned to me, and said, "Fine lot o' books you got here." But with a gesture so foreign, so out of character that I was forced to laugh. She was actually being seductive; and above all, not seductive by the ordinary formulae, but by the dashing hectic formulae of the cinema. It was astonishing. Posed like that, her hip stuck out under the palm of one hand, her slender, rather frail legs Venus'd—one knee over the other—she had become that cinema parrot, a dangerous woman. Even her small face was strained to an imaginary expression before an imaginary camera. Only the awful sightlessness of her eyes betrayed her. One became embarrassed;

48

as at a theater where the famous comedian fails to raise the most fleeting of sniggers from his audience.

"Come off it, Grace," one said uncomfortably. "Come off it. You're not an actress."

She was suddenly chastened and dumb, like a reprimanded pet. The pose was shattered. Slipping off the dressing gown she lit a cigarette and sat herself down on my knee; began to kiss me in a businesslike way, pausing from time to time to exhale clouds of smoke from her small dry mouth. Her eyes might have been covered in cataracts for all the meaning they held in them. Her kisses were tasteless, like straw. "Do you like me?" she inquired at last with stunning fervor—the great screen star taking possession of her face for a second. "Do you reely like me, mister?"

From that moment there is the flash of a sword, dividing the world. A bright cleavage with the past, cutting down through the nerves and cells and arteries of feeling. The past was amputated, and the future became simply Gracie. That peculiar infatuation which absorbed one, sapped one by the fascination of its explorations. Gracie stayed on, and days lost count of themselves: so remote was that world in which I wandered with her, so all-absorbing her least mannerism, the least word, the least breath she drew.

After the first ardors were tasted and realized, she became even more wonderful as a sort of pet. Her vocabulary, her great thoughts lit up the days like comets. And that miserable tranquillity she retired into when she was ill made one realize that she was inexhaustible. What a curious adventure another person is!

I phoned Tarquin: "My dear fellow, you must come down to my rooms on Tuesday and meet Gracie. I'm giving a little party for her. You must come. I'm sure you will be great friends. She spits blood."

They all came. Perez, the gorilla with his uncouth male stride and raving tie; Lobo agitatedly showing his most flattering half-profile; Clare, Tarquin, Chamberlain with his bundle of light music and jazz. They sat about uncomfortably, rather ghoulishly, while I, reveling in the situation, made them drink, and helped Grace to perform her tricks. It was a cruel tableau, but she was far too obtuse to realize it. She played the social hostess with a zeal and clumsiness which would have made one weep if one were less granite-livered. I congratulated myself on my skill in gathering together such a collection of butterflies for their mutual embarrassment. Yes, I chuckled inwardly as I caught their eyes over their glasses. The comedy of wheels within wheels. It was a society of pen-club members who, after being invited to meet a celebrity, had been presented with a mere reviewer. Scandalized they were by the performance Grace put up, cocking her little finger over the teacups, and talking with the hygienic purity of an Anerly matron. (Preserve us from the ostrich.) How their eyes accused me!

Poor Grace was obviously an embarrassing bore. They relaxed a little when the gramophone was started and Chamberlain was compelled by punctiliousness to gyrate with his hostess. He was the least affected by Gracie, I suppose because he was the most natural person there. But Perez and Lobo conferred in a corner and decided that they had an important engagement elsewhere. Lobo said good day with the frigidity of a Castilian gentleman dismissing a boring chambermaid. No manners like those of the really well-bred.

Later, however, Clare danced with her and she seemed to like it. He alone of all of them seemed to speak a quiet language which was really familiar to her, which thrilled her from the start. In fact they danced so well together, and so intimate were their tones of conversation that Tarquin began to fidget about and behave clumsily with his glass.

Chamberlain, who didn't live in the hotel himself, followed me to the lavatory, and kept me talking, his eyes shining with excitement.

"What do you think of Gracie?"

"Good enough fun. Not much of you, though."

"What do you mean?"

He laughed in my face, wrinkling up his nose. Not quite certain whether to be frank or not. As always he took the chance, however.

"This party of yours. An elaborate piece of self-gratification. You must always take it out of somebody, mustn't you? Life is one long revenge for your own shortcomings."

"You've been reading the Russians," I said. Nothing else. It was furiously annoying. I bowed and led him back to the circus. Tarquin was water-logged by this time, and ready to leave. Clare danced on in a kind of remote control, a social communion with Gracie. They hardly spoke at all, but there was an awareness, an ease between them I envied. A contact.

"Well, Grace, I'm going," said Chamberlain with good humor, shaking hands with her. To me, as he passed, he offered one word, in my private ear. "Sentimentalist." I confess it rankled.

That evening I took it out on Grace, appeased the rage that Chamberlain's little observation had bred in me. For a day or two everything about her seemed odious, *odious*.

But all this, one realizes, is simply writing down to one's subject from the heights of an intellectual superiority, à la Huxley. It is a trick to be played on anyone, but not on yourself. The intellectual superiority of the emotionally sterile. Because I am grateful to Grace, more grateful than inky words can express, whatever agony you inject into them. Yet the idea of an audience! The idea of anyone *knowing* that I felt such sentiments turned them at once crystal-cold. Changed them into a rage against my own emotional weakness. And thence into a rage against the object of that indulgence, yclept she. In retrospect the party explains itself simply enough. Was it possible that I felt anything for this little cockney child with her tedious humors, her spurious gentility? Quick, quick then, let me insult myself and her for such a lapse from the heights of intellectual purity of feeling. How we cherish the festering intelligence! But then again, feeling, if it is to be interpreted by emotion is not my province: at any rate if I am ever to write about it. For bad emotion can only produce the terrible squealing of the slaughtered pig—*De Profundis* is the sterling example. Let us thank God therefore, that I do not try to squeeze out such pus on to handmade paper. I shirk the epitaph for Grace, not because she wouldn't understand it, but because I dare not write it.

The carapace of the rational intelligence! I think the reason I loved Grace so much was that I could escape from myself with her. The cage I inhabited was broken wide open by our experience. She was not audience enough for me to hate her. Yet, writing nicely, "love" is not the correct word. For a man like me does not need love in the accepted sense. There should be another word to express this very real state. One hardly knows how to do it without the key word to the situation. Let me leave a blank space and proceed.

Why and how Gracie supplied this provender, it would take me an aeon to write. Her idiocy! Her uncomprehending urbanity! Above all, her stupidity! Yes, her stupidity made me feel safe, within my own depth. It was possible to give myself to her utterly. My desire was as unqualified by fear and mistrust as hers was by intelligence. Sometimes, sitting there on the bed with her, playing foolish kindergarten games with her, I used to imagine what would happen if suddenly she turned before my eyes into one of those precise female doormice of the upper classes with whom only my limitations express themselves. A weird feeling. I had, after all, utterly committed myself: and the idea of Grace turning into a she-judas before my eyes was frightening. Imagine a Croydon Juliet, secure in her knowledge of exactly what *was* sacred and profane love, rising up from my own sofa and scourging me! The cracking whips of outraged romance! (No. No. Preserve us from the ostrich.)

Must I confess, then, that the secret of our love was the vast stupidity of Grace and the huge egotism and terror of myself? These were the hinges on which our relationship turned. You see, I could not *tell* her I adored her. No. My love expressed itself in a devious, ambiguous way. My tongue became a scourge to torment not only myself but also the object of my adoration. Another woman jeered at, whipped by syllables, addressed as "you bitch," "you slut," or "you whore," would have been clever enough to accept the terms for what they seemed worth. Who would have guessed that in using them I intended to convey only my own abject surrender? Only Gracie, of course, sitting in the corner of the sofa, very *grande dame* in my colored dressing gown, deaf and sightless, cocking her finger over a cup of tea! Who would have accepted an apparent hate and known it to be love? No one but Grace, my cinematic princess.

Chamberlain, when he called, was shocked by the knife edge of cruelty that cut down into our social relations. He did not realize the depths of her insensitiveness. He saw only what seemed to him the willful cruelty of myself. He did not realize that my viper's tongue would have withered in my mouth if set to pronounce a single conventional endearment, "my darling," or "my dear." No. I am that I am. The *senex fornicator* if you will. The lutin. *Nanus* or *pumilo*. Tourneur's "juiceless luxur," if you prefer it, but never the conventionalized gramophone-record lover. But I realize that even these weird colors are denied me by my acquaintances whose method is simply to reverse the romantic medallion and declare that what they see is the face of cynicism. "Dear Mr. Gregory," as someone said, "you're *such* a cynic," whatever she meant.

In a way this must be rather a pity, for Grace pines for romance, dimly in that numb soul of hers. Wistfully. Sometimes, on waking her from a trance, I have discovered that the object of her musing was only Gary Cooper. Soit. It has become imperative to present her with a substitute.

Much pondering on the subject had evolved for me an elixir, which seems to do the trick. Thrice-weekly visits to the cinema seem to hack away most of the romantic whale blubber which would poison our relationship; the rest is dissipated by an occasional visit from Clare. He is, as it were, the practical side of romance.

Saturday evenings she goes dancing at the Pally De Dance with him, glittering in a vulgar new evening frock which my charity has provided; baubled, painted, and with a swath of scent following her, a yard wide, like an invisible page. Radiant, one might almost say, were not her radiance the radiance of a rouged death mask.

With me she is still a little uncomfortable, but once outside the flat door she takes on any romantic color she chooses. Out of the weekday chrysalis steps the princess Gracie, owner of a tall dark partner and a latchkey of her own. I would be a fool to grudge her this. Yet it rankles. I grudge it. And again, so unfortunate in my way of showing my feelings that I force her to go, goad her, simply in the hope that she will revolt, renounce the role, and stay at home. "But you must go," I say, when she shows the slightest disinclination. "Clare will be sad. He says you dance lovely." Hoping of course that she will laugh, put her hands on my shoulders, perhaps, and stay. But a more literal-minded little jezebel you could not hope to find. In all obedience, she goes. If I had the courage to say to her, for instance: "Tonight you must stay. I don't want to be left alone," she would as obediently stay; but try as I might I cannot bring myself to say the formula. Poor Gracie. The female thaumaturge. Where anyone else would try perhaps to deduce what I was feeling from the ambiguities of what I say, Gracie accepts the literal rendering of the text and acts on it. In this way I have no one to blame but myself.

Of course, there are solutions. But I am too much the retiring violet ever to try them. I could, for instance, learn to dance. In fact I even bought a little manual of dance steps and trod a grave measure or two in front of my looking glass, wondering if it were possible to take Clare's place in the ballroom. Alas! I can see at once how fatal the attempt would be. The fallacy of the idea. Because what she wants is not a partner, but a romantic ally. Fox trot I never so nimbly, I could not hope to oust Clare.

For consider the disparity. Clare is tall, insolently cat-eyed, black-locked. The gigolo, in a word. His evening shoulders are padded to professional heavyweight size. Bigger than Grace, he hunches protectively over her, singing snatches of the tunes in her ears. He knows all the words to all the tunes, it seems. His movement is a lush, confident seal's glide on the polished floor. Confronted by this picture of him for comparison with my own reflection in the mirror, I am at once disgusted by the fatuity of all this. No. Saturday evenings I sit virtuously alone, a-reading Gibbon, waiting for the clock to strike twelve.

Sometimes Tarquin comes down to see me, all nerves and nonchalance, and sits on the edge of a chair, talking wistfully, until they return. He resents her taking up Clare's time but dare not show it openly. He is scared that they will fall, as he puts it, in love with one another. "Aren't you," he says nervously, "in love with her enough to see the danger of all this?" Naturally, my viscera contract at this open statement of a fact which I haven't ever wanted to examine closely. "Love?" I says to him I says, with my newly acquired Brixton aplomb, "Love, Tarquin?" This with all the chaste control I can muster. "Oh, it depends what you mean by the word." I call up the Nelson touch and nail my pinafore to the mast. "What is love?" It is not myself I am asking, but Tarquin. I dissociate myself firmly from the question. Have I not already signaled my ignorance by a blank space where the word should have been? Nevertheless I am malicious now, because he should try to smoke out the hornets' nest in my brain. Shall we make him wriggle? "Do you love Clare?" I say venomously. "Love," he says, beginning to tremble, *"Love!"* The word is a sort of motor touched off inside him. His knees liquefy and dissolve inside the creased tubes of his trouser legs. "My dear fellow, what do you mean?"

This is the seventh occasion of Clare's visit to the Pally with Grace. By this time we are nearly drunk on claret. Tarquin is almost hysterical and I am seeking about for the right phrase with which to disembowel him. It would wipe out my anger at

Grace's desertion to see *him* break down. But he will not. We sit like a couple of aged schoolmarms and discuss "life." Tarquin's confidences are a little embarrassing because they are so out of proportion. When he was five, he assures me, his little sister pulled down his trousers before five of her girl friends. This he assures me is the cause of his curious psychology. All of which is vaguely reminiscent of a literary outing with one of the Powys brothers. "You can understand the shame that polluted my life?" he demands angrily. He insists on reading me his diary, at any rate those significant excerpts which scald his bowels. Bad prose and worse sentiment. There are little flourishes and bravura pieces which are waiting eagerly for posterity. Tarquin banks his hopes of immortality on this tome: these hypochondriac dribblings!

"Do you keep a diary?" he wants to know; and contemptuously I tell him, "No."

A little disgusting on the whole, this soul-outpouring of his, because so trivial. "We must have sanity, don't you think?" he says wistfully. "We must reduce our lives to some sort of order. I'm trying very hard to get to the bottom of myself. What do you think?"

The anger, the hard bright anger in myself, when I consider Tarquin's tram excursions down the one-way street of introspection and psychoanalysis. "It isn't anything *wrong*," he says, speaking of his love for Clare; "it isn't a physical attachment. I had my prostate looked over. It's quite normal. It's purely a desire for some emotional relationship between us. Gregory, old fellow, you know what loneliness can be, without contact, don't you? Sitting alone day after day, don't you?"

The claret is finished. Nodding with the stern kindness of a medico, I retire to the kitchen and unearth some bitter beer. Tarquin molts by the fire.

"Ever since I was at school I felt the need for love. Ideal love, don't you see? I'm not immoral. The law couldn't touch me if it wanted to. Physically I'm chaste as . . . as . . . what's very chaste?

Tell me the chastest thing you know. Yes, that's right. As chaste as a bloody eunuch ... Ha ... Ha ..."

A little spasm of mixed laughter and tears. The beer produces a series of diminishing reverberations in his bowels; a regurgitation. He spits in the fire.

"I fixed my emotions on friends, on masters, anyone at all. I used to write poems to them. You see? Then afterwards ... Oh, I don't know, why am I telling you all this? I regret it. I'll be ashamed to come again. Why can't I shut up and be silent? Why? Is it something wrong with me? What do you think? But that damned war finished any control I might have had. I was happy in the line. Sounds funny, doesn't it? But happy, old man, I've never been happier. Of course my nerves were shot to hell, but the lack of responsibility, just waiting like cows to be killed. You see one couldn't *think*. My God, what a blessing to sit there in that noise, chewing mud, and trembling, *unable to think*. It'll never be the same again. I try with music now but it's no good. Only sometimes Wagner gives me the feeling, but it's no good really."

Ach! but a truce to Tarquin. He has framed his own portrait in that wretched diary of his. What a monument of unconscious humor and pathos!

The night I told him that Clare had been unfaithful to him, rather that Grace had been unfaithful to me, he was for beating the gigolo senseless. "The world's not large enough for us both," he admitted, starting to be sick. In the bathroom, falling on his knees, he clutched the tails of my dressing gown, and said: "Help me, Gregory, for the love of God, help me, help me."

I helped him to bed . . .

Here ends the extract from Gregory's diary.

*
**

That is a fragment of the tender id of this book: the secretive, wincing plasm of Gregory tangled in his own egoismus; tangled in the green lace of the writing. I do not pretend to interpret. It would be too much to expect of the interrogative ego, the other me, whose function is simply to take a sort of hieroglyphic dictation from space, and annotate it, punctuate, edit. Perhaps add a pert little introduction of my own, and an apparatus of variants.

If I reflect on our individual and collective funerals, here in the Regina Hotel, running side by side in the snow in a chronology which has nothing to do with time—for it has forfeited time for the living limbo—then I am forced back to a picture of Lobo sitting over his chart, his fingers busy, while Gregory watches from a chair. Always the Gregory who does not exist here, the Death Gregory of the green fable. As for the chart, it is the final symbol of this annihilation. At night I can see it on the wall. It contains every principle, every motive, every boundary to which our deaths are subject, in which they are consummated. Plot me a graph of the doom, in which the southern provinces lie! The tunnel of Lordship Lane where my feet have worn themselves down to marrowless stumps in my wanderings. The smoke and uproar of the tin tumbrils passing the eternal windows. The museum clock face is scourged by raindrops: it dies, like a pale face on the stalk of a tower and reminds me of the death of time. . . .

When Gregory speaks out of the darkness I am wandering again in that insane system which is not solar but infernal. The fronds of the sickening trees from Green Lanes away to Champion Hill, where the travelers go at night with their bags and baggages. At Catford, where the blind men dance to the violins, while the wind blows their eyelids over them; and their hands are terrible soapy talons! Deliver me from the blind men of my childhood! Stand on the bridge and let the engines launch themselves at you. Heavy steel lances diving between your legs and the smoke chokes up between the arches. All the signals are set green as the evening shuts down, long rays of evening paralysis over the tenements. Lochia. The houses secret and prim. No sound, no sound of the rigors, tragedies, lamentations leaking from behind the shutters. The door knockers hanging on broken hinges waiting for the Host to lift them. Inside the kitchen ranges flaring, surrounded by steaming clotheshorses. Texts on the wall at an angle. Mantels blossoming out with a sudden soft pop. Letters with Indian stamps on them, Halma, Ludo, Baedeker, Old Moore, dripping, sequel, the green house lit with a green rain from heaven, the haggard fingers stitching a winding cloth for the morning . . . It is difficult to write it. There is a transition from that place to this, where I sit and watch Lobo work at the map he will never finish. But it is immediate. The connecting links have snapped, or been burst into pieces. I live only in my imagination which is timeless. Therefore the location of this world which I am trying to hammer out for you on a blunt typewriter, over the Ionian, is the location of space merely. I can only fix it with any certainty *on the map.*

From Peckham where the children sail their boats, where the lovers play with each other and go mad on the dark common after dark, away to the lairs of Lee Green, where you can smell Blackheath stalking upward into the darkness, leperlike, eaten by roads and villas. From the fag end of Anerly where the tram lines thin away into a wilderness of falling tombstones; Elmer's End, a locality of white stumps in the snow; to the Crystal Palace stuck against the sky, dribbling softly, pricked with lamps. Lawrence knew this world. Look up suddenly into the night. O ponderous phalloi, you have impregnated the world, you are the hostage of these delicate girls whose virginities are hard as the iron rails of the beds on which they toss!

The hotel is crowded with ghosts. Since Edwardian times no one has dusted this statuary, these carpets, these indestructible potted plants. I am thinking now of the Welshman. Morgan stooping along these corridors as if under invisible blows, with a mop in his hand. Or at night, seated by the humming iron boilers in a battered chair, draining his whisky at a gulp, and coughing up a bloodshot story. Morgan found drunk one night, twined round

the figure of a Greek goddess, fearfully excited by its utter stillness. Or giving himself an erection solemnly, to show you exactly
what the catheter did to him when he had the clap. The beautiful
mutilations and barbarities of Wales, the valleys strung with
sores, the religion. And to the seaboard of his world the eternal
beating of the Atlantic, the white races. Morgan's inheritance
is a queer barbarity, a religious anger, which jumps from nothing
along the dents of his face. I am fascinated by him, because to
my own crude struggle against a protracted adolescence, he
presents a bold and solid picture, in large round lively colors. He
presents as nearly as he can the quality of an experience without
dressing it up: puzzled, louring, hooking the writhing words
from his vocabulary like octopods, as he sits there by the boiler,
drinking and yarning. Look, one night I came down here to find
the furnace doors open, the dirty linoleum bathed in flames. He
was working, stripped to the waist, the liquid dust rolling down
his body, the contours of chest and arm frilled in flame, tossing
great mouthfuls of clinkers into the furnace. His dugs were a
tangle of hair and dust. When he saw me he was suddenly leaning
on the shovel in delighted agitation. (Gwen, of course. He has
been shaping for Gwen for months now.) I could only guess at
the reality through his imprecision. "She come down 'arf an hour
ago. 'Ere. By the boiler." *His face was like a flower.* "She come to
me with nothing under her dress. She said: 'Do you want it,
Mister Morgan?' Gor but it was surprising, like. I dint know what
to say. Then she lies down here, in front of the bloody fire, as
God's truth, sir, in front of the fire 'ere." He choked on his own
spittle and produced a grin. Phenomenon. Then, turning aside,
latched the boiler doors fast. In my role of echo I sat and waited.
He was angry now, sort of resentful with me for being at all
interested. Then he ended with terrific naturalness: "She was
what you might call fruity. Draws it out of you, sir." Then, as
if a little bewildered by such a literary figure, he stared at his
feet and blurted out, "Juicy as fruit, sir, and that's no error."

From this epic to the minor myth of Gregory is a step that seems unbridgeable, to me at any rate. Morgan at one uncouth jump reaching beyond the boundaries of our idealism, our dilute passion, our effete aesthetic. I am helpless to do anything but move the green bishop to a new paragraph. Helpless.

**

Here begins Gregory:

The unbearable poignance of being inarticulate—or do I mean only too articulate?—for I have words enough. *"Christ,"* she said to me once lying there covered by my body, *"Say yer love me, why don't you? You never says it, Gregory, you never says it. It's not good without you saying it."*

She had never cried out before; never tried to cross the forbidden territory which lies between us. For a half-second it was as if, to descend to the stale phrase, my heart was broken. The pain of finding her almost within my reach, demanding comfortable familiarity and tenderness, was almost physical. Here, your romantics will tell you, under the left breast. I wondered all of a sudden what it must feel like to sleep with me, to miss the open reciprocation, the crude vulnerability of the passionate mammal: the warmth that Chamberlain revels in: the bowels of compassion. . . .

Faugh! But I'm a saurian. Leave me my toadlike composure. I defend my own psychic property like the Devil himself. (*"You never says it, Gregory, you never says it."*) Poor Gracie, and her lame performing toad! The distance was never crossed. Even now, putting this elegant *ci-gît* over her coffin I do not really regret it. I am that I am.

Here ends Gregory.

**

But it is true what he says before: a phrase as valid for us all now as it was for him when he wrote it.

Everything is plausible here, because nothing is real. Nothing. The warm schoolrooms with their furniture of little round heads, the hunchback, the black car riding out on the midnight to meet you, the desire, the hours I spend at this desk in a vacant room, with only this diary to testify to Gregory's life. The blank telephone which carries your scent into the room, among this literary bric-à-brac, these moldering novels, poems, articles, the statues on the snow whose personality I can feel even in my dreams. To fall upon you in an elegy of frenzy, and feel the circles of snowy birds break from your white prison, burst open your breast and begin, falling across the stony body in prismatic regiments. Forgive me.

We meet at night on the downland, in the last territory of the great arterial road. There is that figure which will break from the dark trees and dance into the glare of the headlights in all gaiety. Leather ankle boots, swished wet in the long grass of the fields. The woolly Cossack hat snuggled firmly to the head. Hair blue-black, smooth, brushed cleanly back over the icy lobes of the ears. Cold the cold fingers which will burrow in the lighted dashboard for cigarettes; and the so faintly painted mouth cold in greeting like the friendly cold nose of an animal. Breath spouting a milky spume on the frozen air. This is the dimension I wander in at night, this and the dimension of history. It is hardly reasonable. The children are afraid to look at my face because they might learn something.

Imagination can depict continents, immense humid quags of matter where life pumps its lungs in a last spasm of being before passing down slowly, sponging away into its eternal type of mud. Things without souls which wander among the mossy stumps, hummingbirds, or pterodactyls with klaxon shrieks, blobs of sperm drying in crevices, or the nameless maculae lairing and clinching in mud to produce their types of solitariness. This in the realm of history when the children are sitting deafened by the silence, and the book empties itself out on the desk in many colored pictures. The carbon forests buried in their weeds and marshes. Pithecanthropus striking fire from a cobble. The rhino calling. The enigmatic fan of planets plotting its graph on the night. The first spark of history struck from a cobble while the ashes of our campfires soften and wrinkle. The children's faces like so many custards! The waters thawing, drawing back. The havoc of the ice ages set suddenly into gear. The earth begins its ablutions. The planets lick themselves clean. The mud of continents scraped, plowed. Forests picked out and tossed into space like patches of fluff. Endless the migration of apes in little boats, with food and skins and nursery implements. Men with bronze and cattle paddling the Gulf Stream into chaos beside their dugged females. Oh, the terrible loneliness of the ape's mind to see the dawn sweep up from the poles in a prismatic snow, shivering a fan of colors. The flakes settling and thawing on the blue water of oceans. Behind them, lost in a void which has no location, a world: before them—what? The rim of water seeking away into the seasons, consuming time. No hand or olive branch to guide them. The snow ices their hairy shanks and the skins in which they huddle. . . .

It is like that, primordial in its loneliness, the mood in which I set out to meet you. The history is a sort of fake I invent all day among the children to nerve myself for our meetings. You are sitting out there, under the sweeping skyline of country, with time strapped to your wrist by a leather thong. At your back the airplane light swivels its reds and greens on to the grass in many hectic windmills. There is no object in life but to reach that lonely cigarette point in the darkness. All day my own movements struggle toward the darkness. Immense massive maneuvers against time, so that I am like the underwater photos of a swimmer, parting the thick elements of gloom with slow hands toward the moment of meeting.

I am alive only in the soft glitter of the snow, the turning of switches, the labored churning of the self-starter. The engine coming awake under my slippered toe, the heavy metal personality of my partner. We are off on the murderous roads, the engine staggering, whining, hot with slipping from gear to accurate gear. The road opens like a throat at Elmer's End. I huddle nervously and press down my foot. Bang! down into the suburban country, among a rain of falling tombstones. A hailstorm of masonry falling away to one side. I am immune from danger at last. The lights are passing and falling away, like lambent yellow cushions, always flung, always falling short. Everything is gone at last, our failures, our shabby quarrels, time, illusion, the night, the frenzy, the hysteria. I am in the dark here in a metal shell, blinding away across the earth, these infinite lanes toward her.

Flesh robot with cold thighs and fingers of icicle gripping the wheel of the black car, everything is forgotten. It is no use telling me of her inadequacy, her limitations; no good saying her mouth is an ash tray crammed with the butts of reserve, funk, truism, revulsion. I admit it. I admit everything with a great grin of snow. But it is no use. If I can find her moist and open between two sheets anywhere among the seven winds, you can have everything that lives and agonizes between the twin poles. Seriously. I switch off the dashboard and let my soul ride out on to the dark, floating and quivering on the frosty air above the black car; my personality has been snipped from my body now, as if by scissors, to ride along the night wind against any cold star. Everything flows out of me in a long effortless catharsis, pours on to the darkness, licked by the airs. This is the meaning of freedom. My money has poured out of my pockets, my clothes fallen from me, every bit of tissue sloughed. Everything is clear in this struggle to reach her. The car humming like a top, stammering, banging round corners with its insane fixed eyes; the carpet of light racing along the dark arterial roads; the distance being patiently consumed. I am in a kind of fanatical imagery now, unreal, moving through this aquarium of feelings, conscious of nothing but the blood thinning in my veins, and the slow fearful heart.

We fall together like figures made of feathers, among the soft

snowy dewlaps of the cattle, the steaming commotion of voices
and cud. The loose black mouth with its voice of enormous
volume. We are surrounded with friendly cattle like a Christmas-
card picture, on the ground, our bodies emptied out of their
clothes. It is a new nativity when I enter her, the enormous city
couched between her legs; or a frost-bound lake, absolutely aware
of the adventurer, the pilgrim, the colonizer. The snow is falling
in my mouth, my ears, my soaked clothes. This is a blunt voyage
of the most exquisite reckoning. Enter. She has become an image
in rubber, not the smallest bone which will not melt to snow
under the steady friction of the penis. The hot thaw spreads raw
patches of grass under us: every abstraction now is bleeding away
into the snow—death, life, desire. It is so fatal, this act among
the cattle. We are engrossed bobbins on a huge loom of terror,
knowing nothing, wishing to know nothing of our universe, its
machinery. When she comes it's all pearls and icicles emptied
from her womb into the snow. The penis like a dolphin with many
muscles and black humor, lolling up to meet the sun. The fig
suddenly broken into a sticky tip that is all female. She is laughing
hideously. The car is standing among the cattle, no less intelligent
than they. Under me is no personality any more but a composite
type of all desire. Enter. I do not recognize my arctic sister. Under
my heart the delicate tappets of a heart; my penis trapped in an
inexorable valve, drawing these shapes and chords out of me
inexhaustible, like toothpaste. The cattle are kindly and interested
in a gentlemanly way; the car urbane as a metal butler. Under
my thews, trapped in bracts and sphincters, a unique destruction.
She is weeping. Her spine has been liquefied, drawn out of her.
She is filleted, the jaw telescoped with language, eyes glassy.
Under my mouth a rouged vagina speaking a barbaric laughter
and nibbling my tongue. It is all warm and raw: a spiritual
autumn with just that scent of corruption, that much death in it,
to make it palatable. A meal of game well-hung pig-scented
tangy. Such a venison, more delicate than the gums of babies or
little fishes. Open to me once like that and the Poles are shaken

out of their orbits, the sky falls down in a fan of planets. I am the owner of the million words, the ciphers, the dead vocabularies. In this immense ceiling of swan's-down there is nothing left but a laughter that opens heaven: a half-life, running on the batteries. I am eating the snow and drinking your tears. Stand against the hedge to snivel and make water while the shivers run down your spine. You are beautiful all of a sudden. Your fear makes me merry. *A very merry Christmas to you and yours.* I am saying it insanely over and again. A very merry Christmas to you and yours. She runs at me suddenly with blunt fists raised, shouting wildly. Enormous dark eyes with the green and red lights growing from them. The cattle draw back softly on the carpet. Her tears punch little hot holes in the snow. I am happy. You will go about from now on with an overripe medlar hanging out between your legs, your womb burst like the tip of the Roman fig. But even this brutality goes when I feel the bones against me, malleable and tender as gum; the eager whimpering animal dressed in cloth opening up to me, wider and wider, softer than toffee, until the bland sky is heavy with falling feathers, angels, silk, and there is a sword broken off softly in my bowels. I am lying here quite ruined, like a basketful of spilt eggs, but happy. Vulnerable, but lying in you here, at peace with myself: the tides drawing back from me, gathering up the dirt and scurf of things, the thawed pus and venom, and purifying me. I am at peace. It is all falling away from me, the whole of my life emptied out in you like a pocketful of soiled pennies. The faces of the world, Lobo and Marney, the children, Peters, the car, Gracie, the enormous snow, statues, history, mice, divinity. It is forever, you are saying wildly, with green lips, red lips, white lips, blue lips, green lips. It is forever. Our lives stop here like a strip of cinema film. This is an eternal still life, in the snow, two crooked bodies, eating the second of midnight and sniveling. We will die here in this raw agony of convalescence, by the icebound lake, the city lying quiet among its litter of whimpering, blind steeples.

They must be saying good nights now all over the world. I am saying good-by to part of my life, no, part of my body. It is irrational. I do not know what to say. If I take your hand it is my own hand I am kissing. The aquarium again, with everything slowed down to the tempo of deep water. Good-by to my own body under the windmill, weeping in the deep snow, nose, ankle, wrist made of frosty iron again. Help me. O eloquent, just and mighty death. The great anvil of the frost is pounding us. The cattle are afraid. Let me put my hand between your legs for warmth. Speak to my fingers with your delicate mouth, your pillow of flesh. I am a swimmer again, moving in a photograph with great, uncertain, plausible gestures toward you.

I have said good night and drawn the car out slowly homeward. There is no feeling in my hands or feet. As though the locomotive centers had been eaten away. Tired.

Hot scent of oil along the great arterial road. There is not a fraction of my life which is not left behind with you, back there, in the snows.

*
* *

In the hotel the lights blaze. The stillness of the little death hangs along the corridors. Lobo is locked in his room, his heavy head bent over the chart. At his back the wireless gives out the barnyard orchestrations of jazz. From time to time he will raise his eyes and let them rest on his pencil box. Not thinking, numb, the iris of each eye focusing its dark vent on the Mayan eternity. He will let the tepid piddle of the music squirt coolly over him, without attending to it. He would like to cry. Next door Miss Venable wrestles with insomnia. Dial. Detective novels. Ovaltine. Teacups. The bad lamp hangs its yellow membrane over her. The novel palls. How easy to pour herself out an overdose of Dial one of these fine winter nights, at the full moon. She tries to think of God. Three stories up Clare is lying in bed. Tarquin stands over him talking. The window is open and snow is blowing in on the floor. The yellow eyes are sardonic. Connie has entered into their drama suddenly and instituted a new order of things. To Clare's salary an increase of three pounds a week; to Tarquin's lorve a kind of internal strangulation, a hernia. However, he is talking largely. The new view of life etc. "Tell me about her," he says bravely, his nose quivering. This pathetic pose of indifference amuses Clare. "Tell me!" He wants to be made to wriggle, to be stung, whipped by details. Nowadays he can feel so little, really. "I want us to be friends, Clare dear," he says shyly. "Tell me everything. Confide in me."

"Well," says Clare in his croaking voice, saturnine, "if you must know, she's a dirty bitch. When I'm not there it's candles, or hot soap and water in a bottle. See? It's a corridor, that's what it is, see? She likes it from behind on Sundays to remind her of her old man Joseph, see?"

Tarquin has to leave before he vomits. In his room he walks about like a shy little girl; he will not speak to anyone. If I had the time and the energy I could be really sorry for him. Connie in that gas-lit flat with the blood running out of her as fast as the port runs down her throat: blood on the towels, the curtains, the bedcovers, the pillow. Blood everywhere—and his little Greek Clare cleaning his white teeth and helping himself from the bulging handbag. Or the night of the party when the gas went out, and you could see suddenly the sonata blotted out by the dark. The piano like a dumb buffalo there, and Clare trying to mount her on the piano stool, with strange uncouth movements. Tarquin locks the door of his room every night now to feel safe from the blood. He plays David and Jonathan with his pillow these days but it is no good. It is no good at all.

It is so very silent here at night: my room amputated from the planet. A laboratory hanging in space where the white-coated intelligence I, clinical Holy Ghost, brood forever among the bottles and the pickled fetuses. Memory has many waiting rooms. The train for the end of space has been signaled. Shall we run out among the cavernous sheds to meet the monster? The truth is that I am writing my first book. It is difficult, because everything must be included: a kind of spiritual itinerary which will establish the novel once and for all as a mode which is already past its senium. I tell myself continually that this must be something without beginning, something which will never end, but conclude only when it has reached its own genesis again: very well, a piece of literary perpetual motion, balanced on a hair, maintaining its precarious equilibrium between life and heraldry. With the pathos of Tarquin's diary I insist that everything must be included. It is difficult. For instance, there is no category of irrelevances. Everything chosen is relevant. There are no canons—should be none. It is a hypothetical prophecy I dream about in this area of the night, alone, chewing paper, or anchoring my hands fast until morning. The difficulties are so enormous that I am tempted to begin at once: to try and escape from the chaste seminary of literature in which I have been imprisoned too long. Everything must be accepted, including Tarquin, and transmuted into the stuff of poem. There is your body, for instance, which rises up over the unwritten book like a wall of snow: the component parts of the day ending in an agony of rebirth—unless you have your period! There are acres of hysteria when we weep together weakly for no reason at all; there is that moist, friendly target under your dress, so mysterious in its simplicity that I cannot keep away from it, returning each time to the heart of the enigma as one might return to a gnomic verse and find a new meaning in the snow each time. All this is such ripe matter for the book that I do not know how to begin it. I am serious. It is such a book as Gregory could not even imagine, could not even begin to *plan*. The little green snowman sitting in his own shadow, keeping the crows off his work with wild sweeps of the pen. Gregory and the monstrous behavior of literature which he used as a cloak for his terrors and realities. Strange chaotic chords which fill the diary. I have been reading it again, puzzling over it, and the realities which it deals with....

***

Here Gregory begins:

That I too have nursed literary pretensions, I will not disguise from myself; that I have now finally rejected them is proved by the airy nonchalance of this journal, ha, ha. By its very fragmentary character, which preserves only the most casual excursions among my memories. Yes. At one time I had accumulated every principle, every canon of art, which is necessary for the manufacture of a literary gentleman. Now I not only despise the canon, but more, the creature himself: the gent. I am a saurian, I thank you, but not wasp-waisted as yet.

The theme of my only book is one which even now occasionally entices me, insists on its formal excellence in a world of shapeless, inelegant mediocrities. I had planned this work as a profound synthesis of life—as an epitaph to the age. Its theme was revelry; its title—if I may make so bold with the sensibilities of the world —URINE. Simply the divinely organic word in gold Gill Sans on white paper. It was to be a small book, about the length of Remy de Gourmont's *A Night in the Luxembourg*. Its simplicity would have delighted that delicate literary fencer. But let me explain.

In Siberia, I have read, there is brewed a drink, whose name I do not recall, but whose potence is due to an infusion of muscarine —a poison obtained from the beautiful scarlet mushroom fly agaric. A regular toper's tocsin. But more. The active principle in the brew, the muscarine, is eliminated by the kidneys, and passes into waste; into the fluid whose name (I am too fastidious to keep writing it down) forms the title of my opus. From this discovery dates a curious and delightful cult. Whenever there is feudal merrymaking abovestairs in the Siberian baronial halls, the servants avail themselves of the waste products of the festivity to do a bit of merrymaking on their own. You begin to see the satanic implications of the thing? Believe me, even now, Olympian as I am, I almost regret having rejected it. Its scope is perfect, leaving no room for those personal reflections of the author which provide the tedium of half the novels published. None of your vague moralizings or contemplative trances. Nothing but the bare anatomy of narrative—nude and pure as a winter landscape. Simply this:

A party above- and belowstairs. Man proposing the toasts, and the servants furtively disposing of the humiliating evidences of its ultimate waste. The link connecting the two planes is, simply, waste. The golden gains for which the furtive valet spoors the chamber pots is profoundly symbolic. Its significance I shall not dwell upon. Here is your answer to every homely commonplace. A carnival party in action. Sluts and sluttishness abovestairs and below. On either plane the so-called action is simply erotic formula—love toasted by the master, the kitchenmaid toasted by his man. The same tocsin warms a multitude of cockles.

Really, I tell myself, really some day soon I shall be enticed into beginning it. Until then, let me offer this title page to your imaginations—what gonadal ecstasies shine beneath the simple symbol, what promises!

URINE

by Death Gregory, Esq.

Here Gregory ends.

***

It is so silent here at night. Above all, so silent. I lie awake: the essential I, that is, from whom I expect response to noise, to gesture. The other, the not-me, the figment, the embryo, the white something which lives behind my face in the mirror, is lulled underground, hibernating. The opulence of the snow steams down my eyeballs. I dare not sleep because I never dream about her. Instead I go to the window and communicate with the statues out there. The plaster outlaws on the grass. Their personalities are a match for me on such a December evening. Cadaverous the trees. A late train draws away across the indistinct haze of the moon, a bright nerve of color. I am full of irrational ideas. I shall go up, perhaps, and speak to Tarquin. Disturb Lobo under the pretense of some important news. But having so lately left you it is as if I am in a suit of armor. Chain-mail reticence. I am lonely but I do not wish to see anyone. A poem, then? How about a fine chop-licking poem about you, about the snow and the cattle? The pen is clogged with black ink. O eloquent, just and mighty death etc. I am too full of you. Let me digest. Let me digest. It is in such a mood that I slip down among the trees, across the derelict pond, to the grass-fringed garage, pausing for a second to count the lighted windows. Lobo still awake and Clare. All night now I will drive the black car under the moon in an agony of escape—I do not know from what. Escape, under a full moon, with the fields traveling away beside me, the silent farms and cottages, the facile ancient spires. If I could reach the sea I would be at rest. Its enormous breathing and sponging the dead body of the stones would quiet me. I would empty you into it without ceremony, the part of you which I carry about with me, living on me. I would dump you like a corpse and turn back to the city with refreshment. But there are only these metal roads along which we scream all night until the moon dissolves and the first stagnant eggs are poached on the snow. The streams are frozen over. I walk beside them on the grass, now stiff with rime, in a million priapic blades; I walk quickly, with a light step, as if to some important appointment. If I find a dead robin under the bushes I slip it in my pocket with a preoccupied air, as if I have no time to examine it. The cattle retreat from me with vague alarm, ducking their great heads and watching me out of the corner of their eyes. When I can stand it no longer the car draws

72

out again, coughing and roaring down the roads in the ribboned
snow. I have a sympathy with this tepid steel hull which I have
learned to manage so deftly. I switch the lights on and off; I open
the throttle with a sudden scream; I sing loudly out of the window.
At nine Eustace Adams will be sitting with the poached sun
balanced on his shaggy cranium. The children will be whispering
and sniggering. Marney blowing his tulip and shuddering. Another day opening from the navel of my misery: from the moment
when we fall, like figures made of feathers, in the snow. It is in
this dawn, running down the long roads to the place I call home,
that I begin again the enormous underwater gestures toward another night and you, spreading the gloom with slow vague hands
toward you. Everything is plausible now because nothing is real. I
am stretched like a violin string, to snapping point, until tonight.

Morning at last, like a fever. The ash trays are full, the lounges
are being swept, the boots retrieved by their owners. The fires are
lit. Tarquin is walking down avenues of cinders with bare feet. I
have no patience with the diary today.

At the bare deal desk I shield myself behind my fists and pore
on the green writing savagely. The children stretch away like a
sea, into the womb and beyond it, like a huge garden planted
with snotty-nosed turnips and bulging swedes. Gregory Stylites,
help me through another submarine day or I shall die.

*
**

Here begins Gregory:

In the dog days there were long effortless phases, spent ex-
clusively together, which make the core of most of my memories.
Not factual—for what ever *happens?* But a kind of aromatic
stretch, forgotten between the leaves of a book for centuries: the
frail delicate veins of our adventure. The hotel was empty; everyone seemed to have gone away or died. It was this death of the
outer world that gave our exclusiveness its flavor. Imagine it.

Whole days in which no one came to see us; there was not even a ring at the front door. We rose late and lounged all day, half-dressed, playing fantastic games with each other. Hide and seek, for example. Upon my honor, hide and seek in the empty corridors of the hotel. Or bandits and police. Or Ludo, a game which I have always detested.

Or, when I was exhausted by crawling on the floor lowing like a bull, while Gracie matadored me with a red dressing gown, I inflicted my literary garbage on her. My novel, my letters from the infernal regions, even the only poem I ever wrote, which begins: "The clouds are my enormous limbs, whose convalescent shape, Dawdle on beds of down, and yet, Invite a further rape." And so on. This lame practice for a literary career, which if I had only pursued it, would have ended my life in the Abbey—or at least in all the popular anthologies. Then there was my diary, the little black book in which the green ink smokes like many jewels. Gracie is the only one who has ever had my diary read to her; she is the only one who has dared to signal this minor eclipse with a long solemn face and a look of utter puzzlement. Yet, sitting there in the armchair, she never lifted a finger, but listened with heartbreaking raptness to every word. *Every word.* Greater love hath no man etc.

"Look," I say to her. "Why listen to all this stuff? Tell me about yourself. Let me immortalize you with polysyllabic taste."

"No, honest, Gregory, I like it. What I understand. It's not everything, but Rachel . . ."

"Ah, you like Rachel?"

"Was you married to her?"

"No."

"Was she . . . a street woman, a bad one?"

"No. She was an art student."

"Did she let you . . . I mean . . . she was a girl of goofambly wasn't she?"

"Her father was a soap king."

"Coo."

"Yes."

"You was married but not churched, eh?"

"Yes."

"The other's not interesting. Read me some more about Rachel. What kind of clothes did she wear?"

"Usually none."

"Haven't you no description of her clothes?"

"None. Look, Gracie, why listen to all this? Tell me your life and I'll write it down in a story. That's more interesting."

"Ooer, my life? What are you talking about? I'm just ordinary. Nothing from the common, I am."

"That's why."

"I'm a bad girl."

"Good."

"But I never took money for it unless I was stony broke, honest to God, cross my heart, mayIdieifI'mlying."

"I'll make a note of it."

There was Bob. On these mild mornings, when the clouds are like enormous limbs sprawled in weariness after an orgasm (acknowledgments), we talk about Bob. Bob is a source of great misery to Grace because he done a flit on her. He was a fine upstanding boy, of a good family. His father owned a radio shop. He took a fancy to her, and she took a fancy to him. They fell. Marriage was on the cards, because in those days, and in spite of her father, Grace was a virgin, entirely educated by the cinema in which orange blossom is always depicted as the right true end of lerve. O.K. he had said, looking as much like a conquering gunman as possible. O.K. But there were conditions attached to this business which she would have to fulfill first.

He was poor, and she was honest. O.K. Then why wait for the mere cash to arrive? Where was the point of it all? Bob used to say, with fine buckishness, snorting cigarette smoke and lolling on his sumptuous elastic calves: "Listen, baby, you leave it to me, see?" And Grace would numbly leave him quite alone and puissant in the territory of ideas. "I know my stuff, baby." He

would continue, "'Ave no fear. It'll all be swell. *You* see. Yes
SIR. Oil say." Rolling his small blue beads. "Oil say." He was a
patron of the Albany when he had the money; a strong supporter
of that Swedish maneater, Greta Garbo; a banjo player of no
mean caliber. Above all, a good businessman. Yes SIR. Oil say.
Saturday nights he would feel her furtively in one of the various
cinemas. And one reverberating Sunday afternoon he deflowered
her clumsily on the golf links where they were "courting." O.K. Or
rather, not quite so O.K. Gracie wept a little bit, partly from surprise, but mostly from pain. But Bob soon soothed her with a
fine line of talk, pleasantly salted with gunman slang. Was he a
cheap skate, he asked indignantly? Was he a hoodlum? No. Then
why all the fuss? "When I says something is O.K., kiddo, it's
O.K.," he intoned.

The following Saturday afternoon found her sitting numbly in
the nearest free clinic for the teaching of contraception. Bob was
a clever lad. A wise guy, see? On her finger she wore, with a
frightened air, a five-bob wedding ring. A hefty circle of brass.
She registered herself as Mrs. Smith, and was initiated into the
priapic mysteries. Well, Bob had solved the one pressing problem,
viz. How to keep her wind and water tight. His tenantry began,
with an option on a ninety-year lease later on.

The option, however, was never claimed. Their affair dragged
on for a year or so, through various vicissitudes. Then Bob was
offered a traveler's job in Manchester, which he took in his stride.
Even then there was the vague understanding that if it turned
out all right etc. etc. and prospects were good etc. etc. they would
marry. Not so. A few months later she got a letter full of interesting Edwardian phrases (Bob was a user of Penfold's Manual, *The
Gentleman's Letter-Writer,* sixpence at any bookstall), calling the
whole deal off. Young people, the letter began, often do things
on impulse, recking not the cost. And a lot more stuff about
taking the gentleman's way out, and quotes from Revelation. The
letter she still keeps in her handbag, along with less interesting
mementos—sticky toffees, film photos, lipstick, and a cheap packet

of condoms. Reading it aloud to me, she moons softly and sadly
on the fate Bob left her to. In an elf's voice she tells me how
upright and honest he was in all money matters. What a card he
was, always in demand at parties. Of course the letter, for all its
tragic news (perhaps because of it), she considers a masterpiece
of its kind.

But it is no use trying to solder this old stuff to the present, to
make it topical. In these dog days nothing is (was?) topical except
the fantasy which encircled us. The enormous nubians in the sky
and Gracie airing her repertoire of games for boring afternoons.
Let me drop the historic present. It is a device that looks a little
shallow after a time: as the conjurer I am self-conscious, yes,
there is the aorist. It was up my sleeve all the time.

Gracie *was* my fate: IS dead. A sort of mirage, this word I
cannot grasp. A tinsel moon on a garish back cloth. A circle of
blackness which blots out all new horizons. A rent in the clean
daylight of her yellow, peaky, little face. O.K. But if one were
to start a quibble about temporal realities would the present tense
justify itself? Is she behind me sitting in the chair, coughing over
the latest Film Paper? I do not turn round, because I know at
once that she is. In bed, worn out, languorous, aching with plea-
sure between starched sheets? Yes. But only when I am on that
borderline of the realities when every abstraction has solidity,
weight, volume. I can lift desire in my fingers like this small bud
of a breast. I can see it, feel it. It enters my experience like a
calamity.

Gracie and her merry tricks! Pranks for wet afternoons! The
time we spend sticking pins in the fuses and putting the hotel in
darkness. The solemn, wholesome enjoyment we derive from that
humorless black telephone. Watch her sitting there naked, playing
one of Bob's hairy pranks on the local butchers. This is early
morning, mind you.

"Is that 'Iggs the butcher?" she says, very ladylike in a voice
like a pat of butter.

"Yus, madam. Hit his." The porky assistant wiping his hands

on his apron. Then Gracie, in a frightfully subtly accented voice:
"Do you keep dripping?"

"Dripping, ma'm? (say, Fred, do we keep drippin'?). Yes,
madam, we do."

And Gracie slowly melting down into laughter, gripping her
fist hard between her knees, the laughter gushing up in the wonky
lung: "Then what are you going to do about it?" The click of
the receiver and the endless soft whewing and crowing which
was her laughter filling the little room. What a rich jest!

Against this medallion I offer you another, later, more puzzling
picture; a Happy Snap taken when reality had at last closed down
on us—myself in a black skullcap phoning for a five-by-two cedarwood coffin. *Ci-gît. Ci-gît.*

*
**

To your romantic, whose mind is clouded over by his false
values, the final tragedy of love is death. Not so. I protest immediately against this idea. Life is the one force which has power
to suck tragedy from us—and however untimely the end, we may
be sure it is not too soon. Life has always finished with us when
we forsake it; death is merely the aesthetic convention which the
sardonic playwright bows to. The final touch which shapes the
piece—too absolute and perfect to have any relation to the play
itself. What book is different for the word Finis on its last page?
De Gourmont is right when he says that he who weeps for
Ophelia has no aesthetic sense. True. What tears one has are
stifled in the spectacle of her madness. Life had finished with her,
poor wretch, before death dragged her downstream, a sopping
lily among lilies. I leave Rimbaud to follow her downstream to
the shallows, the white wretch among the lilies, with the white
lily-face turned up pointless under a thatch of flowing hair. The
imagination is shocked numb by this vision of her floating away.
Analyze it, and you will see this is still the reflection of her
madness.

78

Words. Words. So many words. All this, of course, to impress upon you the essential appropriateness of Gracie's death; the absolute rightness of her lying there, in strained white silence, covered by flowers. On her face, as I watched her amiable father screw her down, there seemed to be a strain; as if she were speechlessly interrogating the silence which had become her master. A pretty simile for a dead prostitute? Hush! We shall have James Douglas on us with his stainless battle-ax.

Death caught us on the upswing of events, before life had really staled. A good shove . . . a scuffle . . . an oath in the darkness . . . and Presto! the lantern breaks to pieces on the floor and goes out. I offer you a cedarwood Gracie, with lovely long brass handles, softly glowing, and—Ophelia did not do half as well—*with knobs on.* This is the real epitaph which she composed in one of those last drowsy moments of lucidity.

"Good night bitch," one had said heartily. "Sleep now and get up well tomorrow. I'm sick of your yellow face. Give us a sign of life."

The light was switched off. She lay there in darkness picking the sheet quietly in long bluish fingers. Knowing her as you do, you do not expect any answer to my endearment as she lies there, do you? The light was off; otherwise the Gracie I have created would lie there and stare at me for an age, expressionless, saying nothing. Perhaps, standing there in the dark (literature! literature!) I write myself down as being *aware* of the impersonal stare of her eyes. Truth is more exciting than fiction. I will tell you the truth.

For a moment no sound. Weary, I stand at the door, about to leave the room. I expect nothing more. Instead I make up a dozen or so hypothetical scenes in which she realizes how soft and quivering the essential me is, inside the carapace of brutality. She says, for instance, "Come here, Gregory," and rewards my obedience with a long kiss there in the darkness. Or she says, "Gregory, don't leave me, I'm scared." Dear me. This is becoming cinema.

79

Then, as I stand there, she gives a single husky chuckle and says, *"And the same to you with knobs on!"*

It is an immense comfort to imagine that in those last few days Gracie did find a clue to my conduct. I would like to protest this point with vehemence. If this were fiction I should describe how I stood there, my ankles turned to water with relief, seeing that at last she understood me, had found the perfect formula of reciprocation.

Perhaps, after all, truth is less exciting than fiction. This is the high spot of the tale, the crux of our relationship. "With knobs on" is the summing up of all our differences, the epitome of our love. The critical point, as when, in any Russian novel, the Christian protagonist, having speculated for pages on the properties of murder, actually *does* poleax his grandmother. Unfortunately I must renounce all those rotund literary effects which would give this nail paring the place it deserves in my history. Take it for what it is. I can only protest feebly, it is the truth. The one true touch of passionate banter which had been missing from the beginning. Perhaps, after all, it is I who am the romantic. Gracie's epitaph and swan song, in one phrase, was this: *WITH KNOBS ON.*

In the West Norwood Cemetery where she lies, you will see nothing but the bare inscription above her. They would not let me write on the tombstone: Here lies Gracie, who died in 1927. *WITH KNOBS ON.*

With the final accurate banality of his class her father ordered the mason to engrave on the expensive marble the immortal jest: *GONE BUT NOT FORGOTTEN.*

We sent her down with an armful of magnificent flowers, as sumptuous as any cinema star's, and this vain promise of memory. What that frail decomposing husk demands from this, my life, is a pound of living flesh. I am paying here, too, however shyly, in green blood. Of the humorous eternity which stole Gracie to add to its collection let me remind myself walking among the bazaar of white masonry, the many tombs, to the one hideous tomb, garish with cherubs and scrolls: I say over and over again to myself: "The real epitaph is WITH KNOBS ON."

*
**

But I have anticipated cruelly. One of the unfortunate things about a personal style, a personal journal, is that one assumes one's reader's knowledge of all the facts. A journal, then, if written for oneself, would be all but meaningless to the world; for one turns, not to the spadework, the narrative, but to the most interesting points in it. Look at me. I am in such a hurry to finish the job that I blurt out the end before the beginning. It is going through me at such a pace that I cannot distinguish the various flavors of incident, in their chronological order. (I am a liar. It is artifice which dictates this form to me.) Or the word death, like the word finis. If you began FINIS. "She died that I may live etc." It makes no difference. It makes no difference. If the title page were Finis she would still exist, amorphous, evocative, musky —a white kelpie luminous on the last page.

(Think of Ion lapsing off the white rock into the sea, which gurgles over her like a solid blue myth. A sheath of water over the hips, the pectorals, the little plantagenet chin. Down, down, turning and bowing among the white chalk of defunct squids and the pedestrian deep water. Ion is death translated in sudden luminous terms by a live myth. Ion is dead, long live the myth. Write a large Finis with the keel of a liner. Ion lives, I say triumphantly, she lives. Here I can put my hands on the warm basalt and feel her breathing grass into my mouth. I am losing the thread. . . .)

One assumes (if one must resort to ordered sanity) a complete knowledge in the reader, I repeat: and simply supplies a few twirls and flourishes—a cadenza in green—to ensure one's personal fame. All diaries have been written for an audience. For the sake of posterity then, let me add a flower or two to Gracie's public posy. Let me supply a few knobs, in all admitted vanity—which is humility.

There is the business of Clare, who, like Blake's stranger, came and took her with a sigh. Knowing Clare, I can imagine pretty well the form that seduction took. Gin the foundation, romance the actual rubble, and a fine tight cement of flattery and tinsel. How often have I seen the same dreary hook baited for the sentimental miss. Poor fellow, he was unhappy. He was misunderstood. There had been a great tragedy in his life—the expression of which was intensified by the gin and balloons. He would not openly talk about it, even when pressed; but as Gracie once said, "You could see it writ all over him!" Oil say! Under his carefree jazzing, his glittering façade of smile and insinuation, you could see vague hints of this secret misery: like patches of damp on an otherwise white ceiling. Poor Clare! It was love that had done this thing to him. The hang of his blue-black head proclaimed it. Singing as he leaned over his partner, the tears would come into his eyes at the stark pathos of the words, the curdy weeping of the saxophones. "Love," he sang softly, caressingly, "Love" (with a four-beat rest) "brings out the gipsy in me." Everything pivoted about love. And Gracie (this is the suburban princess, remember) danced, staring away over his shoulder like a blind cat, knowing only that her breathing was quickened by the pressure of his hand on her backbone.

Sometimes in the spot dances he cupped her breast in his hand and pulled it with sentimental melancholia. The implication being that his own private tragedy made him a trifle abstracted—a remotely romantic playfellow on the lines of Jacques. For Clare even motley was ever so faintly tinged with a fetching misery. A modish melancholy was his evening wear. Gracie was enslaved and enchanted. Several times, a little tipsy after the ball, she allowed Clare to savage her (with sentiment—how else?) in the taxi which my bounty had provided. But all this was mild stuff: a routine performance that everyone expected of him in taxis. She experienced it sedately in the character of almost-a-wife, or married-but-not-churched. It was when he demanded slightly more that the vaguer mists dispersed and left her face to face with the spurious reality which they had manufactured. Here was lerv, after all. And to Gracie Love was the largest and most violent flower of Romance.

Clare, you see, felt after a bit that Gracie ought, by rights, to fall in love with him. It was his trade, was it not? And he ought to fall just a little in love with her—enough to reach the bedroom. This is what produced the mangy pantomime in which the part allotted to me was that of Sir Jasper Maltravers, Bart., who held the mortgage on Grace's little property. My snarls were supposed to echo among their honeyings. It helped Clare no end to have a bona fide villain for the piece, to set off his own gasconading flourishes. Unfortunately when the time came . . . but I anticipate.

On the question of loyalties Gracie was fairly strong. It would be unfair to take my money and forsake me for Clare. "Nao, nao. Play the game, I says to myself. Play the game. Gregory's been a chum to you, I says, and don't forget it." This was nice of her. It was just this self-conscious pinch of honor that complicated the machinery of love enough to make the whole show interesting. When Clare beat the window ledge of the taxi with his fist and snarled that he could not do without her another second, she felt a little numbly afraid. Perhaps (she hardly dared to think it) he might do something rash. He might *do himself in.* And Clare, thoroughly piqued, worked himself up into a rage and began to be scathing. She was gutless, that's what she was. She didn't love him enough. Or did she? Then why wasn't she prepared to forsake all for love? Wasting her life on a little shrimp like Gregory, with no more romance to him than a bulldog . . . etc. etc. Grace was very miserable. They comforted each other after these outbursts and she began to think that she must really be in love with him. They tried every recipe in the cookery book of emotion. One week Clare would grow a little morsel of honor on his own property, and swear that she must remain true to me, and not give their love another thought. And Grace, mutely nodding her head, would squeeze a few loyal tears from her eyes with difficulty and enjoyment. They emoted frequently together, these little fictions adding a real spice to it all.

On the Saturday night in question Clare, very drunk, was more importunate, more fetching, more melancholy, more honorable, and more tragic than he had ever been before. He was furious with Gracie. The fact was that he had met a brewer's daughter in the Paul Jones who had invited him to her Brighton villa for the weekend. Now if it had not been for the spurious love between him and Gracie he could have accepted: just popped his partner into the taxi and said good night. Gracie would have jogged home, while he could have taken the wheel of the sports car beside his little financial corner in Pale Ale. It was this Homeric LOVE that mucked everything up. Forced to accompany his Juliet home he was furious. Gracie must pay the damages. Accordingly he raised hell in the taxi and sent the mercury climbing. Grace was persuaded that they could neither of them live another day without crowning their passion. It became imperative to hand me my little piece of suffering.

I was sitting by the fire when Grace came in, tears in her eyes, sniffing mildly. Instinct kept me silent. I pretended to notice nothing. Sitting down in the chair opposite me she said, in a small, creaky voice: "I love 'im, Gregory. Ooo I love 'im." If her eyes had been less alarmingly blind I might have laughed. Closing Gibbon demurely I switched off the wireless and asked for details, with the familiar sensation of freezing along my abdomen. It was no joke playing a part in Clare's idiotic masque, I realized. So fair and foul a day I have not seen. She told the tale sadly enough. It was when she said, "He says I must go to 'im tonight or it's finish to us," that I became alarmed. Here was my cue. I could see what was expected of me. Either rage—I could kick her out—or calm husbandly understand. "If you think you love this man, Emily, I shall not stand in your way, but pray to God that this passing infatuation will pass and you be restored to me whole . . ."

Actually I said casually, "Do you *want* to go?" She didn't really.

She only wanted to imagine herself going. Ah! How good to break the tedium of domesticity with a few rows, scares, alarms. Yet my pride demanded an immediate vote of confidence. Silly, but perhaps pardonable. As for Grace, as you know, she was just Plasticine. I could have convinced her in a half-minute of the false position she was in. She was simply waiting to see which was the stronger force, ready to be carried away by it. Numb as usual, and a little pleased that for once the elements had decided to break over her head. It was, she felt, in some curious, inexplicable way, tragic. . . .

Everything would have been perfect if it had not been for my pride. That half-second's pause after I asked whether she really wanted to go was enough to outrage the professional husband in me. I knew of course that she hesitated simply because she *did not know* whether she wanted to go or not. She would never know. But to hang fire on a point like that . . . Obtusely I said, "Well you must go, of course, if that is the state of affairs." This, you see, begins my perverse business of torturing myself. "Go on. Change your clothes and run along." (Why did she not protest?) She sat there with her toes turned in and said nothing. I fiddled in a ladylike way with the fire to restore my nerve. Repeated, "Go on, Grace." It was a delicious sensation, like standing on the edge of a cliff. Would she, after all, go? By God, she would pay for it if she did! "Get on with it," I shouted angrily. "Hurry up and change."

She got up slowly and sniffed her way into the bedroom, a little surprised, I imagine, that things were not turning out as she planned. She must have had a queer sensation of losing control over events. Here was Gregory, after all, acting right out of character. He was neither the jealous husband nor the understanding domestic pal. *What* was he?

She changed into my kimono with the parrots on it and returned to find me sitting in front of the fire, deep in Gibbon. I had taken the opportunity of putting on my skullcap. That, at any rate, gave me a superior monastic mien which always worried her a little; and whenever nervousness over a domestic or foreign crisis seized me, I immediately donned, as they say, my little skullcap. It gave me a sort of fancy-dress confidence in myself.

"Well," I says to her I says with hearty monastic exuberance, "you're ready, then?"

"Gregory," she said suddenly, "it wouldn't be fair of me. It wouldn't be playing the gaime."

I pooh-poohed this vigorously. "Fair, my dear Grace, what are you talking about?" Getting up I took her arm in order to call her bluff once and for all. I felt a little sick. We walked slowly to the front door of the flat together. She was puzzled by now—and a little afraid. Her arms were cold under the garish sleeves of my kimono. She hung back slightly, hoping I would prevent her from going at the last moment. Really, she began to realize that she didn't want to go one little bit by now. At the door I released her arm and said: "Quietly, now. Don't let Morgan or Charles see you, or we'll have rumors. Good night." I pushed her gently out, shut the door on her, and switched off the light. Outside the colored panel of glass I could see her still standing, staring in at me, puzzled, unwilling to go. Then, hugging her cold hands in her armpits, she turned and vanished.

Gone! For a second I was so surprised that I could hardly believe it. She had actually gone. And in *my* kimono, too—the final cruel touch! Then I was in such a sudden panic and rage that I could have done anything. The names I called her! Enumerating all those sterling qualities in myself that she had spat upon by this outrageous act, I returned to the drawing room and poured myself out a stiff brandy. Someone must be made to pay for all this! Someone must pay! O.K. I sat down to the piano and began to murder Beethoven.

That night Tarquin called. He had been sitting in the lounge reading the *Criterion* and waiting for Clare to get to bed safely. He wanted to know why they were so late. Had they got back yet? I told him bitterly, "No." For a second I was profoundly shy; and then, rallying, I told him, "Yes," with details. It was his turn to be profoundly shy. His distress accounted for a decanter of brandy. So abject he was, so miserable and hopeless, that I almost began to bless the event which was the cause of it all.

"It's not that I'm jealous," he said in one of his rambling attempts to excuse himself. "It isn't that at all, as you know. Dammit, I'm not a greengrocer. I've read Petronius and I agree with every word. One must be free, don't you think? Yes, I'll take a small one. No—WOA! Don't fill it up like that. Where was I? Yes, freedom. I don't grudge him love, Gregory. I'm as modern as you are. I mean we're not greengrocers, are we? We've read Petronius and we agree with every word. He must be free. It's his spiritual love I want. Try and understand, Gregory, try and understand. You are so self-contained, you don't feel these things. I'm more mystical. Try and imagine my loneliness. Since Mother's death I've needed to be looked after. I've needed care. I want to be spiritually cherished, that's it. Spiritually cherished. *If only that bloody little gigolo would confide in me . . .*"

(Think of Ion among the deep-water statuary, the hotels of the Greek waters, in the latitude of myth, dabbled by the delicate noses of fishes.) I say to myself, I do not care. I do not care. Let the liners go nosing southward, cutting her in slices. "O God, hear my prayer," says Tarquin in private. "O Lord, hear my despair. O Lord . . ." He vomits green like a horse. The piano is playing. The books wink on the wall. Ion is a vase with many dancers. The myth precipitated in milky chalk at the bottom of a beaker. This is the isolation of hemlock. Ion! Ion! I am losing the thread. . . .

The rest you know.

Here Gregory ends.

*
**

Shadows in ink. The hotel with its blue shadows in snow. The convalescent blue of phthisis. Brother, I'll be that strange composed fellow. In the darkness they hang out Japanese lanterns for the festivals. In the pandemonium of the ballroom the bunting sliding the floor in a long swoon of color. Antiques gyrating forever, pictured by the mirrors in their gilt scrolls. The jazz band plugging away in the din; and in the barrage of drunkenness our hearts ticking over, squashed upon each other's in pain. Darkness cut and blanched by the trembling spotlights, seeking the winners. You with the silver mouth and devil's eyeteeth I could rive; press my arm into the arch of the backbone until the lean breastless body thawed and melted, pouring over me in a wave, like lighted oil on water. I locate this night dimly as the one where Lobo sat out in the rainy gardens, under a striped awning, making Miss Venable weep. Onward. Onward.

It is so silent here at night. This tomb of masonry hems us in, drives us in on ourselves. Ourselves! I am getting a little like Gregory, rolling the heavy chainshot of the ego about with him, prisoner. Here in these metal provinces, we are like dead cats bricked in the Wall of China. The winds turn aside from us in the dead land, the barren latitudes. I tell you the trams plow their furrows every day, but nothing springs from them. The blind men walk two by two at Catford.

Overhead in the darkness the noiseless rain is shining down over the counties. The pavements are thawing back to black asphalt. In this room the madness has set in, goading Lobo to finish the chart. Delicate, the dark gigolo Clare treads the mushy street, cloaked and hatted, to a dancing engagement. The heavy signature of the mist glazes the dumb domes of the Crystal Palace: the final assured vulgar mark of Ruskin's world on history. In Peru they hurry to early mass. The streets are baked. The peasants stand with their lice and sores and almonds in the church doorways. And his girl—ah! his hot little Latin world of little black men. If for a second he could reach her across the chart, across the bottles of ink, across the cockatoo on his pencil-box cigarettes, shopgirls, frost, wind, tram lines, England—if he could only seize her and escape . . .

Black Latin Whore! We, sentimental, send our desires to you

across the sea like many furling gulls. But after Dover imagination fails. The gulls waver, tremble, fall, are sponged out by the mists. . . .

In the saloon bar, Connie, the brewer's widow, awaits Clare. (One of her frilled garters hangs over Lobo's bed—a gravely humorous present from one libertine to another.)

Connie possesses thighs like milk churns. Her mouth is an old comb full of many sawn-off teeth. Her laughter sets the froth dancing in her mustache. Dancing with Clare she sweats like a sentimental seal under the armpits, pants, moans, a little sentimental when the word love arrives in the tunes. Offer her a beer and she will sit up and bark like a sea lion. You could balance a glass on her nose as she sits there militarily, her behind overlapping the swivel stool. She sits down on her vulva. Watch her now. So. The circular head of the bar stool is applied to her bottom, penetrates the soft swathes of blubber, disappears. Infinite subterranean shuffling. One imagines the warm endless penetration of the padded stool in her viscera. "Jesus, she's well sprung," says Perez. Then the springs tighten. Giggling, she is sitting up there on her own neck. Her eyebrows perform gigantic arcs across the night. She is gay ha ha. The tank is full of ha ha. She loves the warm herded smell of males in the saloon, wet overcoats and whiskers, rich smell of steam and underclothes and armpits. She has been married twice. Barroom gallantries. "Oh, *do* 'ave another glass of beer, miss." And the shrill drafts of piss from the urinal which comes in at the swing doors. Men, men, men—how she loves the warm smell of herded males! She could take a man in each arm and slobber on him with that wet mouth of hers. She could slip a thick finger in their flies and tickle them. But Clare? He excites that superficial side of her which wants Romance. Oh! the sleek lateral waves in his hair. Oh! the delicate Levantine manners (how painfully acquired by post and study). Clare sucks little purple cachous that his breath, when he blows it on her, may be nothing less than royal honeydew. All the perfumes of Arabia cannot rinse the gin from it, however. He dances gravely with her, leaning on her whizzing exuberant tits with a sort of locomotive paralysis. Thumping, her great thighs propel them. Vast effort, as if they were dancing under water: spurning the floor, the walls, the band, the rotating glass dome which shivers splinters of prismatic light across the dancers. Gin brings out the pussy in her. Gin, and Clare's hoarse crooning. He knows the words to all the tunes. His hand is palm outward on her spine, a genteel Edwardianism.

Connie's eyes are glazed. For the last hour or so she has been diminishing, become steadily more diminutive and pussycat. In the interval, downing her beer, she has become a child of twelve again. "Hair down to here," she yelps, striking her arse, "but me mother took it all off. The dirty old sow." Dancing again, her intimacies are outrageous—even here. She has shrunk up on his breast like a wee girl now, like a bird nestling on his necktie. She peeks up at him with a panting smile, her little lascivious bud of lips pursed up. She can feel it stirring down there, like a live thing. The tight rod he has in his trousers now. She is diminishing, melting down, thawing. Ah! she is such a thumping, swollen, four-teen-stone, *weeny* little thing!

In the lobby she puts her hand on him. "You've got it," she says nervously, as if he might be playing a trick on her. There might be nothing in there. "You've got it, haven't you, ducky? Oo I can't wait."

Afterward he will have to take her home and undress her, layer by layer. She will lie, like the Indian Ocean waiting for him—one vast anticipating grin, above and below!

Shadows in ink, and the strange composure of syllables. The quilt lies heavier on my bones than any six-foot earth. I am living out hours which no chronology allows for. Which no clock marks. If I say I love you I am using an idiom too soiled to express this cataclysm of nerves, this cataract of white flesh and gristle which opens new eyes inside me. I am opened suddenly like the valve of a flower, sticky, priapic: the snowdrop or the anemone brushing the warm flanks of Lesbos. A daemonic pansy opening to the sun, stifled in its own pollen. The delicate shoots are growing from my throat. From the exquisite pores of the membrane the soft vagina of the rose, with the torpedo hanging in it. The furred lisping torpedo of the bee. O God.

It is above all the silence which is remarkable. The last train to the world's end has gone. The last bus skirts Croydon or Penge —what matter? In the tram terminus the deserted trams lie, their advertisements quenched in the smoky gloom. Corralled like horses they await the milk-can morning. Lochia. Rags of blown paper writhe among the snow. The dirty skeletons of the day's news. There is not even a prostitute to brighten the cavernous roads. Hilda has gone. A real old-timer, the only one. Married a commercial traveler to give the fetus a name and status. Status! Extraordinary how sensitive she can be. Alas, poor Hilda. A raven of excellent jest, Horatio. The way she breathed beer and onions on one: the great cheesy whiffs of damp that blew among her clothes! As for the wretched fetus, if it could have spoken through its gills it would probably have dealt as curtly with its ancestry as Gregory. "My parentage is Scotch, if you must know. Well, northern. I am not sure, really. I am sure of so little. At any rate *my soul* wears tartan!"

Hilda, at any rate, swaggering up and down the bed in her pink cotton kilt—Hilda, with the great hanging sporran of red hair over her pelvis! A raven of excellent jest! Perez would take handsful of this rufus pelt up in one hand and blow on it playfully. "What have we here, Hilda? Feathers, my love?" Hilda with the great voice like a bass viol rasping out command and insinuation. Her gas-lit bed is a parade ground, a barrack square; her voice is all history rolled and boomed and rapped out in one's ears.

Like a gaunt rat she lived between the pub and the tobacconist. In the snow she scuttled across the road splay-footed, ducking under the lights of snoring cars, to buy herself a packet of fags.

Hilda, the fag end of the sentimental dreams I cherish! The
memory of her is a sort of scarification, like wounds the aborigines
keep open on their bodies, rubbing irritants into them, reopening
them until the resulting ornament is something to make the whole
tribe envious.

Hilda a-decorating Newcastle. I imagine vaguely docks. Hilda
among the lights and tar and feather sailor boys: the whole fairy-
land of breathing steeples. Forsaken, a gaunt rat by the water. All
night the lick and splash of inky silk. Pillowed on the flood's broad
back, the elastic steeples inhale and exhale their panorama. Morning. The child miscarried, and shortly after the legendary husband
died. Perez, her only real friend, has got a letter from her, inco-
herent, blaring, tear-stained. A poem on violet paper with an
anchor for a watermark. We still read it aloud when we want a
good hysterical laugh. Hilda, and her rich pithecanthropoid contortions! Here, under white ceiling, planning an equipment of
words to snare these hours which are so obviously secure from
the dragnets of language: lying here, what sort of elegy can one
compose for Hilda, for Connie, for the whole rabble of cinematic
faces whose history is the black book? Shall we people a catacomb
with their portraits? The last tram has gone. The epoch from
which this chronicle is made flesh, when I think of it, is an explosion. My lovely people like so many fragments of an explosion
already in flight—Hilda among them, flying like a heavy bomb,
northward to Newcastle. Madame About died in 1929 of uterine
cancer. I, said the sparrow, with my bow and arrow. Tarquin
died quietly while he was pouring himself a cup of tea; and
showed up for dinner without a trace of his death on his face.
Scrase, the golden-haired son of a cash register, himself hard and
tight as a fistful of blond cash, was emptied out of the autumn sky
to keep company with Icarus. In the snow there is a hail and
farewell for Perez, for Lobo, for Chamberlain. . . .

Am I the angel with shining wrists scraping out their microscopic beauties in God's ink? The shirted cherubin! See, I take a

mouthful of ink and blow it out in many colors at the sky. From that fragile column fall one or two figures—these my shining darlings!

*
**

On that portion of time that is a Saturday printed on paper, over a quotation from Genesis, I go and inflict myself on the Chamberlains. In his flat one could sit for centuries without anyone knowing you were there.

Chamberlain himself sits in the armchair with a lighted pipe in his mouth and tunes up his little ukulele. Very softly and nostalgically he sings the following ditty, in one of its numberless homemade variations.

> *Dinah!*
> *Has a lovely vagina!*
> *Why, it's like an ocean liner,*
> *And my Dinah's keen on me.*
> *Vodeo do do etc.*

Dinah is his wife. She says, "Stop that." He stops it. She says, "Make up the fire." He makes it up. She says, "Begin toasting the muffins or we'll never have tea." He rests the toasting fork negligently on the fender, and returns to his art. Very softly he begins, in a queer voice, full of pipe and nostalgia:

> *Dinah!*
> *Can you show me something finer,*
> *Than the portable vagina,*
> *Which my Dinah keeps for me?*
> *Vodeo do do etc.*

A prediluvial world in which I can sit at rest and watch the whole pageant pass. The shadows in ink, the chart, the green diary, the mathematical cones of snow towering up to heaven, the desire, the kingcups opening between my toes. I wish the summer would come. The winter of my discontent prolongs itself into infinities of boredom, and this moment is the only radiant instant recorded on the spools of time. Here, in the pipe smoke and worn books with nothing but the great warm personality of the fire in the room. The muffins festering on the prongs, and the lion-hearted coals. Outside on the steaming lawns St. Francis is picking the lice from the sparrows. It is all gone, I am saying to myself; it cannot last. She has gone away into the country of the frozen lakes and the stiffened hedges. Hilda wrote: "I don't see what I done for God to treat me this way. Perhaps because I been a wicked woman. When the child was seven month on I felt in my bones that something might happen. Now God's torn it properly for my sins."

And the other letter which I carry about with me stiffly, like a withered limb: "It has been snowing and I am lonely. I wish I could cut you off and carry you with me wherever I go, inside me. I could be warm. I lie in bed and imagine it."

Chamberlain reads the single page, puffing at his pipe. He gives it back without comment. Later on in the evening he says: "Other people's love is a little disgusting, why is it?"

Or there is Tarquin, in the character of the great artist, tracing his history in literary cadences which are not bad, considering everything. Art is a disease, he is always saying. Massaging his shining cranium he will read strophe one of his great symphonic Bible to Peters. Thus:

"Where shall I trace those first parents of mine who generated all history by the first faulty contact of sperm and ovum? Where the faulty placenta, the first deviation of the fetus let down delicately on its cord to rock in the amniotic fluid? How shall they be celebrated? Where shall we see the first microscopic flaw in function which gave us the world of fire, of stone, of oxen, of numbers, of terrors—*and of Gods?* Perhaps I was swung between the loins of a troglodyte, natural as fruit though faulty, in the

94

womb of blackness squeezed; my head out of shape, my cretin's eyes pressed out under sweet sickly white lids like those of a fish; my limbs shoved out and shinbones bandied. I am sure my brain was jumbled in its sack, teased by bone pressure, until I laughed, lolling my head back, heavy, heavy, to protest that the sun was night-black . . ."

Ten years' hard polishing have gone to shaping this opus. Polishing of prose, of spectacles, of the great bald cranium. He sits, like a polyp, and waits for applause. A little scared that there will be none. After all, ten years . . . Needless to say, this is the only piece of the symphonic Bible extant. He tries to pretend that there is more of it, but there is not. "It's not in its final form," he will say prettily if you ask. But one examination of his notebooks when he was out one day convinced me that this great artist never finishes anything. Even the diary has its off moments. Or January the 3rd, 5th, and 19th occurs the sublime thought, "Nothing of note."

Well, even I get hard up for material at times. That is what brings me to the snow. It has been snowing again. Again! It has never stopped. When I was small there was a fugitive summer at the seaside with Uncle Bob, and Wendy. Wendy now, the rugged little apple tree, with her soft bark, her solid knotted little stance, the heavy poised apples inside the green shirt. Wendy like a short sharp bite into a sour apple. Pippin-bright face and lips with the spittle shining on them forever. Holding her down in the corn while the yellow corn shuffled over her head and fell in her eyes. When I am lying touching the soft cornfield with my hand I am apt to wake up with an apple between my teeth. Wendy!

But this is a snowscape in indigo, nubian, cobalt, ash wednesday, gothic, Fiume. I am walking in the dark streets with your letter in my hand. All that is coming from me is a sort of saga in answer to it. I can feel it coming from my body. I am so unhappy that I would like to spend my remaining money on a whore—if there were a whore to be found. Alas, poor Hilda.

It is in this area of the night that I come upon Morgan in the dark street. There is blood on his waistcoat, his hands. A strange agitation in his eyes. "There's been an accident," he says, licking the snow from his chin. "At the station." Snow settling on his eyebrows, ears, lying in little drifts against his collar. "For Christsake." He beckons me into a shop doorway. It happened tonight as he reached the station to meet Gwen. A sudden roar and a puff of black smoke. Terrified he was down there on the line, scavenging among the broken carriages before he knew what he was doing. "She's O.K., sir. Missed the train. But what a mess, you never seen such a mess." His hands are agitating themselves about a packet of cigarettes. One carriage copped it fair and square. Five people literally cut to bits. The doctor was sick. Arms, entrails, and etceteras lying about in the corridor. The doctor was young. His great body is restless, turning this way and that. He does not go back to the hotel at once. He wants to reminisce a bit about the war and the messes he has seen. "I've been close to it many times, sir. But never shook me like this." He is quite voluble. "I thought of *Gwen.* By Jesus Christ, running down the stairs." There is blood on his hands. He helped them gather up the loaves and fishes, the pieces of meat, and put them into sacks. We begin to walk as he tells me this. Then, walking down the huge corridors homeward he lifts his head into the white showers which fill the enigmatic space between us and the moon, and says, in an agony of surprise:

"Pieces of meat, sir. They was nothing but pieces of meat left. 'Ot and steaming, as true as I'm walking here."

If it is not too late I shall go up to Tarquin's room for a spell of mutual condolence and misery. Or he will be sitting there at his little piano curiously upright and military. It is as if the music were working him, not he the music. Like a man suffering an electric shock he sits there and watches his own big hands act. His technique is supposed to be flawless but satanically hard (*vide* Gregory). He loves the romantics, dwells on their long snot-curdling melodies with a resigned pathos hanging in his big eyes. Emotion only seems to reach him with difficulty, by osmosis. That is why his taste is so emotional. From the terrific shivers and orgasms of the music he draws some infinitely small private thrill. The rest pours over him. Wagner, now, that is his comfort. In flocks and shoals the heavy volumes pour down over him, filling the room; he sits under a waterfall of music, an icy douche. Like a flower his heavy head floats on the surface. "Wagner," he says breathless, standing up with the music running off him, knuckling his eyes. "Wagner!" And smiling, "Wonderful," panting hard from the coldness of the shower.

On such evenings I am too preoccupied to applaud the maestro, so, recalling that literature is my main interest, he will utter a few lines of the diary aloud, not looking at me, like an incantation. I will ask: "What is that?" I know quite well what it is. "Do you like it?" he will say archly. "Yes. What is it?"

Then we will have an interesting little session of reading aloud. A post-mortem on the psyche, that delicate butterfly which lives behind the pale walls of his abdomen. Or he will read me the famous last chapter of his immense (unwritten) work on Bach, which ends with the terrific epigram: "It remained for *Bach* to make mathematics humane!" He must really write the other chapters one day soon, he says meditatively, don't I think? Of course I do. I am obliged to contribute some form of sociability to the session, because after all, it is his room. I cannot face my own. I cannot face the dead books, the stale sheets of poems, badly typed, the littered drawers. The bed, my six-foot tenement, the ceiling where the fantasies hang like bats, and squeak like a million slate pencils. If Lobo will come for a walk I am grateful, with a real humility for his company. I do not speak much, but it is good to have a companion to walk beside.

On these cold nights Lobo is quite hysterical about Peru, waiting for him out there beyond the ocean. He tells me of the streets with the brothels, warmly lighted, the radios going, the guitars: the innumerable doors with their eye fents hungry with black eyes. The dark men crossing the streets like ants to their assigna-

97

tions. "It is so easy," he says mournfully, "so easy." Compared with this arctic world he warms his hands at Lima. . . . Ah the Rimac twisting under the bridges, the shawls, the parrots (damn those parrots!), the family friends, so many bloodless hidalgos: the whole machine of traditional family life turning over, fault- less. There was a girl friend of the family who used to go down to the seaside with him. Hot sand; his fingers easing out the creamy chords from the guitar, heavy as milk with romance. She was so ardent, so full of response that her kisses scorched a man —made him wriggle like a sandworm. He stands under the loopy tower of the Christmas tree in a window to tell me this. Behind us the even more loopy tower of the Palace sweating a rank thaw from its million menstruous boils. His face is transfigured by the memory of her warmth. Tears in his eyes. "She was so hot," he says suddenly, and shoots out his hand to my wrists, as if his own warmth of feeling could give me an idea of hers . . . "So hot." I always remember him like that: standing in his immaculate clothes under a leaning tower, while behind the street swirled away its drifts of snow and driven lamps in foam and emptiness. We are deserted in an ocean of lights. His face is varnished under the brim of his hat, his eyes superb. "Come with me," he says im- pulsively. "Let us run away into the sun, dear boy, into the sun, my friend." He flings his head back as if searching for new planets, new constellations. Transfigured. His walk lilts. Then, the snow begins to fall, insidious white soot, and his elation is quenched. His face sours. The melody has gone out of his foot- steps. Sleek, the astronomical manna powders our eyebrows. The wind has driven a nail through my temples. I am stifling. The slow, cumulative concussion of a world of frost crowding upon our world. We get into step homeward. Lights burn dimly behind shutters, without festivity. Wax lights, floating in bowls of childish water, guarding the dead faces of sleeping infants. The snow howls and flutes among the immense concrete corridors, smothering volition, desire. A train scouts the uttermost outposts of the stars, tracing an invisible ambit. Venus and Uranus up there, winking like lighthouses across the white acres. The spiral nebulae spreading wider and wider, like pellets from a celestial shotgun. The earth under us, creaking and ancient, like a rotten apple in the teeth of an urchin. Wendy! A rotten green apple, decaying to the brown of a pierced molar under the snow. Wendy, with the heavy apples in her green shirt, the firm warm bullets of breasts in a snowstorm of reason, killing me. You will understand, lying out there among the ironed-out lakes and fields, you will understand this panic of separation that is hardening my arteries with tears.

Invisible behind this aura, which strikes our heads like a clown's baton of feathers, trying to fell us, the red giants and the white dwarfs are at play. Galactic imbecility. It is a season of the spirit in which the idea even loses its meaning, loses the bright distinguishing edge, and falls back into its original type, sensation. Words are no good. If you were to die, for instance, it would mean snow. Palpable, luminous, a shadow in ink. And your dying too fatal to reach me when the wind is up among the trees and there is laughter inside the dark houses. When the telephone rings I say to myself: death. But it means nothing. Like a hot iron passed over a tablecloth—the white fabric of your face ironed suddenly into insensibility. I choose this word rather than any other, because in the past it had the most power over me. Now the idea itself is starched and stiffened back into a nothing of white. The elastic snowscape and this atmosphere which we breathe into our lungs like a rusty saw, is all. Is all. Is all ...

These abstractions crossing and crossing the drunken mind; and we on a planet, buzzing in space across the alphabetical stars: the creak of the earth curling away into the night like a quoit, like the creak of cable and spar on a ship; and only this mushy carpet on which to tread out our footsteps toward the final wedding with loneliness.

Does the endless iteration of loneliness tire you? It is the one constant in our lives. Even when the night now is spotted with shadows whose dapple seems to present a graph of this emotion. Oh, behind it, I know—somehow behind it in a dimension which

I cannot fathom, life still tumbles across the scenes smelling of pageantry, heroic, wet white, blue goiters, clowns, sopranos, fire-eaters. . . . But we shall never reach it.

This is what must be known as a state of war for Lobo. Woman has at last become the focus for the hate and despair which dribbles away, day in, day out, like a clap: in the red postman morning, in the afternoons over muffins and post cards, in the dusk with the returning schoolchildren—at night in his private lair with only the monotony of the gas fire to suggest continuity in a life which seems to have stopped like a cheap clock.

Hilda is my only anodyne against the white leprosy of the frost. Like the fool of the tarot, the crazy joker of the pack, I wander through the events of the way. The imbecile hangs on the mercy of time like a lily on the river. I have no being, strictly, except when I enter that musty little room, frosted softly at night, where Hilda, the giant cauliflower of my dreams, moves about her tasks. Between the artist I, and Hilda the prostitute, there is an immediate correspondence. We recognize and respect each other, as pariahs do; we love each other, but we do not understand each other. Nevertheless we have made a truce. We share the scraps which life pushes up among the flotsam on that bare beach where those other beachcombers like ourselves raven. This room, this four-poster bed is the Sargasso Sea, with the tides hourly pushing up the empty cans of ideas, desire, hunger with sharp edges, hopes, destinies: crowns, trumpets, hymnals, all tangled in the weeds which grope about our bodies in the long nights. Nothing to suggest tomorrow as a plausible reality except a snatch of midnight song leaking from the bulging pinions of a shutter. Nothing to tell us we will rise again on the third day. That we will be made flesh.

The sheets are dirty. The walls are dirty. The soft bloom of gaslight whispers the items of the day's news. A paper lies on the bed. The lying eye, trying to read it, sees the type blowing past the gas fire, out of the window, like a fine sandstorm. Black signal of the world's disease—the wasting disease that calls for more and

100

more calamities, more catastrophes, to scald the nerves. The world's tragedy is Tarquin's tragedy. He can feel nothing. Hilda's tragedy is that she can feel too much. Her great cow's heart thaws at the least thing. An ignorant, blundering Lucrece, she is raped by the first emotion which impacts on her. What? The Turks are slaughtering the Armenian children? O the *pore* little things. Her tears dribble into dirty handkerchiefs, into her bodice, her shift, her handbag, into the moist *torche-cul* which hangs behind the lavatory door. "You don't feel nothing," she says. "You don't feel for them pore children, you little bastard."

"But, Hilda," I say, "it happened years ago."

"It's in the paper, isn't it?" she demands. "If it's in the evening paper how can it be old?"

She has been reading the first of a series of articles which reconstructs war history. However. I lie dutifully and try to imagine the Armenian children. Impossible. Corfu. Refugees. The Ionian curling along the buttocks of the island. Armenian choirboys making boots. The words echo horribly. In the night she cannot sleep. "I'm thinkin' of all them pore kiddies."

Or Hilda like a great bee moving about in the yellow gaslight, fiddling with her cosmetics, squinting in the pocky mirror. A soft cadaverous pollen blooms along her cheeks, along the craters of her face. Every line means something. This heavy horse face is the Bible, the Koran, in which I can see all my victories and defeats epitomized. The whole word of my dreams is written over by these lines and wrinkles.

I have become suddenly soft and malleable inside, these days. Hilda looms across life like the image of one of those incestuous loves on which one's family repulsions are supposed to be fed. I rely on her. I lie and let her wait on me, like an invalid. I am consumed by this wasting consumption of maternal love. I want this slow convalescent childhood to be prolonged forever. Hilda has created for me a shadow out of the sun where I want to rest.

The time runs downhill on iced feet toward Christmas. A plunge into the crater of time which is chaos, original disorder. This great bed is the ark of desire that drifts quietly down the long corridors of water, down the pockets of dreams, through the veils and mists, *waiting for the dove.* Toward Christmas, and I am slowly being rolled homeward again, to the womb. The core of me is bound up like a fetus, a weak parcel to be slung again between the loins of my parent. I am drifting down again into the great matrix of lovers, the sunspot where all emotions are liquefied, blended, alloyed into the one all-conquering loneliness. The pungent misery that alone can make me feel. Everything else is tidied up, swept away—like those pieces of steaming meat Morgan gathered in sacks. Cupid's loaves and fishes. I have nothing now, no emotional luggage, except this quiet convalescent wasting disease, this drawing away into maternity. I give up, am utterly sunk in death. Hilda is the genesis from which I shall be born again on the third day. If I shut my eyes the whole world is blotted out. I live in the womb as a fish in a deep sea. The cool drizzle of blood feeds me. Like Christ in the soft pouch of the virgin's belly, I wait in a slow dawdling, fish-like convalescence, for the moment of parting: bright cleavage, the flash, the cold air like the smack of a palm on my mouth. The lanterns, the heralds, the warm suffocation of animal piss and white breath in the byres. To leave this world!

Lying asleep I try to imagine it. The babe hooked out of the uterus, coming up gasping, dizzy, like the fish who perform the silver nimbuses around the heads of the fisherboys. The sudden scorch of sun along every scale. The dazzle of light from a million crooked mirrors. The yell of delirium and fire. Then the same stale hook baited again and dropped into the ocean of chaos. The brown-armed Jesus sits there, the intelligence running along the lithe rod to the pink mouths of the fishes. The fishes idiotically kissing the hooks that await them. Every tremor, every nibble runs down the line like a current to the nerves of the brown arms. He sees nothing. Only the fingers feel the currents of remote life in a dimension unimaginable.

Lying asleep I often wonder whether Christ was not born of a

102

prostitute. Whether the tale of the immaculate conception was not some showy literary metaphor of the day, which we translate wrongly. The symbol of the fish; the ray of light; the messenger: Aeious Pneuma! How tolerable the world might be if we could face an idea like that. Mary and Hilda, with the breath of plenty blowing in their souls, the gourds plumped with riches. The Christ we have made is a fish: a pale intellectual parasite who has gnawed our livers for an aeon. Son of tragic mother, tragic. The soft intellectual fish of the fairytale brooding in silence on the hooks which he would never have the courage to swallow. Jesus a damp scrotum which has lain for two thousand years on the butcher's slab, under the knife . . .

The great bed drifts on under the stars. Hilda the great quiet maternal body lying here. The bread of life. Her crude paws seeking along one's ribs as soft as the sacramental wafer. Memory has many waiting rooms. We have encountered and passed the spirit which broods on these immense waters. There is no fear left now of chaos. I am like an imbecile child visiting the Zoo. I will never be happier for I will never recover from this soft phthisic paralysis, the absorption into the maternal womb. Hilda is the great comforter.

Or screwing her hat down before the great mirror. The mantelpiece is a morgue of wild creatures, stuffed and petrified in glass boxes. Owls with pained expressions and eyebrows. The gas hangs fizzing on the knotted chandelier. My own reflection in the mirror is turned upside down among Hilda's face creams, cosmetics, underclothes, photographs. The hanged man of the tarot! Hilda's great head is rooted to her trunk with heavy thonged sinews. She turns this way and that so that the cords stand out sharply. She purses her mouth up like a giant sucker to take the color from her pencils.

In the night everything is blotted out except the comfort of this heavy flesh, the comforting pressure of a hand in my hand. I am the infant in the hospital bed: Hilda the incandescent night light which cherishes my death-still face in sleep! Paralyzed. Even

103

the passion itself has become an idea, a figment without relation to myself, the idiot in the truss. Blind, the vast tide spins us on its back, and desire folds up its tent, and misery blooms quietly in passion which is beyond tears. Beyond tears, and gently rocked on the fathomless paralysis of chaos. The night smells as musty as a phonebox. The eyebrows of the owl project a vast travesty of Connie's face across the dark. I am simply a cheap cosmetic touched to the lips in darkness. I provide a color which soon smudges, dims, washes away. The newspaper, like a bomb, lies on the chair among my underclothes. O world, be nobler for her sake!

Blind, in the darkness, the faint images of the world project themselves on the wall. The chart of Lobo. The boundary which we are all forbidden to cross. The passion which winged me until I was an exciting skater, covering the thin crust above fathomless blue water. The wounded gulls for the Latin whore. What have I become at last, that the night has bulged, swollen, burst into pieces? The face of the virgin shines vibrantly out of everything, the virgin prostitute of the fable, grimacing painfully under a throbbing star. A flux of little fishes waits in her entrails, eagerly, for the door to fly open on the world. Fishes with a knowing look —intellectual martyrs!

Here I am crucified at last in the dirty bed. The umpire is the owl with Hic Jacet eyebrows. I am at peace at last, fingering the nail holes, like the mad actor. It was a wonderful house tonight. Seven calls before the curtain, not counting the whole-cast ones. Across the trembling, deflated womb of the vision the curtain slips down giddily, bearing the one apocalyptic word: *Asbestos*. (If any mystics call before I'm through, just show them to the dressing room among the gauds and flowers, will you?)

The great bed drifts on among the planets. The snow has stopped. The sky is familiar again: clean and shining, with a harvest of brilliant prickles. The airs are the impalpable cerements that clean our bodies; the essences of the embalmer soak into our bones. Poor parcels of soft rank flesh, with the wine and

cigar smoke blowing in and out of our nostrils, what should we
do with the souls that are supposed to inhabit us? The moon is
peeled like a billiard ball. Hilda is crying for the Armenian chil- *Cashel*
dren who are really her own. Shall I tell her that she is Mary? She
wouldn't believe me. That her time is drawing on now for the
son of man to be born? One must avoid alarming her. Tomorrow
the door of the womb will be rolled back. Tonight, drift on among
the familiar constellations and dream. Sufficient unto the day is
the woman thereof. Blind, the night has shrunk to the dimensions
of the wasted penis—the hollow reed in which life is carried and
generated: shriveled under the taut stars like an empty paint
tube.

O world, be nobler for her sake!

*
**

Items of our peculiar death. This, in the category of epilogues,
though the show has not ended.

January brings the first raw cleavage of weathers—a blind hint
of the merchandise which begins to fructify under the snow.
Foxes' ears underground, odorous, odorous. From the chalk breasts
of Ion an Ionian asphodel. As always, the weather I am continually referring back to is spiritual. Winter is more than an
almanac: it is dug in invisibly under the fingernails, in the teeth—
into everything that is deciduous, calcine. Winter, as the figures
produced by the shadow of the retinal blood vessels on an empty
wall. I tell you it is part of the spiritual adventure, like our meeting in the snow, and the great arterials stretching away to God
like a psalm; and you, gathered in the snow, a soft cave of flesh.
That is why I am marking down these items in the log of that
universal death, the English death, which I have escaped. It is
lonely work. For each day there is a blank space to be filled. I am
not as industrious as Gregory. One thought of you melts down the
old fount of words, the runic, the mantic, the mystagogic, so that
if I so much as dare to lift a pen I find the nib clogged with a

lump of lead. I suffer your absence, but I cannot reconcile myself to it. It is as if part of my spinal column were absent. I cannot stand erect, but slouch like the Pekin man. All night now I am writing. . . .

Winter morning. The slow painful birth of something raw. Lochia. All hair and embers. A wound across low ridges of cloud. A celestial snail has trailed its slime across this valley. All feeling obliterated. The room, my coffin in immense shadows. At half-past five the whisky has given me such a bellyache I cannot sleep. I draw the curtain and stand before the fire, confused by the explosion of fitful dreams in the consciousness, arms hugged under armpits, watching the morning lift. Toes cold, nose cold, belly cold.

In the vacant bar the ash of the fire must be gray, the empty glasses upended in the sink with the froth stiff in them. I remember with a pang the rowdy company who stood about the blaze, the gold urine fermenting in them. The fine smell of rye whisky, gin. Crisp green pound notes. Acrid cognac that caught one's throat and moved along the veins in spikes and needles of feeling. At one gold tilt here was a crown of thorns for any Christ among us. The shuffle of boots, and punctual tap of phlegm in the spittoons . . .

Lobo is away in Germany on holiday. An occasional post card with an inevitable obscenity on it arrives from him. Tarquin is very interested. "Tell him to *describe* it in detail," he says angrily. He wants details. Tarquin himself lies in bed, with a shawl round him, sipping Bovril. He is hurt because Clare has not been to see him. He will stay in bed until the gigolo's pity is aroused. For weeks, if necessary . . .

On the fifth there is a storm. Lightning and vast thunder running along the ribs of the Palace, shivering fire and quake. A woman killed by a roof tile. Driven slates skiddering in the snow like little snowplows.

On the sixth I wake to find the world finally snowed under. Drifts a foot high on the roads, in the gardens, cemeteries, playgrounds. That statuary coy and naked, ankles rooted in the white quilt. Morgan with a red nose, sneezing his head off. Big fires howling in the lounges. Every visitor who opens the front door sends a great ringing blast of air down the corridors. Death creeps in among the other scents which run laughing from one end of the hotel to the other. A breath of cold as piercing as ammonia eats our nostrils.

Altogether a curious expectancy hangs over this day, as if I am expecting something utterly momentous to happen to me. Or perhaps the world. I scan the paper, but there is nothing to justify this premonition. War has not been declared. The nature poet occurs on the middle page. Snow. Bird and holly. Even this is not the expected cataclysm. All the old invocations served up in meter: I can never understand this frightful brand of Englyshe Countrie sentiment, with its inevitable false rhyme which is so much more annoying than no rhyme at all.

> *The robin hangs upon the bush*
> *A jewel in the winter hush.*

Altogether nothing is happening and there is the huge feeling that something has happened or must happen. Traffic disorganized. The postman dispenses his spurious cheer of dishonored checks and late greetings. A very merry Yuletide to you and yours. Tarquin will not let me draw his blinds. He knows, he says, that it is a bloody day and prefers to spend it by candlelight.

> *The robin twirts upon the bough,*
> *The postman has a nasty cough.*

But nothing turns up; the anticipated Thing leaves me in suspense. Then.

At teatime, buttering toast in Tarquin's room, swallowing my spittle at its appetizing flavor, I am approached by Charles, the deaf mute. On his little tablet he has the hieroglyph: "The flat telephone. A lady."

I hound down those immense corridors like a convict. Everything is silent in the room. I think suddenly of Gregory, I don't now why. Gregory has just gone up for a breath of air. I put the receiver to my ear and it is cold. You are talking suddenly in that pure animal's voice. Gracie is lying dead in the bed. It is unrolling through me, your voice with its queer frigid tones, a fugue of snow and cattle, and our bodies like lumber on the white quilt. I am sitting here like a drawn fowl, feeling my viscera dissolve and flow down over my knees to the carpet. You are taking a holiday, you say. A holiday! From what? And, above all how, when every latitude is swollen with desire and unrest, every meridian poisoned? Here I will show you my wounds like Mercator's projection. A new cartography. Forgive me, I did not mean it. You cannot help the snow. There are four candles in the room. Yes, and the first edition of Baudelaire. Books? Do not send me a book. Not even the Song of Songs. You cannot sleep with a book! No, there's no comfort. Hullo, can you hear me? No, not even poetry. The nerve centers are all dead. Send me a scalpel, a bright new scalpel with the cutting edge of prophecy to it. Send me a poleax, a humane killer. Why do you not speak to me? Hullo. Are you there? Then go on speaking, because I have nothing to say to you. Nothing. I am being burnt inside with the old damnable bruises. To hell with books, do you hear me? I said nothing. Good-by. The Italian towns are lying there crippled among the priests and the Mother Church. Give my love to Keats. Are you weeping? After this I shall go to bed and order a bowl of snow. I shall press it to my face with trembling hands. A month from now we shall meet, you say? If I could believe in eternity as a few slips of printed paper with numbers on them, I might find you intelligible. Speak to me. You are speaking but it is like water squirted over a statue. Say something sharp, decisive. Speak me a scalpel or a jackknife. No, I am quite alone. The laughter? I heard nothing.

As you are about to blurt out something comes the bright cleavage, I return to my buttered toast on the top floor. Premonition fulfilled. I am suddenly aware of the dullness of the evening, the snow closing with its blue breath; old women in their prisons knitting, milk, hassocks, prayer books. Gales of fire in the lounges and old men dressing for dinner. Tarquin in bed, surrounded by the bones of history, dying piecemeal in life, dying. There is no one I can turn to for comfort.

A gale of wind has begun to ripple across the world; the poles are toppling over into the blue fluttering wings of snow like doves. There is a glacier running slowly in my blood. My skin is chapped and rough as canvas.

I could go quietly mad here, in this room, by this three-day cadaver who sits wrapped in a shawl, decomposing. One of these days you will find me lighting matches and holding them to my mouth. The last kiss under the mistletoe, the last druidical idiom of departure on the wet mouth.

"Your rustic besom?" says Tarquin nicely. He is being very tactful and dramatic. He would sell his soul for a mouthful of schoolgirl confidences. I lie to him, but I can see he does not believe me. His nose quivers like a carrot.

Come, you attenuated skeleton, with the razor nose and the one foot in eternity, let's brim a negus to the death of the world, to the snow, the calamity of whiteness, the doves, the harlots, the music. I mean a real toast, with laughter that is not a cheap swindle. This desire was too delicate an infant. By God! we'll make a man of it.

BOOK TWO

If the spring ever breaks in this district it is with an air of surprised green. A momentous few weeks of fruition in which the little unwary things come out in their defenseless, naïve way. The soot and the metal paralysis soon eat them. The canker of steel rusting slowly in the virginity of the rose.

The cold weather drives us breast to breast in these chilly form rooms by the iron stoves. A raw fug of anthracite and unwashed bodies. The children fart incessantly; and in the form room upstairs Marney, the hunchback, sits down before the fire and spreads out the sodden folds of his handkerchief, sniffing. As the rank menstruous steam goes up he will throw over his shoulder some such profundity as: *Es este obrero quien fuma?* or *Somos nosotros quienes hemos hablado al banquero?* All winter he has a roaring cold, and every day his sopping handkerchief is dried at the boiler thus. The children squeak and fart and hold their eternal palavers behind his back. The air tastes faintly of steamed snot.

This is *Honeywoods*. The two suburban houses telescoped into one, gathered, as it were, under the armorial banner of Eustace Adams Honeywood, Esq. Inside these rotting brick walls, in the bare, unwashed rooms, the children parade themselves daily, in a vain attempt to master the principles and practice of big business. Outside, the trams pass, rocking and hooting, cannonading the windows in their loose frames. The big green board is chipped

113

and faded, and whitened with pigeon shit. The gutters sag and the lightning conductor twangs on the wind like a harp string.

All this is custom now. Familiarity has bred, not so much contempt, as a sort of unreasonable love of the place. In the crooked little vestry, which is the holy of holies, Eustace himself lies all day in a sleepy coma. On the door is the decomposing post card on which he has written, at some time before the flood, the glyph: *E. A. Honeywood, Director.* That means you must tap before entering in order to wake him up. Prediluvial, paleolithic, geologic —there is no chronological qualification which expresses accurately the age of this community. It is outside chronologies.

This is a reflection from the little desk behind the door at which I maunder through the day's work. Next door, from the typing room, the symphonic racket of typewriters leaks across the ocean of papers, of files, bills, acknowledgments. The so-called English mistress, with no roof to her mouth, is dictating a few anthology pieces and classics for the typewriters to reduce to Morse.

> *Tomowwow and tomowwow and tomowwow*
> *Cweeps in this petty pace fwom day to day.*

The desks are humming and the inkpots dancing. A mild solo of nose blowing from the Commerce room where Marney is drying his handkerchief and teaching commercial Spanish. Dust along the floors, and a poisoned sunlight along the windows. This is the time when the blackbird opens up her drumfire, streams of soft-nosed dum-dums on the stunned fields. The captive canary in the corner completes its millionth exploration of the world, and falls asleep. It is bored. Spring has broken like a bucketful of pounded ice and we are still working our feet in our shoes for warmth. There is some irrational problem about Keats, and the nightingales spinning silk in my mind, battling with the sleep. The crepuscular morning opening like a vegetable, and this soft decay in which we either work or sleep. At a precise point in the meditation, when I have reached Greece, or Carthage, or the Syrian lions spitting gold dust, Eustace will open one lidless blond eye and say: *"Carm on, me lad. Get on with that letter."*

"It's done."

"Oh." And he will fall asleep again, wringing his ear peevishly with his finger; or else walk up and down importantly, one finger and thumb searching in his waistcoat for something he never finds, fussing and moping, taking off his glasses and replacing them, whistling through his teeth, or sucking the sore spot on his thumb. Eustace is a queer cuffin. If he farts by mistake he pretends nothing has happened. If I fart he is indignant. "Remember you're in a college with young ladies, me lad," he says stiffly. If I reply, "Hoity-toity," he will pretend to give me the sack. This is interesting because he cannot do so. I am his secretary, true, but our agreement is not monetary. In return for my services he allows me to spend three days a week learning typing. A gentleman's agreement. Hence Keats, hence the lions spitting gold dust, hence to long comfortable dozes in which the whole world is gathered up in a grain of birdseed and handed to the canary. From a private secretary to a mascot is a short step. From a mascot to a house-keeper . . .

"There's that smell again!" he says. I take no notice. Keats must come first. The subject of faulty drainage is as old as Noah. "Do you notice it?"

"Yes."

"It's the girls' bogs again."

Faint drafts of cheese or cosmetics or soap and sweat, and then a long curling whiff of this vegetable odor. Someone will have to go into that fetid little tabernacle and prize open the cistern. ("Plunger won't work, eh? Yes. Yes. I'll have a plumber up to look at it.") It is not the first time. Keats' poetry, I say firmly to myself, rattling my knuckles on the desk like the bones of Judas, was the product of his disease. Five more years, three more years even . . . "Miss Ethelred complained this morning that the pan won't flush," Eustace says suddenly. "I can't make out what that girl eats, like. It's *always* her blocking up the bogs. Once more and I'll

115

sue her ma and pa." The faint whiff like a boiled pudding, engulf-
ing Keats, Venice among its floating furniture, Severn, and that
little cock teaser Shelley, like a blob of pus scribbling, scribbling.
Or Hamlet with the incandescent father? "Listen," he says, "do it
just this once. I won't never ask you again. Just this once."

I am glad, for the sake of this mythology, that Marney takes it
into his head to come seesawing down the stairs at this precise
moment, to contribute his gothic charade to the morning. Here,
his hunchback figure, foreshortened, wagging down the stairs.
First the legs and body, all splayed, then the little knot of the
head; like one of those carnival figures they carry on poles in
Italy. His nose hangs down like Notre Dame in gloom. As always
when he sees the hunchback, Eustace finds a vein of broad jocular
humor spring up in him. One has to be like this with him because
he is so vain, so terrifying in his vanity. Quick, pretend that he is
not deformed, that he is a great brisk normal man. We experience
a panic of embarrassment; we become servile in the face of the
gigantic egotism of this little East End Jew. "Ah ha!" yells
Eustace, "so it's you is it, Mister Marney?"

Marney's head sits back on his hump, perpetually cocked up at
the ceiling. In order to look at Eustace he makes some compensating mechanism hold him forward, stiffly, as if thrust out on an
invisible stick. He is smiling his glittering self-satisfied smile, opening and shutting those little pale mushrooms under his nose. He is
snicking amiably now, pulling down his waistcoat hard. "D'you
notice the smell, then?" roars Eustace with incredible joviality; and
Marney, scenting a joke, demands vot smell he means. "A smell
I'm talking of, sir. A smell what's been bothering us today."
Marney is acting for all he is worth, sniffing and pouting, his
vanity throwing up images of himself, now in this pose, now in
that. "It's not me," he admits at last, "it's not me vot's made it."
And from this piece of wit grows Eustace's deep false bassooning
laughter, and the queer snickering of Marney—like someone
swishing a cane. My cue. I contribute a modish snicker to the

party, politely, as befits a secretary who can't help overhearing. We are both nervous of Marney.

The hunchback's dry knot of hair rides his scalp as if in the grip of a hurricane. His face becomes so taut with laughter that one fears it will suddenly fly into a dozen rough fragments, like a canvas mask. He is breathing right in the mouth of Eustace, leaning on the desk, offering his amusement to the blond man, who sits in utter disgust, laughing back at him. Once every twelve snicks or so Marney's body suffers a sort of tiny compensating convulsion. It is like watching a shirt pass through a wringer. His arms are tossed wide, his head comes down. Then the magazine of laughter is emptied snick snick snick. Shall he tell us what it is? he says at last, archly. Shall he? It's the girls' lavatory. They follow each other out into the hall; Eustace is driving him back deliberately now, laughing him back to his room. And Marney retreats with self-satisfied unction, snickering and louting. Projects himself uncouthly upstairs again like a crab, while Eustace keeps him on his way with little squirts of laughter. Then back to his desk, swearing under his breath, disgusted, outraged, humiliated. Marney! Eustace sitting there furious with Marney, in his little polished black hoofs, with his blond hair falling away on each side of his head.

The human comedy! The divine drama of a blocked shithouse all entangled with Marney, the little brown hoofs, the bucket of green ice and the canary setting out like Columbus every ten minutes and ending like Sir Walter Raleigh. The adventure of the ship, like a wooden body, and the spiritual adventure in the tower. I am not trying to muddle you. It is only that I myself am muddled by these phenomena—the snow, and Marney's raw Spanish tulip, Eustace and the impotence of being earnest. If I look at him now he will be a little ashamed, remembering his laughter. In order not to let me see this, he will turn aside to the little mirror on the wall and examine the cavities in his teeth. From the lavatory a boiled pudding; from the hall where the coats hang like the girls' playground selves, waiting for the clock, a whiff, human, sweaty, polluted with cheap scent and rice powder; from Eustace a pert fart—just to show that the equilibrium of his sunny temperament is restored.

It is not what one thinks, I have discovered from the books I read, that is important; it is not even what one does. It is what one is, essentially. That is why there is such confusion when I set out in an attempt to begin this spiritual adventure, because the fine logical borders of my reality completely disappear when a word comes to seize them; I attempt to put myself in jail, as it were, in the padded cell of language, only to discover that the whole external façade is implicated in this process. There is the ego, plus a number of fantastic appendages, with personal pronouns attached to them. My desk, for example, behind the door; my spring, filling my bowels with mushy ice; my Eustace too, my Marney . . . It is a rapacious mechanism which attempts to swallow the world. In it there is no paradigm of irrelevances. Everything is included in this dragnet—as one might set a lobster pot one night and find a continent in it when the sun rises. The hotel breathing quietly in a snowstorm of electric light; the existence here in which there is neither faith, hope, nor charity; Lobo sitting like a disconsolate robin (a Peruvian robin) by the locked door, waiting for Miss Venable to open to him; or Eustace sifting his voiceless farts through his underclothes and hastily opening the window. (And then, to annihilate this confusion of realities, today there is a wind blowing up from the Levant. The morning came like a fog along a roll of developed film. . . . It is a little unreasonable.)

I am sitting at the desk when Ohm appears, agitated, sweating. He teaches economics. His slack black coattails mourn agitatedly behind his thin back. His mustache lies down wearily on his lip. His corncrake voice is deeper by two tones than normal. Imagine a small soiled penguin with a weak backbone and broken flippers. That is Ohm. For Godsake, he is saying, Eustace must do something. There is one of the girls howling her heart out and he cannot find out what is wrong with her. His violet eyes are full of tears. She does not seem in pain but she is. . . . Eustace puts on his glasses and asks, where is she? Outside the door? Have her sent in at once.

She is there all of a sudden, a rather fine-looking girl of about fourteen. Thick bronze pigtails, and her face trampled with weeping. All of a sudden she says, "I'm bleedin', sir." A strange mixture of fear, shame, and puzzlement. Bleeding? The tears are running down her face again; she is giving out enormous male sniffs. Then, with her throat full of fog, she points at herself queerly and says, "I'm bleedin' down there, between my legs, sir." And before we can say or do anything, she falls down as softly and expertly as an adagio in front of the desk, in a faint. The confusion is immediately precipitated like a Morris dance. Ohm beats his own coat-tails in a wild dash to the telephone and starts ringing up a doctor. Eustace and I pick her up and put her on a couch. Perhaps the poor girl stabbed herself with a pen nib or something. For a while we chafe her hands and Eustace calls the English mistress in, who lights trails of brown paper and holds them shakily under the girl's nose. There is whispering in the commerce room, and peeping at doors. The whole school is shaken to the roots. Then someone suggests examining her. "Yes, yes," flutters Ohm like a ballet dancer. "She might be bleeding to death." The English mistress declines the privilege out of modesty. She has no roof to her mouth, and also she is scared. Besides, she could never be able to explain coherently to anyone afterward, supposing she did find out. Well, one of the older girls is called in, and we males retire. In ten minutes the English mistress comes out with a scarlet face, and runs to the lavatory to have a good weep. In the commerce room they are whispering: "What? Her period? What was all the row?" etc. etc. The doctor, when he arrives, gives us the news in stilted throaty medical terms. He is proud of knowing the terminology, it seems. The English mistress asks for the day off to get over her blushes. She will be bleeding next if she's not careful. "It wasn't *that* I was scared of," says Eustace, contemptuously. "Silly little Winnie. Them girls get up to queer tricks sometimes. Ah well."

He is smiling now. Expelling his noiseless laughter out between his teeth with gusts of cigarette smoke. The temperature chart has fallen to subnormal following the anticlimax. Ohm stands there in his soiled penguins and gives a giggle of relief, then catches his boss's eye and becomes flint again—passive, soiled, immobile and very shy. Suddenly remembering, Eustace sits up and says, "Mr. Ohm, sir." The violet eyes sink to the ground as he stands there, waiting. "Do you notice a queer smell, sir, in here, sir?" The eyes flash up to Eustace, to me, flutter and wander out into the garden. He does not sniff or move a muscle. It was as if he were sniffing with his mind. "No," he says harshly at last. "No, sir."

This question of the boiled pudding steaming in its rags! Or Severn drifting down among the floating furniture in a birdcage across Venice. If it were in my choice I would reject a petrarchal coronation—on account of my dying day, and because women have cancers. (This is a spiritual adventure, not the memoirs of a plumber.) "Do it please," says Eustace, "do it for me this once and I'll promise it's the last time." Ohm has trotted away through the yard door, to his desk in the economics room. Inevitably someone must go into that little hole and prize open the cistern lid to make the plunger plunge. Eustace is sitting there leaning forward, with an anxious, preoccupied look—as if he can hear the shit slowly piling up. "Go on," he wheedles softly, miserably.

In the end I take an improving book and retire to this little tank-like lavatory under the dusty staircase. The walls breathe a beautiful moisture. It is as cool as a butter dish. From the high window I am in direct communication with Madame About, with her irregular verbs. "*Cela passe toute croyance,*" she announces suddenly in my ear, graciously. A question is asked. The sounds are all hollow and resonant. The gracious old woman with the ringed hands, and the aristocratic preoccupation in her eyes; the secrecy of things aromatic, leaves, ferns, under the snow-like silences. I imagine the candid profile upon the window, drenched in its own privacy. Everything is peace when the children enter her room. No rebellions, no hates, no hysterias. In the summer

120

afternoons it is like a dream, time slowly flowing across the class-room, the blinds swinging and freckling the girls' arms and throats. Dust on the windows and the trams smothering by, shadows across the window, passing in cinematic briefness. On the dais she has cupped one hand in the other and is talking quietly to herself, tired to the point of sleep. She does not like helping me to read French verse; it disturbs her thoughts, disturbs this oil-on-water afternoon, and the coming and going of breath in her mouth. At four she will sigh and dismiss us with the benediction of relief; screw down her old black hat with long pins, slide her books into the leather satchel, and go, gathering up her skirts like a ballet dress. Down the dark staircase into the sunshine, along the hot pavement by the playing field where the trees crisp together.

In the lavatory I close my book, disturbed as I always am by the reflection of Madame About's inner privacy: the qualitative superiority of aristocracy, which brings out the tradesman in Eustace and quenches the children without a word. I am a little sentimental about her, thinking of the tall black queen treading the new grass of the playing fields, passing down Green Lane like a breath of tranquillity in her bulging patched shoes; the cherries dripping from her hat, saluting the hips and haws, and the new things which bud and stiffen along Ruskin Manor. Passing along the logical cricketers like a premonition of absolute death, shadowing their angel white with her black rustling clothes and silence. It is too real, the drama which she offers to this common, rather mean and shabby reality. Sometimes, sitting at the wooden desk, watching her face set stiffly in thought, I have the sensa-tion of intruding on her, penetrating the façade of preoccupation which separates us. But this process is always taken up short. She is aware of the potential trespasser in me. When she catches me her face breaks into that perfect lazy smile, and I am ashamed of the obviousness of my interest. I am confused by the smile, the flower that opens upward from her throat. . . . Madame About like a black summer hypnosis dominating a form! What I am try-ing to get at is the almost dimensional quality of her difference from the others, as we might be a formula—the same class passing from room to room, teacher to teacher. The teacher a catalyst which changes us. I am thinking of Marney, and the subterranean hate which connects him with the pupils. Marney is a relic of the Middle Ages; there is the feeling that one day a chord will strike, a cable snap, a wheel turn—that the whole class will rise to its feet and stone him. Marney's face is always visible, eroded, weathered, lined with vanity, staring at us from a hundred cathedral gutters, from gothic buttresses, corbels; or running on hands and feet before the avenging stones of the mob. Often, sitting among the form, one can feel the temperature of emotion take a sudden deep curve up, at some small gesture of his, some vain remark; I can feel the hair tighten on the scalps of these thirty girls as they stare at him. At such times, if he dares to make a joke, the laughter is so harsh and bored that one winces instinctively. But he seems not to notice, turning on the gridiron of his own vanity. When they get him properly on the run the rage sets his face small and hard; his nose thins, eyes sink back into his forehead. He is like a bird. And this rouses the girls. They want to goad him to the end of emotion; they are flushed with rage and a kind of sexual happiness. They want him to burst into tears or foam. But the same class will pass into the French room, and sit as passive as cattle, faced with the complete stoical passivity of the old lady. Madame About, celebrating an eternal inner spring, though the heavens are falling; have fallen, I suppose one should write. I was not there on that August afternoon in which one of the many chronologies claimed her; yet I am there, watching the death mask smiling, with the flower in its throat. ("If this is imprecise it is because I myself am muddled.") By the same method she is here, if I brood on it among the islands, the flutes, and berries: among the lambs leaping to the ceiling, little flossy bombs of spring. Among these hesitating pages, scribbled with emendations and images. If you must write there is no forgetfulness, and no memory. The only periodicity is in the time of poem. Very well, Madame About to waltz time, in a new scansion, with a cadenza of death in it. Or

Marney as a dactylic elegy, punctuated by the brassy spondees of
nose blowing. It is not difficult to explain. On the mantelpiece is a
clock. The hands stand to quarter-past six, and it is striking twelve.
By these tokens I know that it is exactly ten past ten.

*
**

At last, the summer has shut down on us like handcuffs. There
is hardly time to dream. Dust, brickdust, sawdust, soot. From the
Parade the city is carved into misty nocturnes; the muslin girls
are out, salt and baubled beauties, each hugging her dream—
romance. The dream which has not come true. Even the trees
chafe, as if eager to up roots and away. And I am entombed in the
asphalt city, watching the summer as if from behind bars. On
weekdays, as an inhabitant of this world, I am glad to escape from
the hotel. At night, racing along the lanes homeward, I wonder
whether this is not a solution to things: an eight-hour timepiece
divided into illogical portions, telling me when to eat, work, sleep.
It is not purely a question of food; I eat, yes. More than that, I
have fourteen horses of my own consummated in bold steel to
carry me wherever I want. Yet I am not happy. All the roads lead
outward; the buses hum and dance along the roads, packed. Slim,
the slanted, silk-stockinged legs batter past me in dust—pillion
riders heading south. They are so certain of their summer, the
eyes behind mica goggles, the man at the wheel, the stern driver.

Tarquin is away on holiday. He is going to find fulfillment these
days, he tells me. It is the key word. Fulfillment! He lies in bed
and thinks about it. "I think if I could be broken open somehow,"
he broods, "it would be good for me." We had a stag party not
long since with a few of the bored local youths, Peters and
Farnol, at which he became screeching drunk. Night, if you can
imagine it—a hot summer night with the hotel mains all fused. We
were sitting there, lighting old newspapers in the grate and drinking. "Sometimes I feel so damn stale inside. Full of stale air and
microbes. I dream I am suffocating. I go into a room with an ax,

and there I am lying on the bed like a plaster cast, full of dust. Honestly. I lift the ax, one two three . . . My head cracks open, rolls on the floor, I break in half; and the room is full of dust, the hotel, the street, everything thick with dust. Then I look at the plaster and *there is nothing inside!*" The little gingerbread gods of suburbia sitting there with a bored look and Tarquin canvassing for sympathies. If you say something really intelligent they will lift their glasses and drink absently, to avoid thinking about what you say. If you fart they will scream with laughter at your wit. Afterward, whirling down the scented country lanes in the car, Tarquin suddenly bellows: "Perhaps I need speed. More speed. I want to get the air in my lungs." And begins to cry out, *"Faster, faster, faster,"* until Clare fills him to the gills with gin and puts the rug over him. Fulfillment!

Clare himself has gone north to stay with his mother. That is why life is unbearable for Tarquin. One day he thinks he'll go to Salzburg for the festival, the next to Antibes, the next to Athos. As a compromise he goes to Brighton, in order to be not more than two hundred miles away from Clare. I see him off at the station. He looks ill and bewildered, standing at the carriage window, as if he were being taken into the next world. His lips tremble. He grips my hand fiercely, afraid to let go, "Perhaps a girl," he says. "Eh? Listen to me, damn you, when I speak to you. Perhaps I could find fulfillment if I married, eh? A girl. I might find a girl, what do you think? I thought it all out the day I said good-by to him. I hate journeys. I feel so damn worn out these days. If I had children and settled down, eh? The pull of domesticity and all that stuff, eh?"

The train begins to draw away. I can think of nothing to say to him. "It'll be all right," I say idiotically. "Don't you worry. It'll be all right." He leans over clutching my hand, drops it, reaches out, smiles. The distance stretches between us, slowly, fluidly, like chewing gum. He cannot let go on the known world. "O God," he whispers, "I don't want to go. I don't want to go." And the engine shrieks. His face moves across the sky like the face of death itself. Fulfillment!

In the hotel the sour carpets putrefy among all that other furniture, real or imaginary I cannot tell. I am no longer sure of the outlines of the real, so that men and women themselves take on a curious impermanence, mixing together like shapes and symbols in a cinema mix-in.

A letter from the underworld, too, which has a curious dusty flavor when I read it here.

"Dear Puck," you say, "everything is altered now with the first spring things, the first delicate flowers. Everywhere there are delicate arteries thawing, and the earth turns over on her side to let the seeds wake in her. The cottage lies quietly in the shoulder of the hill, under the discipline of day and night. When do we meet?"

I am reminded of Ishtar going down every year into the territories underground, the atmosphere of dust and ashes and silence; and the slow vegetative revival of life, the corn springing from the navel of Osiris. The rain dazzling on the enormous eyelashes of April. The English Seasons, so nostalgic in death, cherishing their decay in heavy loam and delicate rain! It is something unknown. Spring under the ledge of the Ionian weather, that is the image which has swallowed the cottage, the April, the drizzle among the corn; your letter reminds me of the sea among the islands, played out, sluggish, inert like a heavy blue syrup. And here? Dust on the window frames, dust on our hands, our eyebrows, and the racket of machines.

At night Peters tells me about his genius, comparing it to the genius of other men past and present. "One must be a man of the world," he says shyly, "like Eliot, don't you think?" I offer him those portions of Gregory which contain nostrums against the literary evil eye, and canons for novices: *"Books should be built of one's tissue or not at all. The struggle is not to record experience but to record oneself. The book, then, does not properly exist. There is only my tissue, my guilt, transmuted by God knows what*

125

alchemy, into a few pints of green ink and handmade paper.
Understand me well. This is the ideal being we call a book. It does
not exist. And when I talk in this knowing way I intend you to
imagine the work of genius I could write if I put my own princi-
ples into practice. Alas! I am too well-read to make the attempt.
Or perhaps well-bred—because in order to write one must first be
convinced that every book ever written was made for one to
borrow from. The art is in paying back these loans with interest.
And this is harder than it sounds."

Well, this is no concern of mine. Gregory's little struggles with
his logical self have a flavor of putrefaction here, at the desk behind the door. Whenever I become too conscious of this suburban
house, this suburban world, whose symbol is the map Lobo is
drawing and never finishes, I leave the stuffy vestry in which
Eustace walks and whistles, adds, picks his teeth, sucks his pipe,
consults his tin watch, and climb the stairs to the room which is
marked "General Knowledge." There is one solitary occupant; an
inky personality which belongs purely to the world of the image.
A negress. Miss Smith.

She sits, carefully segregated from the pallid northern pupils
of the school, working away at The Life and Times of Chaucer. It
is curious. I am compelled to sneak up to the top floor three or
four times every day to assure myself that she is still sitting there,
lost in the Middle Ages, with the window at her back looking out
like a blind eye on the yard wall. Unreal! But what does one expect? You cannot expect her to have the reality of, say, Monday,
Hymnbooks, lunch intervals. She does not compete. As I say, she
belongs purely to the world of the image. Against her there is only
Zanzibar, mandrakes, Marco Polo, El Greco, and the Dead Sea.
Try to make her plausible and you will find yourself mixing her
in a stew of images, torn limb from limb from the mythologies of
Asia. She is my one connection with the lost worlds. I treasure her.
I would not know what to say if she left and deprived me of that
world of myth which I can see so clearly at work in her.

You see, I sit beside her for two hours every morning now, expounding Chaucer's language to her, about which I know nothing whatsoever. This is a concession from Eustace. She must get lonely up there, all alone, he says: and no one really understands that blinking Chaucer but me. "And no mucking about with her, my lad," he adds uncomfortably. "Her father is a famous African judge."

"Miss Smith," I say sternly, "are you aware that this language you are learning will be useless to you?"

She cocks her poll down shyly and emits a snigger, laughing behind her hand, as if she were shy of her white teeth. It is fascinating. She laughs at everything, chuckling shyly in her sleeve. It is pure Zanzibar, tiger tiger burning bright, monkeys, pagodas . . . everything at once. This insatiable giggle of hers gets in among my thoughts, and shakes the world to pieces. A negress in bright clothes, laughing down her sleeve, at a school desk. Chocolate carpets of amusement, hissing between four walls, under a blind window.

Miss Smith powders her face heavily, snapping her flashy crocodile-skin bag open and shut. She plays gracefully with her features above a pocket mirror, like a dissatisfied gazelle at a pool. Her breasts are large and languid inside the European clothes. Her hair has been artfully clipped into the shape of a bob. It reminds one of those stiff topiary privets, clipped into forms, against the natural grain of the foliage. But it is useless. With one laugh I am across Zanzibar, colored stamps, yellow sharks, vultures, Chaucer, lipstick, Prester John, Ethiopia—moving in the rare air of the image, whose idol she is. It is useless for me to say to her: "I have seen women like you carved in ebony and hung on watch chains."

She will laugh in her sleeves. Her eyeballs will incandesce. Her red Euro-African mouth will begin to laugh again. It becomes impossible to walk hand in hand with Chaucer on the first Monday morning of the world. The laughter penetrates us, soaks us, winds us in spools of damp humorous macaroni. Beads of Nubian sweat break from the chocolate skin, powdered into a matt surface. Miss

Smith sits forever at the center of a laughing universe, her large languid tits rotating on their own axes—the whizzing omphaloi of locomotion. African worlds of totem and trauma. The shingle deserts, the animals, the arks, the floods, carved in a fanatical rictus of the dark face, bent hair, and the long steady pissing noise under the lid of teeth.

All she can do is laugh in her sleeve and powder that black conk of hers jutting from the heavy helmet of her head; when she pisses, pressed down, squashed over the sound box, from the laughter spurt jets of hideous darkness, a storm of Zanzibar, like black treacle. . . .

That focus which attracts us all so much is centered, like a cyclone, over sex. You may think you are looking at her, looking at the idea of her, but really, seeking under her cheap European dress, you are looking at her fertility. The potential stirring of something alive, palpitating, under her dress. The strange stream of sex which beats in the heavy arteries, faster and faster, until the world is shaken to pieces about one's ears, and you are left with an indeterminate vision of the warm African fissure, opened as tenderly as surgery, a red-lipped coon grin . . . to swallow all the white races and their enervate creeds, their arks, their olive branches.

Always I find myself turning from the pages of Geography, of flora and fauna, of geological surveys, to these studies in ethos. The creeds and mores of a continent, clothed in an iridescent tunic of oil. I turn always to those rivers running between black thighs forever and forever. A cathartic Zambesi which never freezes over, fighting its way through, but flowing as chastely as if it were clothed in an iridescent tunic of oil. I turn always to those exquisite horrors, the mutilations and deformations, which cobble the history of the dark continent in little ulcers of madness. Strange streaks here and there you will find: hair-trigger insanities, barely showing, like flaws in ice, but running in a steady, heavy river, the endless tributary of sex. They feed those fecundating rivers of seed which flow between the cool thighs of the

Nubian, stiffen in his arteries, and escape in steaming laughter down his sleeve. Look, if you dare, and see the plate-mouthed women of the Congo Basin, more delectable than the pelican. Vaginas turning blue and exploding in dark flowers. The penis slit like a ripe banana. Seed spurting like a million comets. The menstrual catharsis swerving down from the loins, dyeing the black carpets of flesh in the sweet smell, the rich urao of blood. The world of sensation that hums, dynamically, behind the walls of the belly. The slit lips of the vagina opening like a whale for the Jonahs of civilization. The vegetables rites. The prepucophagous family man: the foreskin eater. All this lives in the wool of Miss Smith, plainly visible, but dying.

It is this aura of death which seems exciting to experience, to speculate on, as I watch her sitting in this attic room, surrounded by charts of the prehistoric world in which Chaucer still farts and micturates debonairly. The black and the white latitudes gathered together in one septic focus. Hush! She has no idea of the disease of which she is the victim. Her face is so beautiful among the medieval castles, the hunchbacks, the swans, that even Tarquin is dimly affected by her. From his diary he read me the immortal phrase in which he put down (in clean light Chinese brush strokes) the essence of her. *"Like a black saucer her mind is, shattered among a million white saucers."* And reading it, walked gravely up and down, fingering his temporal lobes. "Hum. Hum. Yes. To judge by the shape of the cranium I am a man of sudden terrible rages. Hum. Hum. I think," he said at last, "I would marry her perhaps, what? Do you know anything about her? Would she marry an Englishman of good family? It would be decorative even if I never fucked her, what?"

I am reminded how, sitting here at the desk, I have persuaded her to read aloud to me sometimes. For preference not Chaucer or Lydgate, but the macaronics of Skelton which she seems to find amusing and interesting. Shut your eyes. Her voice, softly timid, comes hoarsely out of her throat, manipulating the wooden symbols of the English, infecting them with strange distortions, a curious scansion which rings a new nerve in the cranium. Strange colors glow in the lyrics, shades of rhythm like drumbeats, semiquavers, quarter-tones, what not. Nascent, even under the gnarled belching world she explores with its turds and turnips, flows the river. The whole Zambesi, poured through a cheap print dress and a tube of dentifrice. The Nile emptied word by word into a glass of milk.

Next door Marney is sitting at his desk, head in arms, listening to the bacilli gnawing at his spine. His hump softens, slackens, spins, breaks in two, and the microbes pour from his vetebrae chirping. He is fighting his dark angel. It is no good. He remembers the woman in the damp room, the anthracite, fog, dirty underclothes, french letters, covered in jam, holsters and machinery. He is forced to his feet, forced to rock down to the lavatory and stand rigidly over the pan, furiously knocking himself off; feeling his breath patter faster and faster in his mouth, the bullets of feeling riddle him from head to foot. He holds his penis away from him, as if it were a potato being cleaned in a sink. Afterward he is forced to lean his head against the cold wall. Tiny cries of rage and disgust come from him. He is doomed. Tenderly he buttons himself up and climbs the stairs. He is afraid. The dark angel hangs over him. He opens a book on double entry. The cabalistic ritual of the mathematics soothes him. He expounds a problem to himself, moving his lips, fiercely, aware always of the succubus hanging over him. "Yes," he whispers urgently, "yes, I understand it. Yes."

The lament for a dead sparrow rolls across the planet like a wheel, attaching itself to chunks of England and Africa alternately: a superimposition of worlds. Imagine Chaucer larded in spit, rolled in carvings and flour, turnips, maypoles, ostrich eggs, totems; paddled downstream among snoozing alligators, noses above stream; stirred by the big toe of the hippo, and served with drumbeats and dog shit in a feudal castle, under canopies by candlelight or rushes.

I tell you, when she reads the world moves into a dimension of pure sensation. Her giant mouth moves up and down the page, fuddled with language like a gorged bee, producing ever more sharply conflicting modulations, snoring rhythms, hamstrings, incisions, tubers; woodwind . . . And underneath it all, this obsessive river flowing.

I am sitting here with my eyes shut, watching the language cross my imagination, each syllable a color. A visible notation of images thrown up, theme and countertheme, all mixed in a crazy fugue. All pouring down toward that original center of exodus under the colored dress. The lobster pot of the lost races, into which I am poured with the syllables, drumming down like suds in a sink. The flap of an envelope has shut down over my eyes: I am voluntary, submissive, aching. As I swing down into the darkness I am growing gills again, and an electric tail. My penis swells, turns purple, and my brains drop out of it. I have dropped at last through the grating into the river, have severed the cords behind me, am free to swim in the matrix, the black saucer, knowing nothing. Dimly can feel the sluice of rich gravy drumming along my scales, the slow corrupt delirium of rebirth. Am fed. Dazzling, in the flash of this last moment's reason, I question myself eagerly. Is this amusia, aphasia, agraphia, alexia, abulia? It is life.

*
**

Or else at night, in the open car, under the milky brilliance of the sky, confess my sins and ponder on the Logos with the precocity of adolescent despair. I have the sensation of dying, from the roots of the toes upward, being consumed like the asphodels after a late season. These downtown women remind me of you. The contortions of a whore will suddenly open your face brightly for me, with the eyes sitting there, hard, crooked, merciless as diamonds. The summer is like a drain, choked with filth and bloody rags. This desk is the pulpit from which I infect the world with my despair. The auditors are in, sticking a friendly spanner into the obsolete machinery of the school. Eustace has begun his duel with me. If he arrives first in the morning he will put every bill, form, receipt, ledger, voucher, on my desk, and absolve himself of guilt. At lunchtime, when he goes, I will direct the whole stream back on to *his* desk. This game will go on until Petitt the auditor flutters in, with his nose bleeding and quills behind the ear, to settle everything. After that there is nothing to do but listen to Eustace deploring his wife's fertility. "I just hang me trousers on the bed," he says poignantly, "and she's clicked again. It's not logical. I don't know *what* happens. I reely don't."

Then, out of all this routine, this sifting of bills and candidates, comes a wire from Tarquin, asking me to meet him at the station. I find him in a first-class carriage, swathed in a rug, with a soft hat drawn down over his eyes. His face bland, sexless, with the queer stony significance of an Arabic cipher. He moves stiffly about, gathering his luggage, appearing not to notice me. When I speak to him he does not answer. We go out like ghosts together, to where the car is parked.

Suddenly I am aware that there is something wrong. I see his face framed across the corrugated iron roof, the bubble of soot and steam, the brood-mare whinnying of engines. It is set in a fixed frigidity as if he had lost the use of his muscles. He tucks the rug round him and settles down, brooding. The car is gathered up in the lines of traffic. I say nothing. Presently he will tell me what it is in that nervous, lapidary voice of his. Now. His lips open, but he turns his head away silently. Faint graph of his bony cheek against the lighted shops. Then he speaks miserably, folding his virginal lips round the words, as if reluctant to let them escape him. "I had a woman," he says, turning away. A silence. I am absorbed in the traffic. He rearranges the rug, and coughs. Then with a deadly impersonality he begins to speak again. Such an icy aloofness, he might be offering a definition for a dictionary. "I had the wrong idea," he says. "She lies down and arranges her legs like compasses. But of course you know? *Do* you know? Shape of an M. *I have never seen anything so obscene in my life.*" He laughs shakily. "She catches hold of you and sort of corks herself up with it." He gives a little cough and sits there, upright and pale, with the rug gathered round him as if he had received an electric shock. We swing down the long lighted streets homeward, and all the time he is sitting there at my side, whispering and muttering quietly. "I am finished," he tells himself. "Finished. Done for. Ended. From now on it's going to be different." His eyes watch his own reflection on the windshield with the queer bloated look of an octopus. In order not to think I drive as fast as possible. The doom is growing again, the nostalgic panic of these provinces, which kills these men. And Tarquin is here, looking as if he were bleeding to death under the rug.

We arrive, and with the same chaotic imbecility he watches the porter unstrap his bags and carry them up. In his room he lies down immediately on the bed and closes his eyes. The air is heavy. The windows remain shut. Everything is the same; nothing has been touched. The Japanese prints, the microphotographs of the spirochetes, the red handbill of the lock hospital, the pipe rack picturesquely impending with its untouched briars. Dust on the rack of books, Isidore Ducasse, Huysmans, Rolfe, Dowson, Pope, Strachey, etc. His American cousin strains out of her frame like a goose, and recalls that voice I heard on the phone once. "Tell him not to be so dizzy. He's gotten to be a moral leper these days." The cash-register voice of a new continent. His diaries lie on the shelf, waiting for the revelation, the Chinese ink, the Roman numerals, the Gothic script. What will he write?

"You can't understand my death," he says at last. "A fuck's a fuck to you. Emotionally you're a plowboy still. Open my suitcase, will you? In the bottom left hand corner you'll find some eau de Cologne." I obey him. He saturates a handkerchief in the scent and presses it to his forehead. I sit here miserably on the stool, trying to read the names of the folios on the music rack. The light is very dim, shining from the piano in the corner.

"Clare is back," I say.

"How old are you?"

"Twenty-two."

All of a sudden a curious convulsion shakes the bed. The springs begin to twitter. I stand up in alarm and see that the corpse on the bed is weeping. His mouth hangs down, wobbling open, twisted up sideways into a deckle-edged grin. The handkerchief covers everything except his mouth, from which comes this taut, painful pissing.

Immediately I see Miss Smith's red dish of laughter widening, running down her sleeves. The humor pouring from the wet nigger grin like a stream of gongs falling over us in an ocean of discord—until we are floundering down again into the annihilation of the lost continents.

Afraid, I run out into the passage. Everything is quiet with the hallowed quietness of an English Sunday evening. I am suffering from a sort of mindless hysteria. I perform a number of silly acts, without reason, except that I must not think. The hotel with its ant life, its corridors, its somnolent billiard room and lounge, surrounds me.

I open a book and see you standing out there, like a whipped bitch among the apple trees. It is not good enough, my beautiful id. On the title page there is Sappho meditating under the terrific eyeballs of the night sky, the sea curling away under the white rock, the holly trembling at the moon, the silver riders galloping toward Crete. Turn your face to the sea wall, and listen to the noisy lungs of the water under the cliffs. The moon crawling across the warm tiles, and the whole Greek world gathered in a single knot of agony in the left breast. The night moving one way and the sea another, and the body torn in two by them. Or is it Gracie in her English room going blind as a collie among the starched collars? Gracie and Sappho sharing the last dazzling jump into history. The water closing. The tactless sea in many husbands of silver treading the white meat under the cliffs, breathing among the statues and the chorus. Good-by.

In his room Lobo is sitting on the bed in his elegant continental smoking, waiting for the hour to strike. To improve his technique he is working himself in the mirror. "Working," he calls it. "Working" a woman. His eyes enlarge and diminish, registering every insinuation between oriental eroticism and sheer delirium. I sit in the chair, and he does not speak to me. He is absorbed in his own wonderful art: crucified by this technique which he operates from the leering Maya lecher's mask.

"Tarquin," he says at last, absently, "says I was cicisbeism. Hot dog, eh?" He is allowing the supplication to run into his eyeballs like melted butter. Lobo is walking in that void with crooked fingers and the hunger of the woman on him. He is never satisfied, deep down inside himself. There is always this panic hunger which ends in a kind of febrile hysteria or brutality. "When I cover a woman," said Perez once, "when I cross her and get into her—I am home." But Lobo is never home. The womb is his target, but he misses it. Something intervenes, a letter, a bill, a calculation, a fit of weeping, blood, nostrums, fear. He is forever sitting inside the barbed wire, planning new apocalypses which abort; new detonations which fizzle down in black powder. The mirror records his despair for him. I am sitting here biting my nails, trying not to think of Tarquin. So much of his agony in the garden is mine. When he speaks I try not to understand. I try not to implicate myself in the process, the machinery of despair. I try to read nothing but the actual words of the green diary, sans undertone, overtone, rumor. It is not mine, I tell myself, not mine. I have other problems. And yet I can't get out of my mind the details of that holiday in Brighton. The ennui. The slowly stagnating hours of despair which followed Tarquin's experience. It is a little hysterical-making. He went everywhere to try and blot out the thought, to dances, museums, theaters. In a cinema he thought he might be drugged for a while. "Then I had one of my ideas. It was all those people in there, fuggy, lousy, damp, sitting in rows. And I thought suddenly of the millions of jaws of rotten molars around me, the rotting flesh of their bodies: *I tell you there must have been several hundred tubes of shit laid up alongside of me in there, palpitating!*"

His vehemence is terrifying. He is paralyzed. He cannot speak.

135

He cannot move. His tears are clotted in his mouth, his throat is full of rocks, As he speaks he goes across to the washbasin, turns on the tap, and begins to spit and spit, as if he would never be done with it.

In the night, when I watch him sitting at his piano, playing to his brain, I know that it is not the madness that counts, essentially counts. It is the ticking of the deathwatch which reminds me of the true focal sepsis. Death perhaps, the worm trailing its slime across this room, these books, this piano. I am so small myself, so utterly incapable of laying even my own ghosts, that I dare not take the responsibility of his. That is why it is so difficult to write about him—I am by implication mapping out my own scenario of despair when I see him standing at that white washbasin, spitting and spitting. And in a lesser degree the same is true of Lobo, of Perez, of all these antic maniacs who live like jiggers in the soles of my feet. That is why I am sometimes afraid of going mad. I have a blinding second's revision of all that I know, believe, doubt, reverence, adore: your face, his face, the skull in the mirror, the knave, the jester, the fool—and I am afraid.

This idea is perhaps not unfamiliar to you. I have reached a dead reckoning somehow. Sunday follows Sunday like many crucifixions, and I have utterly no sense of progression. On the twelfth night of a year already ancient we have rain, rain in a long line of opening razors. It is threshing down the grain, raping the orchard where the apple trees stand like Caliban; where you are lying no doubt with your womb full of loam and the foxgloves touching your nipples. Nothing passing across the arena of smudged hills but the velveteen gamekeeper with the beaded steel gun. It is always the old year here: an old year—"a blind old bitch, gone in the teeth!" The bodies of the wise men sifting down their essence of action to apples and grain and cider; the green counties lifted up to me like the mouth of my girl. The churches solemn among the lichen graveyards. In Memoriam; on the grass the marble stumps, like a mouthful of rotten teeth.

In these days we are wild: a drunken, whoring, perilous crew, aimless as lunatics, racing our own magic from place to place, sinking and smiling among the dying bottles. Laugh and the world laughs with you, suffer and you suffer alone. I gather your face up like a goblet of brandy and drink it solemnly, mouth, eyes, hair, nose, lips, canines, lobes, dimples, tics—everything in a gulp. Tomorrow—what is that? Today there is an amputated centrum in which all activity is devoted to itself. Tomorrow there will be fresh air on my jowls, there will be children squealing, papers, ink, slovenly work meaning nothing. Madame About gathering her defensive guts round that knob in her womb. But tonight I am absolved, in a kind of paralyzed way I am free. I can brighten my lips with spittle and shine forth like an ogre; I can choke you in images, who are only an image yourself; I can smile among the candles and the bottles that taste of sand. I can grovel in my own sick and devour my own dung. I can die—or sleep.

Page by page this noctuary gets completed. Images. Clouds. Shadows in ink. Frankly, I know not what I do. There is Miss Smith, wearing a moth-eaten muff in midsummer, and Lobo in his natty suiting with the subdued stripe. They are going to Canterbury for the day. Blessings on you, my children. Behind the altar screen, the great resonant goth glooming over them, the Abbey with its blue grays, its tooth-white, curd-yellow. In this aura of prehistory he tries to kiss her. She stands solid all of a sudden, turned away, petrified. He is giving a few Peruvian groans and kissing her fingers. All of a sudden she starts hissing. Her mouth is open and vermilion. Flights of geese spit and whirl among the arches. She is closed up by an invisible spring. They go out in agitation and enter a tea shop. He is afraid she is mad. She laughs incessantly all the way home, touching her shoulders with each ear, this black goose spitting in her own handbag. At night he sits in his room with dumb perplexity, asking why she laughed. Why? "Is she virgin, dear boy?" He is tremendously interested, angry, piqued, sore, puzzled, keen. . . . I can see that he plans to add her to the album. For fun I tell him a few lies. "*Virgin?*" I say with fine indignation. "*What do you mean—virgin?*" It is good to watch the interest, the exultation, drain out of his face like water out of a bath. His mouth is open. Everything is pouring into it, draining away. In that case, he says, she was trying to make a fool of him. Can you imagine it? The negress standing in the Abbey, a laughing logarithm, flapping her wings and laughing. Bah!

At night, perhaps, if there is nothing else to do, a visit to the corpse that inhabits Tarquin's tea-green dressing gown. We sip Bovril with genteel affection, like a couple of spinsters, or play cards at the green folding table.

"You are grateful, you say, for being made to think, to weigh, to analyze?" asks the hero in carefully simulated surprise. "You thank me for the death I am transmitting? I assure you, my lad," and so on. I accept these morsels humbly. Humility and divinity—are they not the same thing? Consolation! Courage! One day when you are a big boy *you* shall have a teddy to play with.

"Your trouble is that you are young. Your ideas are eoan—you see false dawns breaking all over the place. You actually hope. Until the platonic poison is out of your system you cannot begin. Stop imagining an impanate Christ, first of all. Bread must become bread, nothing more or less. This tea tastes of urine, does it not? No, it's your turn. Contemplate the world which has created you, my dear, and see where you stand."

There is no answer to this except that I know nothing of the world which created me. Nothing. I am a sort of ticker tape, through which life runs its ribbon of shabby pulp. What is written on it I cannot tell. A love letter perhaps, or a report of famine, or a poem, or a description of a new disease.

"Dear Puck," you say, "the guest has come without warning, so that I am afraid the house isn't ready for him. Spring. By the lake you can hear the copulation of the frogs, like smooth pebbles being rubbed together. They are dying in quantities, their veins are shot with blood. It is good when we lie down together to keep remembering the death all around us, in the clouds, in the lake, in the woods where summer is chained up like a blind man. It is death that makes our love adult, the death of the grain. It is so

138

bitter when we are together, but, like salt, really nourishing. Death is a wonderful discipline. Do you understand me? Good night."

You are no longer afraid. The spring is your ally. The one season you properly understand, answer in your bones. But now that the blind man summer has broken his rusty chain and got free—what now? Shall we make some fine alkaline poems to neutralize this dust, this soma fever?

Dear Alan. I am alone again. This book is not a statement of a path, but a quarrel with destiny, that is why it is necessary for you to understand it. The summer is largely responsible—not to mention the little death. I was thinking tonight of those summer days in the shadow of the priory. They seem to belong to another world—a world of shapes which included such colors as warmth, charity, love, etc. A whole dormant Platonic principle which, in its essence, is England—the marrow and bone of England. This is a very necessary valediction, not only to England, but, if you like, to the world. It will hurt you, but it is the truth. I have looked into my account—the account that seemed so full and heavy with new cash —and found hardly a coin that will ring properly on wood. There was nothing for it but to empty my wallet into the dust and take the road again: without dramatics this time, without heroics—not to mention lymphatics. It is queer to remember that this decision was already shaping itself that afternoon, when we stood on the southern tower of the priory, hanging in the breeze, breathless and exulting like sea birds. All that was the island then, was represented in that humorous razored profile of yours—the predatory nose of the Middle Ages, the Goth singing in your blood, the music you gathered up in those nervous fingers and transmitted, crazy with your own enthusiasm. Southward, like a green beating heart, the flats stretched away into the mist. The myth weathering softly on the corbels, the fragile spines of the windows with their armorial bearings, the buttresses flying into an eternity of childish history. We were hanging up there, like flies, over the Saxon river, watching the tonsures cross the leads in meditation. Irrational thoughts and feelings wheeling up over me, whewing like gulls, somber. It was in that time that I began dimly to see the equation which was finally printed in my brain here, over the Ionian. It was the temptation of the devil, the vision of the cities offered to me from an immense mountaintop. The devil! What should be more plausible than that you should be the Black Saint himself— panurgic, long-nosed, calculating bastard that you are! You were offering me, in your oblique way, the whole of England—the masques, the viols, the swans, the mists, the doom, the fogs: you were offering me a medieval death in which I could live forever, stifled in the pollen of breviaries, noctuaries, bestiaries: split silk and tumbrils, aesthetic horses and ruined Abbeys. The lament for Dido opening up such pits of emotion in my brain that I fell upon my knees, and shattered in little pieces in the hearth. The forest opening its eyes of frost, the unborn morning of the world, the dew in a sheet, the trees stifled in feathers. The great orchestra hymning gruffly among its ants, gathering and breaking in time to the sea. The hot lick of the winter rain, blinding us all from coast to shabby coast. Or Pat going quietly mad among the sprained spires of Oxford. Your room, with the gramophone like a broken womb emptying Beethoven over us. This is the world which was implicit in our extravagant gust, our laughter, our tears, our poems. That is why, when I tell you I have rejected it, I want you to understand clearly the terms of that rejection. That is an England I am going to kill, because by giving it a quietus once and for all, *I can revive it!* This is not a flashy paradox, but something I have experienced, something that I have suffered. Understand me. It is not very difficult. The gulls are wheeling again, in their soft terror, the rooks are uneasy. In the gloom down below they light the candles and begin—the soft elegant litanies of religion. It is an apocalyptic moment, between heaven and earth. We are hanging over the minute, crawling town, while the bells open up. Under our feet the tower rocks at each impact of the vesper bell. A train snores outward, along the hills, into the past. The decision is made. I am no longer softened by tears or doubts.

I have become as hard as a bronze medal. What it cost me to maintain this terrible equilibrium, to become responsible only to myself for what I am—that is not the important thing. The important thing is this: if I succeed, and I will succeed, then I shall become, in a sense, *the first Englishman*. I tell you this in confidence, because afterward, when the great struggle is over, and the whole psyche of our nation—our world—is thrown back into gear—then there will be plenty of time for understanding, analyzing, wondering. It is now, while the duel is on, that your understanding is valuable. This is all I can say. From that rare latitude, which I carry with me wherever I go, under the Equator or over the Poles, I write you this valediction *and greeting*. Affectionately Yours, Hamlet's little godchild.

*
**

The death damp is creeping in again. In the autumn we escape occasionally, like moles, into the upper air, and brood on the extinction settling down over England. This is chiefly to enable Tarquin to write his musical poem: *To England*. He is participating bravely, he tells me, in the death under the shield: the death which he swears is fattening itself on our very bones. Go to the country, he tells me, and describe it all for me when you get back. He does not want to see it for himself; is happier in town. That is why you are beside me again, alive to the sweet particularities of the island's doom, warm of wrist and knee, ankle and elbow. . . .

Cornfields falling away from the thread of the road in dusty garrisons, leaning, gravid, heavy in the ear. Sunk in them almost submarine, among the gardens, the beautiful farmhouses with the beetle in the wood, churches with pointed windows, mellow stables. Tudor half-timbering, scribbled with creeper; plowland and arable in jaundiced yellows, mold-browns and purples, spinning away under your fingers in gentle undulations. No, I am quiet and serious. It is all laid out like a page in Gregory's diary. See, from one end the pen begins to bite, you turn up a long

141

furrow on the paper—a green furrow. The fingers tug slowly like a team of oxen. Behind the steel tooth green figures are coming alive, stretching their arms, and looking around. In this way everything was created.

I am recalling again the terms of our separation: the calendar lying there with the broken back, offering an infinity of smoky evenings. The oblique wishes and hopes of a lifetime gathered together and spent in the space of a few weeks. And now, it seems, I have no more hopes—only acceptance. I keep my mouth shut because my jaw would fall off if I tried to speak.

I am out walking again with Chamberlain in the long evenings: corridor upon stone corridor opening up before us until, for a breath of air and a personal glimpse of trees, we are forced to turn into the park gates. Or else peering at the faded portraits of the Elizabethans in the gallery, while my companion talked vehemently about Lawrence, and his prediluvial madhouse. ("Tut tut, Lawrence? Too vehemently eoan, my dear. Tarquin.")

Rowing on the lake in the mist; or in the hot nights watching the shadows pass and repass on the walls of Hilda's bedroom, lighting the washstand, the shelves of belfries, the hanged man in the mirror. The glare of headlights withering her naked body. Reaching you at last over a café table, touching fingers, one's heart bruised and swollen with despair. The long stabbing waves of parting under the airplane light. The green mouth climbing away upward through my world like a torch, burning away the tissue, the bone and cartilage, nosing among the twittering nerves, annihilating me. Hilda's big toe, left over from the evening's entertainment, posted above the bedrail to rot away through eternity, like a traitor's head on London Bridge. Or Perez whimpering on the table among the students while the current ran like vinegar up his anus. (Rabelais' curse: May the fire of St. Anthony fly up thy fundament.) Beakers of urine turning milky, throwing up their white filaments. The catheter budding, blossoming. Chamberlain's drunken face, dazed with the myth he is creating around himself, asking impatiently for the new book of revelation.

All this has made me a little somber, a little lunatic, to be with you again at last, shut up together in this moving shell of steel. There is an edge on laughter, or even the common topics. I am a little proud of my control. Soon I shall say something, and you will begin to tell me everything—the whole quavering saga of your life—the life which has just begun. You will begin asking those insane questions, where have I been, what have I done, what have I seen, why do I look at you like that, where will this all end? If I am honest with you now, if I give the impression of sincerity, it is because I want something. Inside I am weeping for my generation. I am devising in my mind a legend to convey the madness which created us in crookedness, in dislocation, in tort. We are a generation enwombed. A stillbirth. Like blind puppies we are seeking the way back to the womb, we are trying to wipe away the knowledge of our stillbirth, by a new, a more glorious, more pristine event. We have been expelled from the uterus blind and marrowless, and we grovel back toward it in a hysterical regression of panic. Look, I am burrowing in your lap with my mouth, like an animal. I am hammering down the doors of the womb. Screaming to get back. I would gather myself up like a snail and crawl back miraculously if I could, stuff myself up to your gullet for safety, anywhere, anyhow. This is at least honest. Do not accuse me. When I go mad, and rip the clothes off your trembling body, when I bite your nipples and groan, it is this expiatory half-death I am consummating. It is so necessary and so poignant to fuck you like that, when you are like a tumbled featherbed; when your mouth is clammy with stars, and your soft cunt breathing its velvet, musky pollen over the earth. Then even the trees, the hills, the towns, seem thrown into soft, perfectly defined focus for me. I am absolved. I have thrown up a support trench: a wall of the womb stands between me and the world. Let them probe, let them probe. Let them sound the walls of the belly, let them switch a searchlight on the vagina, I am secure. All my savagery, all my gust, has been thrown down in a little parcel of seed, emptied into this yawning throat of silk.

Now I have recovered my control, I am masterful as a bantam, I am cruel. I am the monster you told me about. Very well. Turn your head away. I stand among the trees in my shirt, and smoke. I abhor you because you do not understand my weakness, though you see its symptom. Then you will turn with those stupid, uncomprehending eyes, and say why did I do this, what made me do that, etc. Your mouth hanging open on its hinges, your face shining with sweat and spittle and tears. I shake you off masterfully, disgusted by my love for you. I am hungry I tell you. Yes, when I act in this heartless way it is because I want to make use of you—or because it is teatime. Choose for yourself. Yes, if I have not given you syphilis it is a miracle. In the car I suddenly catch sight of that geological hammer. You brought it with you to do some fieldwork? I am laughing now as if my mind would snap. The whole country is waiting to be tapped with it, sounded for depths! Fieldwork! My humor is restored immediately, I am guiltless, free, the best of friends. And this puzzles you. You cannot make it out. There is not an atomic trace of the monster in me—not a trace. You try to hold out, be severe, austere, reserved, sulky, but I am infecting you, I am permeating you. I lean down over you, and in a breath I fill every artery in your body with psalms. We are shaken with a fit of hysterical weeping. The car wobbles from side to side. The country swings up and down among your breasts with magnificent lamentation. We are so happy that tears are running down our faces. You are given utterly now, captured and trodden and submissive, and if my hands would stop trembling I would light you a cigarette, I would talk somberly; I would hang on your mouth like a broken jawbone . . . What a thin border between love and murder!

We slide off the arterial by Banbury, and down the gravel lanes, infinitely serpentine and bumpy. The avenue of chestnuts hides the old mill. A hunchback bridge in red stone. Lolling over, as the springs toss noiselessly, we can hear the clean thumping of the millwheel, sinking to a bass hubbub, and then gone, switched off, snuffed. We do not speak any more except by the language of action. The hedges are alive with insects, and visible drafts of honeysuckle.

The car becomes all of a sudden a gauche relic of another world. A preglacial monstrosity with its sweaty stink of petrol, and hot injections of oil on air so pure. We ditch it in a gravel pit and run out together, hand in hand, spontaneously, down the slopes past the Duke of Cumberland. Yes, downhill in a kind of hectic nympholepsy, the grass snapping at our ankles, the clouds deafening us, and the distant cathedral spire swimming up as if to impale us. The seven winds drummed while we were coming. Now they are silent. Our ears are alert, twisted into little helices of attention, but the valley offers no sound. It lies there like a toy.

We are transfigured, burst open and relieved. We have penetrated the outpost and entered into the novelty of Tarquin's vivid death. It is hard to believe, so I do not mention it. If you can understand the fable that this country is creating around us without drawing on false sentiment, you are to be congratulated. For we have become suddenly heraldic here, where the sunshine plays like august lions and the river rides like a clean collar among the parklands. A hectic post-existence, say, in the ballet of countryside, among the Georgian houses weathered to blood, myopic peacocks, dirigible napery of floccus. It is when I think of what the result was that I am disgusted by the energy we spent, the passion, the tears—to produce this music, which he plays to us one winter evening. Tarquin throwing himself into an interesting attitude, holding the sign manual of death in his fingers.

To England should have been an abstract of all the hours we spent together in elegy. In a decorated world, confused by banality, by tears and recriminations, they should still put forth an image in the music: as faded photos, or pressed leaves in a book, can surprise by their evocations.

That night, huddled by the fire, listening to the tone poem, its melodic squirts, its lapses into pathos, I realized that he had not managed to translate his legend of death. The death under the shield had become the death of a Wagnerian swan: a romantic

145

confection—the one thing he was trying not to do. The piano was full of galvanic ballerinas, falling in splashes of fluffy extinction around him. The swan with the goiter singing Wagner, its arse keeping time, its mouth full of toothpaste. But the real—death if you like (these abstractions bore me), the doom which he saw settling down over England, which we smelled out and reported true for him—that he has missed. I suppose he will never be able to create it, because he is too much a part of that declension himself. And dead men tell no tales. But when I see the material, the rough slag lying ready to hand, the exploded components of a world gathered ready for the artist—then I am ashamed. If there were not other things to be done, I would try myself. Sheerly punctilio, as it were, dedicated to a rape under a cherry tree and the smell of sperm; and that incomprehension in your eyes. Magic, you say, it was magical? The past is always magical. Store me the images in a velvet casket among the letters with ribbon round them. If I began would you hold the bucket under my head for the vomit of Englishry—the images?

When the children are silent I sit and brood over the crude magma which we wasted on Tarquin. The manufacture of death, if you please, with a few chromatic runs and tremors. If I could write I would gather a mouthful of bone-dry fiddles harsh as scrannel, and out of their monotonous algebra construct a theme. A dry contrapuntal rasping of marsh toads. Nothing should escape, nothing. Every wrinkle of the motor cortex translated into this withered, picric, asp-dry fiddling; every convolution of the brain fibrous with music . . .

(The Friary where the Middle Ages chops wood. An immense man, bearded to the navel, with laughter like the north wind, and hands of horn. Bones which manipulate the creased flesh with difficulty, as if in gloves. The folded effigies in the crypt among garnished floors and ancient bones, weeping and sweating between cold walls like paralytics agonized for movement. Jesu, Jesu, in the rich hymn, crawling up the walls, putting invisible rings round the pillars, until the doleful arches respond, in diminishing

146

polyphony, "Jesu, Jesu," and the choir is shaken with sobs—blanched almonds—and the candles go out, and the Thing walks.

In the charnel house lanterns smearing chrome along the walls, where the dance of death twitches men by the ankles, or an invisible hand shuts off the drafts of air to their lungs. The Middle Ages holds his lantern for us to see; an imperturbable Noah, secure in his Ark of salvation. His voice can laugh in this place without fiction, and the north wind blows in and out of his nostrils. Here is enough matter to assemble a hundred poets, a hundred thousand cabinet ministers, a tithe of whores, a swath of pimps, a bevy of ladies, a congregation of plovers, an exalting of larks, a true-love of turtles, a chirm of goldfinches, a rout of nights, a pride of lions, a state of princes, a charge of curates, a prudence of vicars, a superfluity of nuns. When the gates are locked at night, and the Friary sleeps, the figure steps down off the walls and begins to assemble them, numberless bodies, false arms, false legs, wrong jaw and backbone (shaking the serpents from them) . . . But what matter? I imagine always Schiller's beautiful teeth, grinning at the lanterns, his head turned this way and that in the fist of friends. A ventriloquist idiocy, but no fard on the taut bones of the cheek.

In the Friary we drink valedictory ales, thin but good, and say good-by all round. A great air of tranquillity about the pointed buildings, printing on heaven; Noah lumbering at my side with the keys. Outside in the road the car waits.)

The three of us are hunched in the front seat of the car together, and Lobo is speaking suddenly, with a kind of panic, about death, and women. How he could never marry. When he was at school history frightened him, he couldn't think or speak. And when his sister died he went running down the road to Juanita, and fell on the bed, trembling, until she put her hand on him, and drew the panic out of him. They were both trembling as they came in the aura of death, the positive affliction of stillness. The twin pins of the headlights swirling away toward London; and we three, hunched over the engine like witches over a caldron, while the

147

hills retreated in the distance, and the road was bitten into slopes and crevices. New pairs of lights came out of nothing to meet us and all the while he talked superstitiously of Ponce de León, lying down there in some coral grot, with sea slugs in his eye sockets, and his armor gnawed by water; and the new world opening from his navel like a gash in the womb of humanity. All the salt in the Dead Sea could not weep it away, or recall the enterprise which had caused it; and in some way all this—his ideas of the Pacific falling away among the sands and armor and pikes and burnt sienna ruddocks; and a skeleton of Ponce de León, clothed in water, flesh dispersed, his skull a birdcage for hermit crabs—all this, I say, seemed to have some relation to the charnel house with its heaps of puzzled bones lying in jigsaws all around. Why, I cannot tell. But all deaths were made real by that visit of ours. Its scope included every example of the human machine's ceasing. Where he saw Ponce de León, I could see those millions of others, the puzzled apemen prodding flesh, or grunting under memorial granite. The Mediterranean deep-water bursting with the bones of seamen and fishermen. Bubbles in streamers easing from the throats of Greeks. The continents rising at the tap of my companion's hammer, obedient as elephants, to crush down the drifting slosh of bodies into a convenient pulp. All this vast energy hangs behind his legendary voice; like some immense paper mill sucking in refuse, old strips of rag and street flotsam, the planet softens us all into scurf, mashes and flattens and gouges the unfeeling vessels into convenience, and then from the matrix produces and creates an endless roll of toilet paper, coupons, poppies, doilies, cartons, cellophane. "Why do we want to live?" he asks nervously. He is thinking of the age I can see: the refuse going into mill and being converted into the twentieth-century symbol of death. It is useless. Death takes us one by one. What do we leave for your children, etc.? When Juanita had her first child she was transfigured, swollen with delight and anguish. She became like an animal. She wouldn't sell herself to anyone. "It belongs to him, see? Everything I've got belongs to him. My

148

Juan. If you had married me and the child was yours I would share him with you." He tells me this with tragic sorrow. He would hang around her lodging. If he could be alone with her he would try to feel her breasts, and she would shake him off with savagery and disgust. The child! *El hombre que ha hecho esto* etc. etc. Sometimes in the night he gets her scent again, and he could kill himself. I am reminded of Marney in the upper room, repeating over and over again, in that strangled duke's voice: *esta hoy mas enferma,* or some such oracular glyph, the meaning of which I long to know. Or Eustace squeezing out his spots in the mirror before going home to lunch. If he doesn't do it, he says, his wife will do it for him. The glass is covered with little spurts of pus which harden, and which he will scrape off with his fingernail when the visibility gets impaired by them. All this is mixed in the image of the paper mill, the planet killing us, and reincarnating us in pulp and discards. Alamort, alamort.

But even Ponce de León fades when, that evening, we three weary travelers creep into the crowded Abbey pews, weary with the exploration of ourselves—the old world of the self—and stand, our faces turned one way, like blind things, under the wild concord of music playing along the slats of the organ pipes. And from the pulpit the derision of a single voice, plump and round with practice, intoning, forever intoning, until our souls are sick and begin to reel under the sheer pressure of pomp. Light, high up there, where the slender pillars buttress one another, fossilized swans, falling in diaper and arc and floss: now crisscross, now lateral, now shafted, coiled, pendent, leaning: O Jesu, Jesu, enough to make the crypt sweat and the autumn cinquefoils flutter among the graves. Our sweet white choir hanging to each note like synchronized corpses in a gallow dance. Breaking rollers of sound, crushed like perfume across the poor shabby things which creep in here like rats, to snap and choke on the poisoned bait. The communion bowl awash with a red sea of bacteria from mouth to mouth slopping dismally; the wafer sticking like gelatin to the roof of the mouth. And above all this noise, above the noise swarming from rafter to batlike rafter, from beam to bolt to nut to beam to bolt to nut to beam, the roar of the chorale; until the sympathetic metal whines along the pulpit, and the whole catacomb tilts, struggling, swarming with our clement souls, sick for sanctuary, with a "Jesu, Jesu" downward into the bottomless basin where the white Thing washes its feet among the lilies —and the pontifical catamites lour, and set up a whizzing like gnats. . . .

The negress is clutching my hand, terrified by these barbarities, like a child. The light of the cross is shining on Lobo, in his eyes, on his forehead, like a brand. Everywhere we are surrounded by insects in white. Anselm is standing before the face of the Lord in his dancing fighter's stance, his great golls working like pistons, his jaw like a ham, his eyes pure shrapnel in their black orbits, Anselm clean of the clap and the drink, fighting the good fight with all his might among the soutanes. It doesn't matter, he is telling me in a whisper. It doesn't matter. Juanita burned up her sugar too fast, her teeth fell out, her eyes swelled up. He is terrified the negress will understand what we are saying, but she is in a fright at the Host; her ears are laid back like a whippet's. I am afraid at any moment she will streak for the black doors. He would never have married her anyway, so it didn't matter. In the name of the father, son, and Holy Ghost. Yes, it was only accident they met. He never really cared a damn for her, as her. It was only that she was there at every crisis in life, so that after a while it seemed that he would never be free of her. One is never free of one's past. Amen. She had become, by identification, everything, Lima, the dead sister, the panic, the gulls; and now among the northern ruins he turned back to her, regressed, whimpered for her like a child. Amen.

Afterward, when we go out through the great doors, it is as if the night had burst open in a dark fruit, so immense and pithy it is, so silent and unshaken. I know then there are no questions to be asked any more, there are no queries to be put to the Host. Everything is washed clean in the stream of faces from the gold doors, the beards, the sacristan, the verger, the whore, the fillock, the slut, the gentry-mort, and the lusk. The light is leaking out among the blue gravestones. Sacred to the memory of Lawrence Lucifer who died this day of August. Offer a candle or a sprig of holly. I am a gnarled backbone of stone, speaking in many hectic lichens, a remote powder in a sheath of tepid lead, out of the reach of iambs or fugue. The whole question, in essence, is acceptance, the depersonalization of self, of the society which one has absorbed. It is not only a question of art, but a question of life. You are altered, affected, transmuted by this orientation. Whatever was your antecedent, your history, that no longer matters to me. I can no longer whimper when your head goes down like a hammer on the white pillow. The strange accidents of bone, the syntax of muscle and cartilage, exist in a relation to something that is no longer history or ideals.

"Lie down and die, frail helmet of dust," I wrote once; and dying that way you were Sappho, you were Beatrice, curling up like a petal in an Egyptian evening. Death among tombs. Death like the salt whips and discord of the winter sea on the first day of desire. Yes, I am serious. What you are now is a lowest common denominator, agonizingly held for an hour in my vise of bone and blood. Believe me, I have taken nothing from you; or rather, by taking everything from you—everything irrelevant, confusing, historical—I have made such an unbearable poignance of you, that just to try and utter it would send me mad. That part of what remains, when cupid's loaves and fishes are gathered up, I keep always inside me, like a reserve of strength. I need it in life. I cannot destroy it by writing it—and destroying myself in a pattern of contagious syllables for the dull world. Never, I promise you, never. That much belongs to life. Amen.

*
**

When the drums begin, and the opaque lightning trembles in the night sky, I become a child again, in revisited history. I per se I, Lawrence Lucifer. In my dreams there is only one possible protagonist. I am moving across the scenery of the world on noiseless castors; my hand is held, but by whom I cannot tell. O per se O. Among the soft fermenting pastel green of the Himalayas Father Paul whittles his sailing boat from stumps of deodar; the hills breathe snow over the deserted playgrounds, a Tibetan panic of winter. The passes glow with eternal malevolence, and the river moves in soft packs of ice, or curdles with green velvet. On the highroad the lamas pass, twisting their tin wheels in their paws, murmuring; in the soft ferns of the hills the pug marks of the bear. On the treble slopes of the foothills the snow is gathering in clouds, the first dour caravans are wheeling up the plain to meet them. The duffle-clad Bhutias huddle in their sheepskins and grovel among the colored cards on the flag steps of the churches. I am alone weeping over Everest. Somewhere over there, eternally veiled in blue, the forbidden City is lying, glowing like a stone. Lhasa where the great horns are braying and the devils jump one by one from the cliffs. I stretch out my arms and fall in the snow; the clouds gather, the avalanche walks down the hills in a toga, throwing petulant boulders. The wind opens up volley upon volley of empty words which drive past me like refuse. All that is locked up in a dream of Lhasa, is driven down into the river among the ice and the serpents. Nothing remains for me but the deaf-mute syllables of a tongue I have yet to learn. The priests are conducting the thunder of the litanies. In the Palace they are clicking their beads and smiling the canine smile. The slopes are writhing with flags; and the colored paper horses gallop over the precipice, clipped with life-giving scissors, swept away as soon as created. The late voyager gathers his cloak in hi: armpits and bores his little pit of air into the hurricane. The antelopes gossip and quiver, their eyes molten, their flanks stiffened to the wind; and the man drops slabs of butter in his teacup and swallows a pill of sacred dung.

I am standing at the window watching the storm gather. The lightning is so smooth and trembling that it lights the room with a queer sustained glint of green, as it might be an aquarium, and I standing here, on the carpet of weeds and slimy rock, waiting. I am thinking of Tarquin's music, and realizing that of all this fear and turmoil it has recorded nothing. From music we demand our whole life if it is to move us: every modulation of dream, despair, love, yearning. It is the past and the future, the first rapture of living, and that future going down into the tomb; the descent of Ishtar among the soiled roses; the entry into the chamber of the cosmos; the first kicking in the womb, and the last elegant spasm of cessation, lull, status.

Tomorrow the earth will be drenched, exhausted, and born again from this orgasm of water: sopping and juicy to the hilt, the roots of the bush. The penis buried and shriven, sliding back into hibernation, curling and somnolent as a taproot. The quickened walls of the cunt lined with quilts and membranes of gum, resin, foxgloves, puffballs, wheat. We will go out together on the steaming arable among the cattle, by the river, and re-create the legend of the kingcup which Tarquin missed. It will not be difficult if we practice humility: humility from the roots upward, all-devastating, all-devouring, omni-passionate. If we have wounds we will show them.

This morning it is Chaucer. We are following the pilgrims' way southward. It is in order to refresh the negress that I am compelled to come out here with you, to taste again the prehistoric world, and reflect on its quietus; because in that stale room, overlooked by the charts, by the blind wall, I have been impregnated with the data of an epoch which is the subject of all contemplative dope. I am stifled in it. I mean the vellum and ground ink ages, the patient, beautiful work, so complete and formal within the limits it set itself. The first presses groaning out their rich black ore of literature. Caxton, Mallory—the simple cunning of widowed children. Wiry paper smelling of candlesticks and glue. Choirs writhing with goblins alleged sacerdotal. Trefoil, cinquefoil, and the whole body of perpendicular gothic gray in the spires aspiring. Minted coins and humorous rapes. Inlaid hilts and beautiful women with the gummata growing in them. The Green King tied by the derelict barge to his mother's breasts. Tertiary noses carved on the laughing faces of the court hunchback. The swans flying backward and the breviaries pullulating in heraldic animals. All this beautiful stuff circulating in the veins of the negress, poisoning her. It is in order to destroy history that I am compelled to experience it, all of it. But behind it all there is the image of the paper mill, the great domes of pulp, endless spools of marrow and garbage and cloth, woven into daily papers, sanitary towels, toilet wafers, blotting paper. I am again on the high tower among the sea gulls, shaping the decision, when I watch this beautiful stuff poured away down the sewers. Somewhere the line has been broken, and we are wandering among the staggering nebulae, in a region of consciousness so cold, so rarefied, that we want to scream aloud for warmth. A region where the healing mythologies are so etherized that they float away elusive, before the mind can grasp them and burn them for fuel. This is the proper No Man's Land, crammed with plenty and radiant steel, where the heart screams for pity, where the viscera contract at the smell of money, multitude, masturbation; where the warm thoughts, the feelings, the delights are stunted from the womb, vaporized and snuffed. Ephemeral Between Golgotha and the slaughterhouse where day-long one hears nothing but the hollow screaming of pigs. There is no quietus; no bodkin, dagger, bullet can ever a quietus make. The dance is on, eternally on.

That evening I was so certain of the age which lies beyond all this, the new dimension, the novel being—a dim gnosis. I have seen the tonsures moving along the leads at Christchurch where the Saxon river drags its sherds of ice all winter, lame of foot; have seen in peacetime a rosy Abbot come down in the dusk to fish the glacid water for trout, while the lights jump one by one to the tall windows.

Last night Morgan was sitting by the boiler telling me about the asylum in which he was an attendant. Juanita was prowling the corridors, her hair in her eyes, a chopper gleaming in her hands. Lobo was whimpering softly as he smoked. They had arranged a rendezvous by the foothills. It was the last attempt on his part to bring her round. He would rape her there and fill her mouth with sand. He was not quite sure whether he would kill her or not. But when she was there, with the child on her arm, lousy, hungry, red-eyed and sore with prickly heat, the whole focus of normality was restored in a second. He knew then that his weakness was too great ever to make him a murderer. He took the child from her and buried it up to its waist in warm shaly sand, so that it could not escape. And she saw at once what was coming, and began running away from him, groaning as if she were stabbed. He was gaining on her, murderously exultant, almost in reach—when suddenly she threw herself down like an animal, and gathering a handful of sand, scooped it full under the shabby dress; filled her cunt up with it, and lay exhausted, panting, utterly without a word, waiting for the tussle, like a bird. He was so unnerved by this gesture that he began to weep, to bluster, to protest, to shout. And all the while she lay there saying nothing. He exhausted every gesture, every threat, every shade of feeling between madness and death, and still she did not answer. In the end he had to go away and leave her lying there as she was, gathered up like a ball, waiting. Speechless. Terrified. Victorious.

What is history beside this unrolling reality which Lobo offers to me with emotion and cigarettes? The progress through the guts of a beggar. When I am covering you my cranium is packed with images, the whole body of the lost worlds is being poured down that narrow slipway to the absolute; history is launched suddenly for me like a dreadnaught, the myth, the prophecy, the gloze, the glyph, the haunted hexameter, the dactyl, the pastoral. The world is crying for it to be restored, but we are offering it only a regression—an escape out of the geometrical rattrap which is really only temporary. It is not only a question of going back to a myth. The myth will come back to us. That is the tenor of this rainy morning; that is what it is telling me, among its polished components of town and valley and farm. In such moments I can tell you for certain that this is the breakup, the cataclysm, the drop curtain on the world. A new language, a new deity, a new indulgence impend from heaven. No, they are already slipping on us. Forms are dying, becoming obsolete, falling aside. Everyone save the antiquarian is afraid. The man of learning has become a cipher—epicene, neuter—with the equipment of a book reviewer. Everything is drifting up in the Sargasso of progress, swathed and shot with weed, tangled in the fins of fish, bibles and lavatory seats, turds and turbines, shuttlecocks and battledores. In the Abbey they are still marking the places in the hymnbooks, oblivious of the fact that tomorrow we shall have forgotten how to read; in the hospitals the forceps are snapping at the sutures of the child; in the Sunday papers the great men become retromingent, pissing backward into the mouth of the public and talking about the shapely subsisting beauty of tradition. In London they are dancing round the Walpole, the Faber poets are marking time and ushering in the millennium with a series of elegant squibs, the Lesbians are onanizing with squeals of buttered sperm, and the noise of the cleaver is lost in the nervous orgasm of a million women novelists. In Rome the papal nuncio announces the use of the fountain pen in such cases where the penis will not work. In Calcutta the black sweep is wandering with crumbs in his eyes, touching the untouchable, and eating the uneatable. In the Ghetto the streets are full of juice and the pavements slippery with haddocks' eyes. In Lisbon there are women as inexhaustible as the Indian Ocean, lying with their legs apart, watching the express hurtle toward them on its metals. In Iceland Eric The Red sets off for the last time with his cargo of skins, wheat, chessmen, cider and porpentines. It is all being washed up toward a madness never before seen. The heretics themselves are appalled, are building themselves Arks from the flotsam of the imagination, and hanging their viscera out for sails; they are trying to escape, choosing what is frugal rather than countenance the ferment here, where life bubbles with the effervescent rhapsodic idiocy of soda from the siphon, and the continents fall away bit by bit, and the weakening Jesu Jesu booms in the Gothic whales—the skirling of Jonahs shut out. Relentless, the watery navel of the world claims everything. The Sargasso of weeds and creepers, where the wise, the children of light, the poor in spirit, the aseptic intellects, the various, the rational, can congregate and put their brains together in a stream of atoms. Not a nimbus is grudged, not a funeral note. Only the sea sucks in its toll of cider bottles, cigar butts, sandwiches, daily papers, and imperial turds. And the snore of the faithful is as murderous as the metronome . . .

*
* *

In the hotel the old men are dressing for the last supper. Mr. Nicholas is lying in the bath licking his whiskers and playing with himself, while his keeper is turning on the cold tap to cool him off. He will appear, stiff, sanctimonious, legendary, in faultless duds, with a carnation in his lapel. His keeper will feed him and guard the old ladies from shameful remarks. Afterward he will sit in the lounge, upright, staring at the wall, as if he were being rowed down the Styx, fighting motionless campaigns in his skull. When the postman knocks and the skulls come clattering through the letter box he will wake and be led, whimpering, to his room. Tonight followed by tomorrow, followed by tonight. In order to avoid the definitive date I take refuge in books, in photographs, in memories of you.

Nothing is topical except this monkey house of elderly people, and the fantastic loneliness which tells me that I exist. I sit for whole days in a vomit of images, re-creating every gesture of yours, every pose, every remark. In the stale library I devour mouthfuls of paper with words written on it. Sirius, the Dog Star, rising on the dogdays; the Book of Kells, and the soft Irish mouths shaping the script, etc. Tarquin diagnoses this malady as fear: "You are not as strong as me, my dear. Look at me. You would think me fragile, would you not? Yet I support the most *tremendous* psychic crises without breaking; and here you are, quite strong and healthy, unable to bear your cross without fighting against it. Be a stoic, laddie, be a stoic." Well, God damn my eyes, I am. At any rate I do my best. On Tuesday I call on Hilda in the late afternoon, and find her sitting at the window among the Victorian relics, trying to write with a crossed nib. Before her on the desk lies a printed Last Will and Testament form. The dusk is falling and the ink is running out. "Listen, ducky," she says all of a sudden, "you better run along and have a blood test, because I copped it at last." I stand there looking into her eyes in a frozen perplexity. I am aware all of a sudden of the effort she has made, of the immense patience that has driven her to this desk. Her hand shakes as she writes, but her eyes are quite steady. She has got fifty quid put away, she says, hence the will. She wants her sister in Lincoln to have it for her kiddy; that is the sister who turned her out of doors. "Just in case," she says, meaning every word, "it's just in case, see? But I'm healthy for me age. Not much chance of me popping off just yet." She is not afraid, but numb. The invisible crisis has softened her up suddenly. She is very mild. Sarcoma, sarcoma . . . the word is flitting through my head.

The night is hot with dust. I can think of nothing to do, nowhere to go. After an eternal walk among the bone-bare streets I drop in to Chamberlain's flat. The dogs jump up and lick my hands. She is alone, sitting in the armchair reading. Chamberlain has gone to some musical festival or other in the north, will not be back until tomorrow. "I had a feeling you'd come," she says. We sit together for a long time in the musty little flat without speaking. Something is happening: out of the hot summer inaction, the lethargy, some decision is shaping itself in us. I try not to think. Presently she switches off the light and turns on the wireless. The room is ringing with a symphony. I sit there in the dark, trembling, expecting I do not know what. Pitch darkness and the strings slamming away at some obsolete figure. Then I put out my arms and touch her. She is standing in front of me in the dark, and as I touch her she topples softly to the armchair, breathing shakily. The skull and crossbones goes slowly down to half-mast. "You won't say anything, will you?" she whispers. "For Godsake, you won't, will you?" I promise her faithfully, trying the effects of a sardonic grin on the darkness. I am filled with a profound weariness and disgust. I go through it, yes, but with this gnawing misery of disgust. I don't know why. The whole room smells of Chamberlain. I am stifled in his musk. His books, his bed, his dogs . . . Even when she is whimpering like a crazy woman in the darkness I am so agitated that I force my hand over her mouth. Her breasts are rocking with tears. It is a beautiful, satirical ballet we are acting together, like gorgeous toads; the motive is hate in some obscure way. Afterward I shut my eyes and try to forget that she exists. I will not speak to her, and this puts her in a rage. I suppose it is comfort and tenderness she wants— well, I just haven't any. Not a scrap. "You've made use of me," she whispers angrily. "Go on then, why don't you go away? You've got what you wanted. Go away, go away, leave me alone." She begins battering me with the pads of her fists until I fetch her a sharp slap on the cheek. It is so ludicrous now that I want to giggle. Scuffling like this, tearing the bed to pieces. We lie for a long time in silence, side by side. The air is hot and charged with weariness. I am afflicted with the thought of Chamberlain—this place is so charged with his personality. Even she, whatever she does, seems to carry his stamp about on her, as paper will retain the mark of print long after it is stiffened into ash. The wireless is playing in the other room, the dogs are whimpering softly. They do not know what to make of this situation, any more than we do. If I put out my arms and comfort her it is Chamberlain I am petting: to fuck her is like an act of sodomy with him. Finally I can stand it no longer. I get up in the dark and dress quietly. She does not move. I go into the other room, switch on the light and turn off the wireless. Then hesitate. Shall I go in and say good-by? I am so overwhelmed by tenderness that I turn and open the door. She is lying there quite still, staring with glassy eyes at the ceiling. I begin to apologize, sitting down beside her on the bed, but she does not answer. If I touch her face with my fingers she turns aside. "Go on," she says at last in a low voice. "Clear out of here."

I sit there silently, staring at the floor. I do not want to leave her like this, without something, some act of friendship. We are both consumed in this slow permeating hate on the summer night. The cars whirl by on the asphalt outside, the first streetlamps are being lighted. "Listen to me," I say. "Come out and have dinner with me. Let's have a post-mortem on this. I'm not trying to hurt you, genuinely." She turns her face to me, and the light strikes it sharply from the outer room; hard white electric glare melting over her features. Her eyes are sunk back into her forehead; her skin is puffy, her mouth drawn up in disdain. I see she does not believe me. But there is such misery written on her expressions that I repeat it over again, more gently. I feel sorry for her. Looking at her face like this is like looking at the moon through a telescope for the first time: the craters, the light playing on the continents, the dry oceans, the deserts. If it were not for my feeling of tenderness I would leave her and go home. So long as I need not touch her . . . She says: "I loathe you," without any real conviction, but because she is still not sure whether to trust me or not. "There isn't any need," I tell her. "Dress now, and let's have dinner."

We leave the flat together, the best of friends, and take a bus northward. Dinner together does a great deal toward putting us back into our customary places. Afterward, strolling in the dark park together among the whores and the lanterns and the policemen, she says: "You know I really didn't want to. That's why I hated you, do you see? It was something I had to do; I've been feeling sort of dead these days, from the hips upward. Now I'm happy again. Thanks for not leaving me. I should have been miserable. Now I'm glad it was you and not someone else."

The balance restored, we take the bus home, hardly speaking, but comfortable together, as if we were old lovers. This is an item:

latterly in a moment of weakness it was confided to Tarquin. His amazement and delight were huge. "Chamberlain!" he kept repeating, as if he personally had scored some immense triumph over him. "My God, and she being fucked all the time! *Stuprum in oestis*, ha ha, *stuprum in oestis*." Stuffing chocolates into his mouth, and sniggering.

All this is an evasion of the true disease, the disease which I try and drown in books, in bright pictures. All day long I pace the museums, inspecting the relics of our history, all carefully laid out and labeled in scholarly hands on post cards. At night I meditate on the quantities of pure gold which we house so carelessly in glass cases, unaware that this same putrid stuff is decaying in our arteries. Is it possible to keep the vitality of the centuries in a bottle, with a post card on it to hint at an identity long since lost? My own history, my present, is confused by the death which I see gathered around me, here a jawbone, there a femur, here a wedding ring, there a pickax. I cannot live because the decomposing bodies of my ancestors dog me at every turn. They are not living in their myth, but dead, influencing my *dying*, not my life. That is why action is so erratic, so full of extremes, because the hypaethral universes which should live in us today are dead, and behind glass. Instead of nourishing us they are the umpires of our defeat, our decline and fall.

The circuit is complete. We have put our myths in the cellar and must start building again with new implements, a new tongue.

Morgan was telling me last night how he had squeezed out the flaccid womb with his fingers and buried the etceteras in the yard. Little Peter, the Tsarina's daughter, had a head like a melon with the sick, fish-like eyelids of the microcephalous idiot. That was the regal idiot who was more of an exile than she knew: not only from Russia but from the world. She spent all day with a pencil writing on the walls, the table, the floor, compiling, as she said, a history of her race. And what she didn't know about history wasn't worth knowing. She could explain with complete lucidity the diseases of

161

the Norman barons in the tapestry. The arrow had fallen in his eye, and he was tugging at it, as if it were embedded in a log of wood. Harold, she meant. The whole saga was written on the floor. She strikes me as a beautiful symbol of our tactics: a true twentieth-century practitioner of fable, scribbling on the table with the wrong end of a fountain pen, the wall, the floor. The Normans took their women gently, she told him, in spite of their armor, very gently and regally. They sniffed them quietly, like a dog examining fruit; then very gently they bit, until the juice spurted. That is what made him trap her against the wall, and poleax her as he did. The value of these experiences is that he regrets nothing. He himself is always part of the phenomena which puzzle him. "Can you imagine," he is always asking, "me doing it? Can you imagine me believing a thing like that?"

When I think of Tibet lying out there among the snow craters, the Golgotha of the dead races, Minoa, Japan opening like the tail of a peacock, or Ethiopia where the lanterns swing darkly over pools of blood—then I know that the myth which hangs so heavily on us is not dead. It is coming back slowly into focus, its power is being restored; wherever we move we knock against its shapes— permeations and diffusions so vast that there is not a square foot of earth without its compulsive magic. Dig where you please along the craters of this battlefield, and your spade strikes gold. The ground is stuffed with it, loaded, grape-heavy, waiting for some cancerous spring to release all this shot and shivered rubbish to burst into crazy bloom around us. It runs in the water from the taps; it stiffens and breeds in the columns of water standing in trees; it permeates the granaries, runs in the seed of the corn- fields. It is everywhere. A shovelful of bones will uncover temples to Quetzalcohuatl and the horrors breeding in them; the bathtub from which Netzahualcoyotl, the poet, stared out across the infant world. The tombs in which even the mummies are dead, and wait stiffly for the resurrection. Caves with the rufus bison dancing on them; the Aurignacian dipping his finger in electricity and tracing the fugitive phenomena of the heraldic universe; the Pekin wonder, the age of lithos, lithos, lithos. Apes with extosis, and the forty-foot dinosaur with toothache. Patrol of the serious mammoth between the ice ages. Saber-tooth changing his diet; crows' feet left on pitchers. Minos. Byzantium flowering drably in Athos, practicing a tradition so formal that fifty years killed its novelty, and after twelve hundred you can still smell it, like sardines gone bad in a tin. Faith, you are always saying to me, ultimately one must have faith—but what degree of it, of shining will, is necessary in order to give these relics a decent burial? And anyway, when you say "Faith," how do I know it is not one of the defunct idealisms under whose banner you are crusading? If I am foreign, it is because I am trying to accept the world, not deny its positivity; or build it up on the shaky armature of an ethic. I have quarreled on this subject not only with you, but with Alan, with Peters, with Lobo. I shall continue to quarrel until my own position becomes, not hypothetical, but definite. Then *vale:* the days are too empty and the nights too long. How can I spend the rest of my time here once I am convinced that life is really imagination?

At night I dream. It is a queer sensation. I am killing everything around me, the ages I have visited, the epochs I have endured, the pilgrimages I have been making—lonelier than any Jew could be, more lonely in race. I give up and let everything pass through me from the age of Bronze to the age of Demons. I ride the wave to the height of a million light-waves, skimming the vertebrae of the canon, articulating the skeletons of old systems to examine them, and destroying them again. This fiendish activity has left me alone in a treasure of images, so barren in their value, that just to write them makes me weary: the filter, the pentacle, the necromance. Everything. The mild faces of the astrologers charting the planets. The stark equation of Good and Evil worn like a halter. The tympana writhing with little horn fellows—myctyres, oxyrhyncs, cirripedes, holothurians. In my imagination I follow the myth wherever it burst forth, in Tuscany, Sparta; where you can still see it living in the stiff green candles of the cypress, the contorted silver of Byzance. The robes crusted stiff with apostles, jewels, and fossils. Metamorphic beards sharded in limestone. It is a form of escape. I identify myself with anyone and anything who has escaped death for a vivid history. I tell myself that I am an alien, a foreigner, a pyknic from Mars. I say this, not because I am lonely but because I know it will come true sooner or later. I establish my ancestry as greedily as any suburban householder, grabbing at the lost men, the scourgers, the writers who ate whips and breathed scorpions. In the severest extremity too, even the brothers among the caves, the troglodytes, the men with the green-stick backbones, the murderous syllables that were not words but spoken actions. At such times I might be God for all the world does to me. If my head were larger I might adopt a skullcap like Gregory and a feeling for language equal to Tarquin's feeling for piano method. (*'Touch?' I say to him. 'Yes. So delicate my dear Tarquin as almost to be rectal!'* I offer him brandy before he has time to flinch. Gregory.)

Well, at night I decide it is no use. Escape is the endless theme of our contemplation, escape, escape. The city is beating around me like a fetus, chromium, steel, turbines, rubber, chimneys. The nights are dizzy with the fog, and the trains run amok. After twelve, there is an approximate stillness during which I begin my journeys in Time: the only anodyne, the only specific. I wander from house to ruined house of the Zodiac, or else narrow travel down to an abstraction which can gag the nerves and spread soma along the vertebrae. The world is speaking outside me, in the night, luminous with snouts of vomiting steel and chimneys. The new world, whose choice is strangling the fragile flame of the psyche. Chamberlain is asking for a mythology: no new mythologies, I thank you, we are insulated against the myth. The arteries are stiff with machinery, the spine is folding up like an umbrella. Across the fatal pantheon of the panic world, so irrationally mourned—not for its own sake, but because we have no pantheon of our own—slides the figure of Mickey Mouse, top-hatted maniac with the rubber pelvis, as blithe as the gonococcus in the veins of

Dives. Because I tell myself I adore you, because when we fuck such vivid abstractions seem to jump from our bodies, I would like to offer you the traditional silver lining. But it is no good. When I hear the great chorus of the common people singing the nostalgic hopeless songs of the silver lining, I know it. It is no use. There is no way out. The inky slit between the legs of Miss Smith tells the same tale as you tell me, lying drawn down like a dog or leopard, vulnerable. Remote as the moon craters, the plumes of sunspot, I can only tell you that your fertility is going bad while you sit there, smoking, or reading the paper; it is falling away into the limbo of all this beautiful useless stuff which I am fighting, in order to try and break free from: in order to re-create and re-enter as a new gnosis.

This is a reflection on that night when Tarquin was sitting at the keyboard like a ghoul; and the music—the music flowing like bile into your small alert ears—was so rancid with the truth that I was almost ashamed to look at you. I knew then that the whole thing was a fake—the legend that Tarquin is trying to create, the myth which Chamberlain hourly expects to speak from his stomach like a devil. The Gadarene descent is so violent that most of us are still unaware that we are moving, so rapt is the illusion of stillness. Where is this new myth coming from? Where is the great heroic figure on which it is to be shaped? The causeways are sinking deeper into the marsh, the future is growing a heavier and heavier burden; the past is cut off like a gangrenous limb. Where and what is the avatar—giant or dwarf? Where is the sterilized paragon of the new epoch—the clinic worker and Holy Ghost combined? Give it time, give it time, Chamberlain is shouting. A few more hospitals, less hours of work, more time for the pursuit of higher things. We must clear the ground first. (He is celebrating his own febrile gust in a whirl of wishbone fantasies.) The door of the Lock Hospital is green. The door of the antenatal surgery is white. Green again for the door of the maternity clinic. The fetus is disgorged like a turd from the infinitely distended red rubber neck of the cervix. Let me breathe, I am dying for air. The mask fits very close to the mouth. Filter my food through the placenta and watch my mother devour it afterward. Chamberlain says we must clear the ground. Chamberlain says we must be more humane. We must love our own guts. Above all we must exterminate the politicians who poison humanity, whose souls are as the toes of old boots. Very just. We must make the way straight for the appearance of Mickey Mouse, who will arrive together with his invisible penis which he is never allowed to pull or twang. Chamberlain says, castrate the man who knows too much and is too little; do not mistake the cultured man for the man who is merely well-informed. Grab at the treasures of the passional life. Chamberlain says we must be born again. Tarquin says we are all born dead. Friends, Romans, Countrymen, there were physiologists who did not believe that the hymen existed; and here the fishermen are ashamed to run about naked though the fish wear no clothes! Nothing but fracture, schism, madness remains. *Imprimis,* Lawrence Lucifer, I per se I, standing on a high tower over many delicate counties, feeling the arteries in my limbs stiffen with weeping and lamentation. We, who are sitting outside in the dark, the great unorganized body of creators, know for certain that it is our own tenderness that is poisoning us. The ingrowing cyst of the love which we dare not offer to the world. That is the germ from which the new martyrdom springs: the stripping of the body, fiber by fiber, the branding and cleaning of the soul. I am remembering Hilda's great rufus vulva like a crowded marketplace; the great conduit choked with blood and paper and cigar ends which we must accept before we can go any farther. The great luminous symbol of the cunt, glowing softly in history like the Grail, the genesis of the living, the blithe plush cushion of life. Hilda lying there like Tibet, glowing in her convalescent secrecy among the snow-bound craters and jewels. (There are so few of us left with the murderous gift of love, so few.) And in that music which Tarquin made, as he said, for us, there was no love; there was no hate even—that symptom of love. Only the terrible enervation, the dead loss, the recoiling of the spirit before truth. I said nothing to you then, because I could remember nothing to say; if I had begun to speak I might never have ended. I thought of Morgan, down by the boilers, with the marks of the catheter on him; Madame About and the smell of her womb; Lobo weeping over the knife; Gregory standing before the death squad, facing the green bullets of words: I thought of us wandering that day by the river, among the elegiac kingcups, busy with dreams so trivial and bright that we had no idea of the doom settling from heaven on us like a floor of soot. Yes, when I said we had become heraldic I meant a painted annihilation which you are still constantly mistaking for life. The country was alive in the sense that a playing card is alive. We were entering into a fiction, and all this is merely the paraphernalia of ballet, the insignia of clowns or swans strutting before some too stylized backcloth. That is why this writing had to become ballet and ape it: not the emotion of personalities, but a theater of the idea. Ourselves, if we still had "selves," as the projection of an idea tossed under a spotlight to spin and dither like Japanese waltzing mice . . .

Hush! We have fallen like statues on the grass, footsore, sundrunk, blind. Your face falls on my sleeve like a petal, the words empty themselves out of it into the silence. No continuity any more in the fable, but the warm naked statue under the dress. Heraldic? Time shut off, as sure as the invisible hand in the charnel house shuts off the breath of the dead. As the bee hangs, softly trembling above a flower, then lapses between the lips, a furry torpedo, so the fingers of their unique dream of logic follow the dumb curve of the statue downward, moist, to the final terminus of dream. Gently your body rides out and hangs above the lacquered river: an image not sponged out, or carried downstream among the Ophelias. They say we love only our own reflection in the faces of others, like cattle drinking from their own faces in a river. The heraldic Narcissus in your face has learned something at last. The true meaning of chastity is knowledge.

The long planes of water run through us like seed or spears.

Here is a beautiful pupa stiffened in the crook of an arm, over-looked by a cloud of amazed corn. The music? What has the music to do with this moment in an old world? Nothing. We are as if dead. Death, but there is something left behind, which blows in and out of the nostrils, washes from the throat in a soft wave of invisible ashes; there is something here which dims candles in churches, evanescent—suds or spores or smoke. You have three sets of lips superimposed on one another softly. Such a thing as a kiss would melt, falling from dimension to delicate dimension of sense; the bland face in its surprise could play no part in it. Queer to think that we, who are here on a playing card, fixed forever in an exclusive memory of desire, now share the "necro-biosis" (Tarquin) of the age. It is so easy to burst through the temporal stuff and delude ourselves. You are warm and ripe under the garish dress. I have entered you quietly without fever. The rain rattles among the leaves like dust-shot; the unwinking river is flowing at your head. An instant's vision of the underwater girl, thighs drawn back in an arch to admit rape, tangled in the flowing weeds and fucus. I am with you to the hilt now, Excalibur bedded in the warm stone flesh, pushing open new continents, new vistas of emotion. The inexorable reaping penis stiffened in a field of parched corn. The trees are dragging their heads, caught in the wind. The river is glacid. The kingcups shine and shine, and scent of the crushed marshflower enters us. You are weeping now with delight, and everything is washed away in this effortless, happy weeping. The river has sponged away the dust, the recriminations, the platitudes, the agonies. We are caught in a loom of feeling, woven to water, to rock, to plant by this action. The axle of the world wavers, trembles, and begins a faster, a more nervous rota-tion: we are spun round with rocks and hills and chimneys. It is all so effortless; a warm plural moan—and the long still entry, shut off, drifting to harbor, home, The womb emptied like a bucket of musk into silence. The river flows. The kingcups shine and shine.

Now that our accidental separation is over I walk for whole days at a time in the aura of the life you carry under your dress. I rub my throat on it like a cat. I caress it. It is like a small baffling center of blackness, of magic, among days and ways too easily understood. That is only one of the reasons I went across to the piano, snatched up the score of *To England* and slung it into the fire. Let us have done with all this once and for all. Let us stop all these corpses drinking their own pus like this. I am tired of Tarquin, sitting there in his rubber gloves, playing the wet modulations of the music. If this is an epitome of the English death, then I can make a better one: as an umpire, an onlooker, not a participant. If I find all this difficult to justify, it is because I am young, miserable, and looking for the way out. "My score," moans Tarquin. "My beautiful score, you little vandal." Whereupon there is nothing to do but sink into the armchair, and go into a sulk. I could kill you for the look of surprise on your face. No compris? No speek English, eh? Well, let us talk Lettish. "Fuck? What is fuck?" I remember you saying. Now you have the same puzzled look on your face. O.K. then, I deny it all, I revoke it, every ounce of it: the corn, the dust-shot, the river. You can take the music and stuff it up that windpipe anus of yours . . .

*
**

But you have resumed flesh: into the black car we stumble like coal miners, hot and dazed. Absolute silence over the bridge, like a dialogue of the Holy Ghost. The night is thickening.

Out there the familiar world running away toward that playground of concrete where the lights bloom. Hang on my weary arms. Faint line drawing of a face against the window. We are being drawn homeward on the long thread of the music into the meaningless circus peopled with fanatics, fairies, and clergymen. See! Trains running out into the night. The world is bleeding trains. Soft bars of maniac jazz pant from the doorways. The face of the people is a great grinning disc, revolving meaningless as a record. The domes stacked up over our heads. Laughing mustaches in barrooms sucking the stacked froth on the glasses. Did you see Anselm come out of the doors of the Lock Hospital, collar turned up, hat over his eyes, fugitive and disguised?

The advertisements warm to life. A bulbed Scotchman drinking a stiff rain of bulbs and winking. Anselm has disappeared down the street, rapt in a player's hide. In the bar they are lining up at the trough. Come, we will sit in a café over cups of coffee and eat each other alive. Your wrists incandesce when I touch them. Burn a strange white: molten filaments, Eyes mad and meaningless, turning here and there, burning in their little crucibles. Is there a temperature chart to record the rise and declension of this fever? In the hollow station Hilda is waiting, as in the tomb, for the door to be rolled back, and her man to step from the train. The engines whinny, and there is a fire between her legs now, for the signals glow. In a little while Morgan will gather up the pieces, *steaming.* In the meantime let us try to forget that the bacilli are creeping up on Camden Town. Red-eyed scavengers in millions. Here, devour my fingers one by one. The fingers of buttered toast taste like ashes. There is a drama being played out in our bodies, but what it is I cannot tell. A fury has distorted that white face of yours, which will end in tears. Take my handkerchief. When you weep your nose is drawn back to your skull like a bowstring. Tears burst from nothing. Your mouth hobbles with reproaches. Eyes like rock crystal. I do not have to strike you to make you gush. This is the beginning of my power. My knees are loosened and my ankles are bathed in your blood. Forgive me. I enjoyed it so much.

The music has led us at last back to the very door of the hotel. Tarquin is sitting with the predatory hands, melting his piano down to treacle under the sign of the swinging spirochete. Let us open a nice fat vein and relax in the bathtub to watch the filaments of blood hang between our ribs. You can still hear the cars screaming along the black road outside? The ring of the postman in the empty house? The wires alive with news from all over the world? The housemaids bulging from blind windows? We follow them like dogs, Lobo and I. The salt bitches! At eleven they hang about the letter boxes in slippers. Yes, as Tarquin says, the only letters they seem to post are french letters. On Saturdays you can see Perez standing up against the wall in shadow like a dog. On Tuesdays you can see him on all fours, on a table among the rubber-gloved elite of the hospital, whining like a dog. All this is a little remote from your white sleeping face, whether I lie on your breast like a sleeping dragon, or whether I tongue you into surgical shudders, it does not matter much. Admit it. When you look into my eyes are you not appalled by the little meaning there is in them? The double-barreled microscope offers nothing but a minute iris-image of yourself.

"This is a new beginning," says Tarquin. "Up to now I have been floundering, I did not know my direction. Now it is all quite different."

He has discovered that he is a homosexual. After examining his diary, having his horoscope cast, his palm read, his prostate fingered, and the bumps on his great bald cranium interpreted.

"From now on it is going to be different. I am going to sleep with whom I want and not let my conditioned self interfere with me. I have finished with morals, don't you think? I am that I am, and all that kind of stuff. One must be bold enough to face up to oneself, eh? I am grateful for Science having made it possible. I shall let my female half come out in full view. Untrammeled, what do you say?"

He has bought himself a few cheap powders and face creams, had a false tooth put in where the canine was missing, even wonders whether a wig . . . Well, we do not discourage him. There is something frightening in the idea of the skinny, epicene man parading about his room with a little rouge on the cheekbone, a touch of eye pencil, and a composition tooth. It is the beginning of the disintegration which he has been announcing for so long. The nymph is bursting from the wrappings. The dance is on! He has already learned a few conventional gestures of the hand, a turkey-like movement of the head and shoulders. He minces down to dinner very prettily these days.

"I shall revise not only my moral but also my intellectual life.

171

From now on I shall commune only with the great *pure* minds like Strachey, Murry, and Euclid."

But as for physical communion, he can find nobody to help him out. Sunday morning is the only time off his Balham cinema attendant can get. He lies on his bed hopelessly and twiddles his thumbs dismally in the counterpane.

"I say, why don't you try it," he asks, "why don't you try being queer? How do you know you don't *need* it? Don't listen to that bloody little womanizer, Lobo. He's just a damned fool. Look, do you think it would damage our relationship if I sucked you off?"

The gramophone stops in amazement at this proposal. He sighs and feels his head, imagining a luxurious crop of hair that he could *toss*, my dear.

"I had a lovely policeman on Thursday. Go on. Why don't you let me? Shut your eyes, you won't know anything's happened. It'll be like being confirmed. Go on. Christ! There's nobody around here with any guts."

At other times he is lost in moods of contemplation which last for days. In this he is, as he says, gathering new phenomena. He has become a vast storehouse of scientific formulae, historical data, hieroglyphs, runes, dogma. His bookcase has become a library for the book which he says he *may* want to write one day.

"One of these days I shall open a nice fat juicy vein, lie down in the bath, and begin the book. No. I don't know what it'll be about. I think a huge book of a new philosophy. *My* philosophy, what? No. I haven't bothered to work it out. It'll all come once I start. Sometimes I get all my ideas clear at night, and start to write them down, and then I think . . . O fuck, what's the use of it all anyway? And I go to sleep. And next day I've got to get a shave, or my lover calls, or something. I never seem to have time."

He suffers, he says, from the expanding moment. It is always there, and always the same, and whatever he does he never has time to write anything but the vague notes in his diary.

"Wednesday. Laid Dicky as usual. Three times a night is too

much. I hold that St. Beuve was blaspheming when he said: *La prostate c'est une amygdale dont je ne vois pas la nécessité."*

A part of his time, too, he spends in London these days, taking an interest in the literary life of his time, as exhibited by the goitered belles of Charlotte Street, and the flat-chested winnies of the Fitzroy Tavern. Occasionally he brings one of these conventionally epicene geniuses home with him. Toby is one of his catches. For us simple provincials he has a healthy disregard, being the only one among us to have heard of Hopkins. As a reviewer he is making a name for himself, having cultivated an analytical style tame enough to pass as brutal, and an infallible sense for literary dogfighting. He stands in front of the fire like a young blowfly and rubs his hands together. There is some talk of a new paper. Yes, Tarquin must contribute; it is going to be devoted entirely to the study of genius in relation to the prostate. Claude will weigh in with a few of his camera studies of great big Nubians. Cyril will contribute line drawings if his hand can be persuaded to remain steady. Toby himself will attack everything in sight. And Tarquin will write an essay on the Flagellation Motif in Modern Poetry. "I'd get you some space," says the hero, "if only your stuff weren't so juvenile. The minute you strike a woman you start behaving like a chambermaid. You want more of the—the what is it?—what's that book of Lewis? Yes, the hard male chastity of thought, or something. Emotion is vulgar, my dear."

Lobo is very impressed by these preparations. He sits attentively, his head on one side, and listens to Toby declaiming poetry. He has got the idea that the paper is going to be an obscene one: "Will it be full of hot things?" he inquires ingenuously. Tarquin is very annoyed with him.

For a time it seems the expanding moment has become the expanding hour. Tarquin has bought a typewriter and has found something to do. Consequently he is happier. Also, as he says, it is nice meeting new people and so gradually having more and more people to *have,* my dear. His rouge smudges a bit, he is so engrossed in his new profession. He has bought a wig and an eyeglass but is too shy to wear them, although we do our best to encourage him. The wig he wears only while he is writing. It is a sort of symbol of his artistic personality, the new man who has emerged, "hard and clean as a statue," from the old scarecrow of doubts and fears and remorses. He looks terrifyingly hideous, sitting at the machine, his pale face screwed into a knob under the too perfectly groomed wavy hair.

The summer has gathered like an avalanche. I sit in the armchair watching Tarquin's fingers at work, possessed by a dreadful agitation, why I do not know. In my mind I am composing my will and testament, arranging about the distribution of my few books and poems, planning the last vale in ink of a red color. In the name of Beelzebub, Amen. *Imprimis,* I Lawrence Lucifer bequeath my soul to hell and my body to the earth among you all. Divide me and share me equally, but with as much wrangling as you can, I pray. And it will be the better if you go to law for me. . . . That is the dusty note of all testaments. Or perhaps: I Lawrence Lucifer, sick in soul but not in body, being in perfect health to wicked memory, do constitute and ordain this, my last will and testament irrevocable as long as the world shall be trampled on by villainy. The shadows are gathering in the inkwell, the dyes are rotating with the faces of my darlings, Lobo and Morgan, Anselm, Farnol, Goodwin, Peters, Scrase, Marney . . . I am not sure yet whether there is a postcript or a prelude lying in wait for me. I am uncertain what this color holds, afraid of the faces that would appear if I started writing. Tarquin tells me to tell you that he is happy. Sexually mature, my dear, and fulfilled. How long it lasts I cannot predict. But we hope, dear reader, do we not?

This said, he departed to his molten kingdom, the wind rose, the bottom of the chair fell out, the scrivener fell flat upon his nose. And here is the end of a harmless moral.

*
**

174

There is a delicious impermanence about the days. We eat and sleep now carelessly, as if we were on a journey, expecting the ship to drop into port at any moment. The graph has curved up again into anguish which it would be easy to mistake for delight. The summer is retreating again and leaving us, stuck like monoliths, in the mud. This is the last fatal spasm before the body and mind are forced back into their autumn forms: the last hemorrhage. I can smell the chilly metaphysic of the winter approaching. The tidemarks of the old philosophies are our constant companions. But there is no nourishment to be found in them. "By space the universe encompasses and swallows me as an atom; by thought I encompass it." In the asylums they are knitting, knitting, as if they too could smell the deciduous season. At the Blind School my body is laid out on the reading desk, while the blunt furtive fingers spell it out like ants. Pressing down the ball of the eye, learning the rib and femur, lifting and dropping the drugged penis. In the garret the douche bag hums and whirrs millions of potential personalities into an enamel slop pail. The eyes of the travelers are turned inward, becoming dimly aware of the visible chaos, the garbage heap of the soul. The problem of the personality grows like a stench in the air, infecting the town with man's essential loneliness. Rib to rib, face to face with the absolute heraldic personality which wakes in each other's eyes, even the lovers tremble, and become sick with horror and emptiness. The air is misty with the breath of cattle. The wayside pulpits erupt in a fresh crop of maxims. Christ! can you not smell annihilation breathing in at the orifices of the cracked personality? Madness is in the air. "I fuck and fuck and fuck," says Perez, with the net of arteries standing drunkenly in his spine, "and it's no good. I feel I can't do enough to them. Women! Piss on, shit on, *draw blood.*" His savagery infects the bony figure of our friend on the bed. I am afraid he will kill Hilda one of these nights, but the madness is contagious. We are being slowly suffocated now that the season is ending, being drawn down like decorous blinds in dead houses. In the hospitals they are working feverishly to keep the corpses fresh. Gay mummies stand in the living rooms of Americans. The white ambulance flutters from house to house, fuddled with blood. The clown draws back his trouser leg and lets fall a false cloud of raucous hair. Beds creak in a million rented rooms, loaded with immortality. Slowly the white principle of the body is melted down, softened into passivity. Chamberlain's face is flushed with fever. He talks loudly and ever more loudly about being born again: so as not to hear the hearse draw up to the door, and the footsteps ascend the stairs. Morgan sponges the tidy limbs with cold water, shaves the slack jowls, trims down the black bush and fingernails. Where is the old woman who threw herself on the body and clutched the penis? Isis where are you? Had she never heard of the *rigor?* Things might have been most inconvenient. The tablet shall be in the best of taste, yes, with a quotation from the Holy Writ. . . .

Turn your face away, I am tired of looking at it. Open your legs and let me be sucked up into the bloodstream, poured from the aorta in a simple beat. I am weary. Do not speak to me, because you can only utter imbecilities. Shut up and function, you stale fucking block. Would you be happy if I went for your carotid with a razor, and showed you the nest of tubes and bladders which live disgustingly in your white throat? "Your poetry," she says in the letter, "is wild and unformed. Concentrate on style. And I don't understand *how you can both love and hate the same woman at the same time.*"

Let us admit it frankly, then, the summer is dying. Come, we will go hand in hand, down the lighted streets and turn in at the doors of the cinema. I will let you stand me a one and threepenny dope. What a fine plush womb we have escaped into together, you and I. Yes, we are in time for the mob fetus to be born. Fancy the amnion having lighted walls and mock-Egyptian frescoes on it. We can send out to the clitoris for an ice. What fine strong whiffs of peppermint. But it is the plush walls of the womb I can't get over. They are so cozy, so homey. A lovely dim wombland where we can cheer Conchita, the maneater, and sweat together. Jesus, how that girl eats her lovers! Let us pretend I am your lover, honey; come, masticate me downward. Chew each morsel thirty-two times. Like a heavy cat she eats her heavies heavily. Suck my blood, dearie, it's only ink. Christ! If you stretch those tongueless kisses out any more I'll go mad. . . .

"Desire is the great problem," says Chamberlain. "It is the real absolute you hear these casuists mistaking themselves about, eh? The focal point of living is sex."

I can hear the ink running in the veins of Miss Smith. The batteries running down under the print dress.

The imitation crock-skin handbag is getting heavier and heavier to lift. The problem of desire eats into us like a chancre.

I am obsessed with the fear of snow. Waking in the morning, I run to the window, though I know it is ridiculous, to see if it has fallen during the night. The insane geometry of the statues seems to breathe premonitions of the winter. The ghost of the black car haunts me, riding against the moon. The blood on the floors of the slaughterhouses has not congealed as yet. The winter of our discontent is delayed; I am so beside myself with apathy and self-pity that when I stand here beside the bed, my delectable platypus, and watch your feet reaching the ceiling, I have the sensation of being a bomb: the explosion of a crammed world reaching down over you, to cover you in splinters, fragments, thorns, ashes, peelings. There is such an urgency in the air we breathe that I am on the point of exploding and littering the room with a heap of plaster images . . . solicitations, condolences, comforts, desires. I am participating in a disintegration of the personality, he tells me. The soul is entering a delirious syzygy. Hilda, like a great moon, and you whose cancerous wrists turn white against the streetlamps with a voltage as yet to be scientifically described.

Forgive my imprecision,* but it is as if I were packing to go on a long journey. Hilda lies open like a trunk in the corner of

---

* This is the recurrent regression motif with which everything seems to end: another back-to-the-womber's allegory.

the room. There is room for everything, the gramophone, the records, the cottage piano, the microscope, the hair restorer, seven sets of clean clothes, manuscripts, a typewriter, a dictionary, a pair of jackboots, skates, an ice pick, a crash helmet, a sheath knife, a fishing rod, and the latest Book Society Choice. There is even room for a portable God, if you rope it up among the canvasses. With these labels to assure me of my distinct and unique personality, I step down into the red tunnel, to begin the journey. For the purposes of simplification, let me be known as Jonah. With Hilda as the whale, there are implications in the Bible story which have been altogether ignored until now. Very well! With that knowing look I always imagine the spermatozoa to wear on their faces, I slip down toward the womb, carrying my belongings with me. It has all been arranged, I am going to be walled in. Womb, then, and tomb in one! Plush walls, naturally, and a well-furnished house. All the genteel possessions of the cultured owl. Sherry on tap, Picasso on the wall over the piano, and the rockiest Latins in the bookcase, glossy with age. Presently the embalmer will call. It will be Morgan, dressed up as Santa Claus; with the sharpest of his kitchen knives he will open the abdominal wall, and extract the guts, cure them, wrap them in brown paper parcels, label them—and put them back. Meanwhile I shall be swilled out with grape juice. The brains will be hooked out through the nose and the cranium stuffed with chewing gum. Then I shall be ready to partake of eternity, sitting in a chair, with the good Ezra open on my lap. I will be just in the mood to lend a stiff ear to the felicities of Cavalcanti. Meanwhile from outside the work will go on. I will be completely bricked in. . . . But what am I talking about? I *am* bricked in! There, by the door lie the ice pick, crash helmet, and skates. If I had known beforehand I should never have brought them with me. It is always the way. They are quite useless. Such a thing as a motorbike is unheard of in this limited plush world. In it there is room for one thing only—*pure thought!* Even memory is getting a little dim. Soon there will be no past. Already I have forgotten

178

Madame About's face: I know only that she carries (*carried?*) a
cancer about with her like a hand grenade. Gracie, Chamberlain? . . . A strange procession of symbols across the consciousness. I do not know any more what they mean. It is useless to
interrogate my jailors—the mummies which line the corridor, the
stiff-bearded winged gentleman who guards the bookcase. They
live in the dimension of thought which is space. To speak they
would have to inhabit time. Soon, I too will lose the power of
time-speech. I can feel the heavy bulk of barbaric words in my
brain coiling up and dying for want of use: the maggots of a
large vocabulary eating each other for want of brain tissue to
live on.

The air I breathe is pure and sterile, and reminiscent of a tube
station. I am fed through the wall, in which lies a sort of filter,
embedded. Once every two hours there is a gush of synthetic food
which passes into me without my realizing it. I am happy because
I am nothing, an idea which is a little difficult to express. This
little plush world imposes a routine on me which I respect. I am
fanatically regular. Between meals I sit and brood. Somehow the
books are no longer interesting, because I am forgetting how to
read. I sit with my hands over my eyes and feel the waves passing
in my body. What they say I cannot as yet tell. It is a language
totally unfamiliar, which runs along a dimension of sensibility I
have not hitherto cultivated. Sometimes I take a little stroll up and
down the chamber, repeating my own name to myself. The absolute deadness of the lithographs on the walls no longer depresses
me. I have got beyond revolution, that is to say, beyond God. For
a moment there was an obstinate nerve in my breast telling me to
take the ice ax and smash my way through the red wall, but I
resisted it. I am so happy in my weakness really. I do not even
regret Pater. My glyptic jailors wait stiffly for me to address them
in their own language. I must hurry up and learn the grammar of
waves, the curious syntax which passes between them like a current. There is a supreme logic behind this life which I can sense
but cannot understand. Concentrate, then, I must concentrate. If

I did not feel I was being stifled the whole time, it would be easier.

As for the whale, the exterior universe which was Hilda (the name now lichenized, sponged, scurfed, dimmed), God knows where she spins, in what logarithmic water, over the Poles, her great flukes flashing blue, reaching up almost to the moon. God knows what deep-water fungus grows between her fins, what ice drums on the outside walls of my prison. Jonah, I say to myself, quietly, persistently. It is the only word left over the dead vocabularies. The only sound which I dare use in this red balloon, where I am inhabited by space. It has become my JAH. On the strange numen of this sound, left over from drowned languages, I shall shape the contemplative myth. The nucleus, myself. Give it time and it will become lichenized over with fables, crusted in jewels and parables, fossilized, filtered, crushed, bathed in spores, made more vegetable than empires, snowed under with divinities, Konx Ompax. Never ask me the precise latitude and longitude of heaven. It is as remote as the great rolling whale, whatever ocean she crosses. There is no language, not even the new spatial language which can do justice to loneliness. To the remote Jonah, shut in this furnished bladder, blinded away from continent to yellow continent, across maps as yellow as coin, deltas, swamps, green belts of fertility.

I sit here, secure in the interpretation of the phenomenal world about me, fed at regular times, absently picking matter to pieces. I have a book in my hands, but I do not know what it is any more. There is nothing but this red mist rising from my ankles and choking me. Very occasionally it seems that I can hear fugitive noises of the old world, real or imaginary I do not ask. There is no reality. Only phenomena. I give them up to you as they occur: drumbeats, the rouged faces of dolls, my lover bleeding at the mouth, a toy pistol, fireworks, the abrupt goat face of Pan squealing in a red mist, a packet of french letters, a dustbin, dog's blood, newts, roasted carvings, fly buttons, musk, lilies, the logos. Phenomena in a mist of vaporized blood. At times it seems that the

red walls are moving outward, becoming larger and larger. I have
no sensation of change, however, of becoming. Only the dead full
weight of *being*, of IS! No doubt somewhere in the arctic the
black whale, Hilda, curves and plays, steaming at the moist
nostrils, with a passionflower at each ear.

This must be the end, the terminus. I am waiting forever in
space. It is time that kills one. Space is more durable than logic
can suggest. If I thought I were going to be born again I should
begin to whimper, to pout; imagine leaving this plush-lined niche
in the forever. Another world? Don't be ridiculous. As the fetus is
reported to have said: "I have been here so long I've sort of got
attached to the old place." Konx Ompax. The less said about it,
the better. If I were to try and translate this existence into terms
more easily understood, I might say that this happiness, in which
I am nothing, is simply the turning off of being: the entering into
of IS! An equation which cannot really be rendered, even by
Arabian figures. Enough to tell you that it is from this springboard
that I must make the final dive into divinity, hell-high, with my
body prepared to ride time as gayly as a cork. . . .

The whale blinds away across the charts, covering them with a
flick of the tail, and the little Jonah sits locked in his cabin with
never even a porthole through which he can distract himself with
imaginary worlds. By now, of course, I am blinded with blood.
My only entertainment is in softly walking round the walls, repeating up my own name, and chuckling quietly. I am happy. Such
great thoughts pass through the chewing gum in my cranium that
I long to perpetuate them, but there is not a scrap of paper. With
my knife I carve a few of them on the walls, but it is tiring work.
My boots are full of blood. The final image of the prespatial world
has passed before me and gone. That was last Wednesday—yes,
the solid Wednesday of the new Zodiac. It was the heraldic vision
of Miss Smith playing on the musical sponge, while to the right of
her a sunlit man was pissing a solid stream of gold coins against
a wall. Symptomatic of disintegration? ? ? And why the hell not?
The last nerve in my body has been touched. I have given in,

folded up. In thy orisons may my sins remembered be. Perhaps somewhere the whale will come up with a mouthful of chewed liners, water lilies, crowns, octopods, grand pianos, and pincushions. Who knows?

But the less said about *that,* the better. Konx Ompax. Mum's the word and I duck under.

BOOK THREE

The great question, then, is action, the perfection of one's actions. This is the problem which gnaws at us in these long winter moonlights: a problem under which the personality struggles, and sometimes seems to flower; to take on distortions, shadows, printed negatives of the flux outside. In myself I am not total. There are so many chinks in the steel that the outer shapes of things intrude, eat in among the orifices like rust. It is the endless duel with one's anonymity that weakens one. See what Gregory says:

*
**

Here begins an extract from Gregory's Diary:

My imagination has become a vast lumber room of ideas. There is no dogma which does not find an echo from myself. I admit all of them. There is no necessity to move because I cannot escape. I sit here by the fire with a book open on my lap and the wireless turned on full, and try to establish my identity—that myth which is supposed to exist behind the scuffle of words in my brain. This green diary, which began as a sort of pawky literary fanfaronade, has taken a sudden upcurve on to the graph of emotion. It has become necessary to me. De Profundis, etc. etc. But I do not believe in God. I have endured many imaginary things, sitting here with my little book, alone, and afraid of making a fool of myself.

185

I have written hundreds of tragic parts which I shall never be able to act. I shall never express anything. Pity me, I was born dumb. Death, the most gracious playwright of emotional scenes, has failed to devise even a walk-on which I am not too nervous to play. Laugh if you want. Since she died I cannot bear the darkness. I cannot bear the eternal self-examination of my actions. I cannot bear the moon's intrusion, wandering like an empty skull and afflicting me with the consciousness of self. Myself, that loathsome guest which I carry on my back, like the old man of the sea. You see, there is not, has never been, and never will be, one morsel of spontaneity in me. My actions are not determined by the wind, by the thunder, by any natural selfless spirit, but by that locomotive apparatus which I carry in a tin box under my waistcoat. I am an insect. Tonight I undressed before the mirror and examined my body very carefully, with a loathing that I am incapable of communicating to the paper. The ribs hanging there like a bagpipe! The small legs, slightly bowed; the flaccid dugs, the belly, the breastbone! I am infinitely outmoded, infinitely secondhand. A secondhand piano in the Caledonian market could give my teeth points. As for the image of the eyes, under their arrows, what an aquarium of fishy reproaches!

Destiny has been altered by her death. Yet she is not the figure I am afflicted with on these winter nights. It is always myself I lament, my own death for which I mourn. I think of her as the addict thinks of his drug. Perhaps Gracie was the one spontaneous action in my life. Flawed, yes. Crisscrossed, eroded, but an action in itself. Are we, then, so precise? Let me use a phrase that even the critics will understand. Gracie then, took me out of myself. In her, within her own ignorance, I created for myself almost a new personality. I was convalescent. "One would 'ardly know you since I come along," she remarked once. "You used to be so shy like, Gregory. Not like the same man you aren't." I was unaware that there should be this, the final attrition of being.

I have looked inward at last, honestly, as I have never done before, as I shall never do again. I looked inward, as Epictetus directs, to see the warm light of my own genius, to be satisfied by it, filled. But all I can discover is these strange figures of grief, this masque of the lost Gregories, which live out their submarine life behind the watery blue eyes in the mirror. There is no audit at the end of time which can ruin me any more. I have drawn a stroke across the paper. It is finished. An autonomy was supposed to exist in me. I petted myself with the idea, I fattened myself with it. Under the interrogation of the moon and the hot jazz I have been forced to admit that it was all faked. There is nothing in there to speak up for me. Only these strange figures of grief which parade across the paper under the squeaky nib of a fountain pen. "Nourish your grief," said Chamberlain, "it is good to be broken down, made defenseless. Let the tears out if they want to come." I am cork. A bundle of hysterical wires sitting here. Do not make me repeat again that it is not primarily she I mourn. My disease is egocentric, and therefore mortal. I am lamenting that perfect action which I shall never have time to do. I was born tongue-tied, you see.

Last night as I walked the corridors of the hotel I came across a door which was ajar. Stuck to it, white and altogether bony, was a hand with a wedding ring on it.

This impersonal cipher reminded me at once of my marriage to Grace—the fantastic quixotry of the idea. "Do you really mean it, mate?" she asked me with that curious quick breathing she had when she was surprised. The answer to the question which you are about to put to me is simply, pride. I realized that, staring at the eroded yellow circle of gold last night. My friend Tarquin had said to me with a snigger: "You're losing your reputation, my dear. Living with a tart quite openly here. It's all over the hotel." I knew then that the game was up. England is the one country where the word "freedom" is used without cynicism. By statute one is free. By opinion one is treated like a cretin. In a place like the Regina there is no law, only opinion. I give you the picture of Mrs. Juniper complaining to the manageress on an autumn afternoon. Such a shame you could not meet the lady. A virginity of brass which handcuffed her military husband and kept him down for twenty years in the wilds of India. Since he died her only interest in life, in the felicitous phrase of Chamberlain's wife, has been to twist the knackers of everyone in sight. She nearly twisted mine.

Tarquin came down with the news one night, and listening to his account of the faction which was ranged against us, I was surprised at my own fantastic rage. Even lice, after all, do not prey upon one another. A petition had been drafted and circulated with the names left blank. My sins were so well known and of such weight that it was impossible for one not to know at once to whom the paper referred.

Tarquin had been approached for his signature and had supplied it—a fact for which he felt a little guilty. Chamberlain did what he could to help. This consisted in bursting into the lounge after dinner and saying in his most indignant tones: "I've just heard about this scandalous business and I'm disgusted at the cheap behavior of all you old bitches. What you need, Mrs. Juniper, is a papal bull." Naturally, this was more a hindrance than a help. His wife was insulted in the street by Mrs. Felix, who was quite clear about whose side Jesus was on in this fray. Added to this was the anxiety that Gracie would have another attack and have to go to bed for a while. Tarquin heard Mrs. Robbins announcing to the lounge that Gracie had a nameless disease. All this, of course, one bore with phlegm. Even when the doctor said he could not attend her again for fear of losing a lucrative source of practice, I could find nothing withering to say. I had become granite. Gracie herself burst into tears, put her tail between her legs, and said that she must either leave me or we must both move. It was exactly this point that screwed down the lid properly. I will not be interfered with. I will not be touched by the unclean. I will not. In the kind of mood in which murder is so easily committed I told her she must marry me. It was then she remarked, "Do you reely mean it, mate?"

What a bore loyalties are. "Of course, you little fool."

"Gregory, I've not been a good girl," she said, "I'll make you a bloody awful missis I will. But if you reely want me I'll try."

"Want you?" For some reason I was angrily contemptuous. Then I saw that the little charade must be indulged in. It was too much part of her social upbringing to see its ludicrousness. A blind spot. But the damage to me, to my pride. . . . You see, even this was not selfless. The wretched responsibility of our lives! Action always in response to outside forces. Never a pure irresponsible action, the theme of the Taoist meditation.

Well, the marriage was solemnized if you can use the expression. The registrar was bald. The witnesses were Lobo and Chamberlain. The day was cold. Gracie coughed endlessly. The reception consisted of a tea in the tiny flat where Chamberlain hatched his schemes. The forced solemnity of everyone, the ceremony, were deplorable. Only Chamberlain was gay, and proposed the health of the blushing bride in a short speech. Gracie, called upon to reply, said: "O no I can't, reely I can't. You all been very very good to us, haven't they Gregory?"

From remote regions of ice I called myself back. And heard my own tinny voice remark, "Yes, my dear." My pride was finally wounded. The victory remained with these good-natured oafs who were trying to be so busy and so jolly, don't you know. Make it easy for them, don't you know. Try and pretend that nothing has happened. Put them at their ease, don't you know. I walked home bareheaded. Followed a dinner at my flat (our flat) at which a great deal of wine was consumed; at which Clare allowed Tarquin to fill his glass; at which Gracie became alarmingly the piercing hostess, and remarked, "Oh, do have another portion won't you, Mr. Chamberlain?"

After they had gone and the washing up was stacked for the char, Gracie came into the drawing room and announced, "Well that's what I call a lot of reel sports, don't you think?"

Shall I go on and recollect what a failure it all was? I had ended it all so nicely with Gracie dying in the little bedroom. It was planned out superbly, wasn't it? The telephone ringing. The half-second of eternity when the light was switched on, and Gracie lay there goggling at the ceiling. Yes, it was all set. Even down to the last little touch: going up slowly to the front door, up the stairs, outside, to where the snow lay thick; the soft lamps; gate-posts bathed in whiteness; hedges cut clean, fretted coal-dark against the powdered trees. Going up for a breath of air, I had intended to put it. Standing shivering at the gate to make water, while my whole life lay before me, written in the snow. Lies, all lies. My disease is the disease of the dwarf. To make myself plausible I am forced into a sort of self-magnification of action, of thought. I am forced to make myself transcend reality.

That is why Gracie was so wonderful. So aptly cut out for you in green ink, shaped for a fine slick tragedy. To tell the objective truth would be to cut my own throat. That is not how she died. But each line I add to this makes me more and more reluctant to finish the job. Hara-kiri. A knife turned round in the bowels—but not the bowels of compassion. The bowels of pride. If I could get at the ulcer which has poisoned my actions I would stir it with my nib until the black bile and pus and splinters gushed forth. Pity me, I was born dead.

There is no room for the classy irony with which I have treated the theme hitherto, which is almost my only literary wear. The moon is shining on these pages. Your genuine ironist is never grilled solely on the iron of pride, as I am grilled. The green fountain which starts from this pen is poisoned at source. False irony; a mask baked down tight over the real interplay of facial muscles. God, to find words which would bite down, right down to the pure lustral source from which perfect action flows. This ultimate purification is the theme of my meditations all night long. I try, believe me, I try. When the wireless shuts down I anes-thetize myself, my own body, my own quintessential self, and watch it carried to the theater. The amphitheater is crowded with advocates. Under the waxen arcs I see the cloth spread. I am wheeled on the great soft trolley to a point of vantage. Strict white automatons parade with necessary apparatus. The masked face of

190

myself leans down over my body, selects an instrument, and begins. A long bloodless slit in the band of yellow. A sound as of a
razor cutting silk. A quiet hiss and splash and infinite masque of
movement among the white figures, busy as ants. The gutters are
slowly, noiselessly brimmed with blood. Discarded livers, kidneys,
tracks of colored guts drop away from under the sheet and plop
into an enamel pail. The yellow envelope of flesh which is my
belly becomes ever more flaccid, more empty. I tell you this goes
on all night, every night. I am thoroughly opened and explored.
My guts are emptied. And to no purpose. It is no good whatsoever.
Today I am still what I was yesterday or the day before. It is no
good.

Here I am, I want to say always, take me and rip me open.
There is a prize offered to anyone who can find the essential
Herbert Gregory, alias Death. These stammerings betray me, but
no matter. I am writing for the public of the damned. Let this
become a piece of superb cartography. Let me be laid out here in
relief, to be pored over by professional students of the soul's
geology. See, strata by strata: the most delicate laminations.
Suffering, dear ones, has made me marmoreal. You will find
written on me all those symptoms of strain that you can see on the
faces of old actors. There is no variation from the magnetic north
of artifice. Touch me, there is absolutely no charge. Observe, I
am utterly metamorphic, I fall away in long rotten flakes.

Sometimes I imagine that it is not I, not really I, in which I
read these sympToms of decay. It is my world dying on me, with
me, in me. Strange tunes seem to blow about the snow-lit drawing room these days.

Gracie, when you died, when you really died there overlooking
the sea, could you imagine that I, turning from your little
pinched-up face with the knowing gamin grin on it, should wring
my hands together in an intense grief. *Not for you! Not for your
dissolution, but for my own?* You poor white symptom of my
world, did you know that the trite mask of sorrow I wore hid the
great merciless fear and rage which your death forced on me? You

191

could not guess that, recoiling from your dead mouth as from a branding iron, I was recoiling from myself—the infinity of empty I's who had yet time to walk, talking of ordinary things in ordinary places.

No, I say to myself, let her be. Don't think of her. She is just a pawn in this philosophic game which you are playing and which is going to kill you. Let her be. The accent is not on the commonplace loss of a body, of a laugh about the house, feet on the stairs, warm body in a warm bed; it is the loss of the embryo Gregory which was born in her, and which she took away into death with her. I was with child by her. I was kicking in the womb. What right have you or anyone to judge my sorrow, not for her, but for the irreparable loss of my germ? The real struggle was not between us but in me. Let her be. Death is just one of those mathematical constants whose value we must accept as approximate—to ten places of decimals. She used to say to me, after we were married: "Gregory, we're not pals very much, are we? I mean we don't like the same things, do we? I don't care for a lot of old books like you do, and you don't care for the pitchers and Gary Cooper and all. Do you? Oi, answer your missus when she talks to you, or I'll clout you one."

"No, we don't very much, do we?"

"Then I tell you what." That with a serious tone. "If you'll come to the Pally once a week with me, I'll read one good book every week and get improvement. I'm not very brainy, but I'm quick on the uptake, amn't I?"

If I had not been nourishing myself on her, this idea would have sounded less frightening. So we were to establish points of reference between each other? I was to learn the rumba and she help herself to slices of improving Gibbon. Perhaps Voltaire, or Butler. (I would like you to know that I am well-read.)

The charm of these little scraps of gossip is in their completeness. Their completeness of falsehood. The process, alas, is too simple. Take a thought from its context and you can make it mean anything you like. You see, when Gracie married me, it

192

was as if she had died on me. The metamorphosis was alarming. While I had been an equivocal, a rather queer and undependable lover, there was always a pinch of good salt to season the dish. There was always a head chef, in fact—your humble servant. But an economic dependence on a husband to a person like Grace means a complete social independence. She is irresponsible, anchored finally by a strip of printed parchment, and a few lame words mumbled by a bald-headed man. Therefore she is free. It began almost as soon as the wedding guests left: a critical survey of the flat, and a careful enunciation of its limitations. "We'll get it all fixed up," she said, "so it'll look nice and dinky when your friends come. I want to work hard for you, Gregory." That was how it began. I give you full permission to recognize this as comic relief. There were curious additions to my tasteful set of furniture. Hideous bamboo trolleys, bead curtains. My beautiful sofa was called inelegant; it was suggested that we should have it covered in red damask, *with tassels.* "We must get the parlor shipshape," she remarked once or twice, and I recognized a new note in her voice. There was the ring of the Penge matron coming to life in her tones. It is difficult to admit that I began to loathe her. I loathed her because I was in love with the ordinary, uninhibited Grace who was sure of nothing; and who by obedience alone maintained her precarious hold on my affections. As a stranger she was a paragon. As a wife she produced nothing but this crop of warty furniture, a few copybook aphorisms (old-style), and a bad temper in me. If it began with the parlor it could only end with my friends. Tarquin was to be slowly dropped. "He's a kind of pansy," she remarked. "I don't like it. I seen that kind before. He's a winny." Next Clare. Not that he was ever a friend of mine. But now that she was a respectable married matron she was angry at the thought of him. She resented him. Lobo and Perez passed muster. Their manners were so lovely. But Clare might yet try and shake the economic stability of marriage by a revival of their great love. He was to be cut dead from the roots.

There were rows, yes. There were great tearings of checkered sofa cushions, wilfull smashing of the chinoiseries with which my spouse had lined the bookshelves. But to my horror I found that Gracie was not to be cowed any more. She was a wife, by Jesus Christ, and she was going to give me of her best whether I liked it or not. And all the glorious misunderstandings on which our love had been built now came forward and contributed to the frightful domestic uproars. Trying to explain, with my usual scholarly precision, just what it was she was doing, she would enrage me with a burst of sniveling and the accusation: "You try to make me out a little tart, that's all. You think I'm not classy enough for your wife because I don't speak proper. I tell you Gregory, I'm doing me best, aren't I?" If I pointed out that that was not the point, she would whimper: "You just want a prostitute here to use. You don't want me to try and give you a home." Bang! another piece of Tottenham Court Road china. All this was unbearably tragic, unbearably comic. What was really fatal to our relations, however, was the slowly altering cosmography of our social life. There is nothing like pride for giving one the interpretive faculty. I flatter myself I can play the social astrologer as well as anyone—shall we say Proust? The glance, the lift of a forefinger, the attitude before a mirror, the hair-trigger meaning of a word—these constitute the furniture of a world in which I am too much at home. All this, of course, is a pretty way of saying that our marriage was not a success. The enterprise was undertaken as a defense against the rights of an individual. It was to end in estranging me from all those who had backed me up in it. The brightly colored tesserae which formed the mosaic of our lives—and so on.

In the beginning, let us say, Gracie was an asset to the menagerie. She was amusing because there were no signs of seriousness on my part. She had a certain chic; as you might say, a pet marmoset might have, if it were worn on the left shoulder of a Charlotte Street genius. It was a case of: "Come along and meet Gregory. He's so original, my dear. He keeps a performing woman." Something of that sort. As soon as the maid became a matron the whole angle of vision altered. It was no longer I who was quaint. It was Gracie. *I was poor little Gregory.* And she herself was not so much quaint as boring and silly. Her affectations, her knowingness, her fatuous little clichés. It was impossible, in fact, for people to come and enjoy my company, without being forced to go through the ultrasuburban palaver which Gracie insisted on.

And then, how those bamboo pieces rankled! But I would have furnished the flat in chintzes, if only she could have been prevented from poisoning the springs of relationship. Chamberlain was horrified by her stolid and utterly ladylike composure. "What a little Magdalene," he remarked, as usual never slow to say what was most truthful and most inconvenient. "One of these days she will say, 'Mrs. Gregory to you, young man.' Seriously Gregory, where does this tram ride end?"

Can you imagine me remarking, "I think it's shortsighted of you, young man, to expect me to help you criticize my own wife?"

The Chamberlains hardly ever called after that. One gets used to being very much alone. However I missed the fine rolling arguments, the eternal questions of desire, marriage, etc.

Of course, there were spaces between the stars occasionally. When she was ill, weak as a kitten, there were rarer moments, when our lives seemed to burn up again, twist up into red shapes of real fire and tenderness. Passion flourishes on tears and self-reproaches. But the contact was tenuous; a precarious crossing from island to island over immense gulfs. Superimposed always across our world was the notation of the disease, with its movements up and down the chart, unpredictable. Yes, it was my world dying, I can see that now, in retrospect; falling away into wanness and death. Without any sort of emotion we were waiting for the last convulsion of matter, the last shaky dredging out of the lungs, bright spurt of blood, untying of fingers and knees.

I would give anything for it to have been as I wrote it. In

spite of my defects the potential emotion is there, you must admit it. It should have been a mouth-to-mouth affair with an elegant epigraph and a cracker motto for an epilogue. Gracie died just at the time when I had no emotion whatsoever to spend on her: dingily, surrounded by nurses and heartless starched blouses, in a Bournemouth nursing home. What thoughts went through that silly little head at the last one does not know. There was no movement in the room, except the prodigious movement of the sea. Mist, and the rain hissing along the concrete marine parade. In the silence you could hear the waves combing up across your thoughts, washing them, sucking back the impurities as they went back. Not even the fashionable numbness, I assure you. Lightheaded as a bell. The rigor had set the bashed face of my little tart in a Christ-like grin of pure imbecility. In my imagination I fell upon the corpse, and enacted a whole scene out of a Greek tragedy. There was nothing moving in the room except the gigantic sea licking the windowpanes, and my thoughts in their heroic mime. All my life I have done this—imagined my actions. I have never taken part in them. It is the catharsis of pure action which is so wounding an absolute to contemplate now. Invultuation! Daily I pierce the image of myself, and nothing happens.

(I am obsessed by the imaginary triviality of all this. Is this just another tic born of diffidence? Am I concerned, here, privately, standing on my own soul's ground, with the creation of literature?)

History is a study which has none of the venom of reality in it. Your protagonist, your chorus, your crowd: everything on the stage has no more personality than an old pack of cards. But autobiography is another matter altogether: if you are honest, a continual, a painful kinosis. If you are dishonest, an eternal fear.

I have been rereading these pages; a little weary and disgusted at the way I prey upon myself; a little horrified at the squeals which go up from them. Memories of De Profundis!

Since I returned from Bournemouth—alone, the very word is like a bell—I have had all my time to myself. I see no one, except

196

occasionally Tarquin, occasionally Morgan. There is nothing to
do, nothing to be done. Yet, this is a lie, because this time has
been the most critical in my life; the most vital, as far as the making of decisions goes, I have ever known. I have been glad to
be alone, to revise the vast catalogue of thoughts and actions
which have been born in me. My body is here, like a vast unused
library in which no one has interested himself for years. Aware
all at once of the battered volumes around me, I have been in-
dexing them, estimating the mental and spiritual caliber of their
original collector. It is fearsome work. Here an Ella Wheeler
Wilcox, there a Freud . . . further on an old Moor's Almanack, a
Baedeker. But where is the Black Book—that repository for all the
uncut gems of creation? I grope along the shelves, blind.

This is my forty days in the wilderness. There has been time
to revise, to annotate, to gloze. Fiat voluntas. On the manuscript
I shall draw a Phoenix, with its feathers in flames; a raving piece
of heraldry to insist on the eternal desire in me—to confess and
be assoiled. Meanwhile, I wander along in my private wilderness,
broken-mouthed with thirst, humming the Te Deum, envying
everyone. Yes, the butcher, the baker, the nun and the candlestick
maker. The porter who brings me my meals, and stands like a
carving with the glass of beer held in his paw. Even Tarquin
whose struggle is not with the Holy Ghost but with his own
weakness.

Gracie's father, now. There is a subject for envy. My wire
brought him down the following day. Small, muscular, with one
of those fine ascetic heads you see in Renaissance frescoes: a
helmet of small fine bones, pressing down in planes to the temples.
His words were gnarled and twisted, it seemed, by the shelf of
pearly false teeth which they had to pass. His first hoarse query
as he stepped from the train was, "Is she still fresh?" Walking
toward the waiting taxi I explained that she was. Silent he walked
beside me, with a queer jauntiness, as if propelled not so much
by the movement of his muscles as by an explosion in each foot
as it touched the ground. In the taxi he undid his soiled gray

muffler, and produced an old tin case with cigarettes in it. We smoked in silence. "I didn't bring her ma," he said at last; "she's queer, you know. Yers, a little queer."

In the silence of authority we were shown into a little room, where she lay, amused, like some obscene flower dragged out of the underworld.

Her father advanced toward her with a series of noiseless explosions. "I must say," he observed, "they made a fine job of it. A fine job." Tap, tap, tap, went his fingernails against the wood. Yes there was no doubt. It was a first-rate job. As if contemplating some definite gesture he turned to me, then stopped and resumed his nonchalant assessment of things. I was somehow afraid he was going to shake hands with me over the body, and compliment me on the fine job I'd made of the whole business. He stared down with his watchful, slightly bloodshot eyes.

But it was when he lifted the sheets, and started to examine her more closely that a spear entered my left side; there was a quality of curiosity in his pose whose meaning I could not guess, but which made me somehow curious of myself as an interloper, almost as if I were intruding on the unpleasant poignance of a private domestic scene. I turned to the window and lit a cigarette with profound embarrassment. It was all in extremely bad taste —Gracie giving up her ghost so easily, lying there so wan; and this little nut of a man running his blunt workman's thumbs over her body, as if he were touching marble, considering its smoothness. No movement in the room, but the sea. I was stifling slowly in my own cigarette smoke when he turned and said, with decision, "Well, that's that."

If there were any private thoughts locked away in that bony skull of his, I did not get a glimpse of them. For the night he had taken lodgings, he said, in the commercial hotel—the Caledonia stern and wild—which was at the end of the road. Turned on his heel after a civil greeting, and left me staring after him, down the long rain-shining streets. I walked up and down the dark parade until nearly morning, trying to sort out those fragmentary impulses, emotions, which weighed me down, and put a fog across reality. Nothing echoing in my mind but the vast reports of the waves against the concrete, the drizzle of rain on my mouth. And her father? More than ever an enigma: self-contained, airtight, damp-proof; locked in silence under the shabby overcoat and soiled muffler; behind the fine plate of bones in his skull. One could beat against his personality again and again, with a sea of queries, advances, intimacies, and the stability of his position was unaltered. Over and above all this, like the very lunge and swing of the dark sea, there was the sad recognition of my failure to mix the real and the unreal, my failure to make imagination life. It was only then that I could have wept: for myself.

Turning away from the graveside, beginning to walk with that explosive action of his, he said, without any sort of emotion, "Well, what's done's done." But the sigh he fetched from his very lungs expressed something more than he would ever be able to say.

We said good-by in the sodden square of the town, somehow reluctant to part from each other. He had a train to catch, he said. There was no time even for a drink at the Plough. I think he was afraid of any sort of intimacy. So off he went in his wet muffler toward the station, like a little dancing master.

Retrospect! Retrospect! What a hive of memories I have become. There has been time, in this wilderness, to account for everything: to excuse my shortcomings, to re-enact my failures, to adjust my differences with destiny. Above all to make the great decision. To be or not to be has been the question for too long. I am determined to answer it in the negative.

Walking the streets of Bournemouth I came upon many faces I should know, many places I should remember, many moldering old houses which my essence visited in the third cosmos. (Metaphysics is the last refuge of the actor.) Trees, shapes, smoke from a cigarette in the dark—strata by strata my memories were laid out across my dead body; wheeling and skirling with anguish like gulls across the nerves. Love me, I whispered, love me and take me from myself. I do not want the gift of freedom—it has become a prison. At night the sea beat like a hammer against my temples. The lights of cars wheeled across the bedroom walls. I had become an inhabitant of a private pandemonium.

On the hill, its garden hidden in spray, was the house in which I lived when I was a child. My mother lives there for eternity among the chipped statuary, the unweeded walks. "Herbert, will you ever sin?" The white round face of the woman above me, and my own voice, "Never, Mother." She used to say: "We are such friends, aren't we, my darling? I know every little thought that passes in your head." From that remark my life begins, a solid unbroken line of dependencies—at home, at school, at the university. Behind the bars, serenely unaware of the flood outside.

Regard me, I used to say to the world, I am the average Englishman. I have never left school and I am proud of it. I carry my virginity and my self-satisfaction on a string round my neck.

Shall I outline it all with introspective precision? I am not a Powys. Shall I explore my garish literary life? Why, I have written disparagingly of Shakespeare in an advanced review—and then returned home to my guardian virgin as the snow and dressed in horn-rimmed spectacles. I have critically disposed of Pascal, Molinos, and Ronsard standing at the bar of a Red Lion Square pub. Once I even lectured on the sexual aberrations of Lawrence to an audience of vipers as learned as myself. In the final audit how heavily will these weigh against me? "You were born to spit on the delicate things," said Chamberlain once in a fit of fury. And in my little cackle of laughter he added, "Because you have learned how to spit on yourself."

Alas! in this personal limbo from which I letter out my fragmentary diary, I see that this observation is very just. It is not the world that is poisoned so much as the people in it. It is my world dying because I am dying—of an intolerable brain poisoning. Pity me, etc.

These nights are very long. I sit here in the laboratory which

I have made of my ego, and listen for the familiar sounds, once foreign, now local. At two the boilers are stoked. I brew myself tea, light a cigarette, yawn, take a step, remember an anecdote of Lobo's, and laugh. I am always aware of myself as an actor on an empty stage, his only audience the critical self. I dramatize my least action, make it studied, calm. I have the eternal illusion of being watched; of being visible to an audience before whom I must be careful not to break down. The late trains drizzle outward across the snowy landscapes, across the hills, the valleys, the dark blue bodies of the counties. I am alone, but no more alone in the spirit than I have ever been. Now that the moon has gone I am able to stand at the window, staring at a star of the third magnitude. I am acting my head off. I chuckle and scratch my head. I lift my cup to my mouth with the air of a dowager. Lycidas is dead, dead ere his prime. In the corner lies the long svelte horn-gramophone. I select the most moving records of "the master's" Op. 61 and play them one after another, as fast as the turntable can rotate. The violin scamps like a cat, poops and squalls and gutters. It is a capital joke. "A violin in an empty house, remote in its meditations as a ghost." That's what I wrote once. Now it micturates like a wombat, hurtles and squeals, winces and foams. I lie here in the chair, chuckling to myself, and let the discords play upon me like jets from a hose. I revel in the anguish of that quivering fiddle. Metaphorically I spit on Beethoven. Mentally, physically, from my very soul, I spit on his misery. I would like to take up those shelves of folio music, throw them in the grate and piss on them. . . . When it becomes intolerable I go and look at myself in the mirror. Standing there in my peacock dressing gown, with one of the smashed records in my hand. The revulsion sobers me. I light a cigarette, shrug my shoulders in infinite contempt, and sit down at my desk, to add the paragraph you have just read.

This morning I receive a visit from Perez. He is a little angry with himself for neglecting me. He says he is only just back from the country, which is a lie because he has been back a week. "A woman?" I say to him archly. It is almost our only subject of conversation. He diverts the conversation. Lobo has the flu. He lies in bed all day, like a little black imp, strumming on his big inlaid guitar. Perez is wondering how to condole with me in my sorrow. He is a little disgusted at having to show any sympathy over the loss of someone like Gracie. A little contemptuous, too, of me for getting entangled with such a one. I can see it all written in his eyes. At last he blurts out: "I say, Gregory, I'm sorry to hear . . ."

"Yes?" I say, demanding my pound of flesh.

"Gracie . . . your wife . . . I've just heard," he mumbles shamefacedly. "Very sorry for you."

When he goes, I return to the piano, pour out a glass of sherry, and sit down to Mozart. My fingers ease the chords from the white soft jacks, like heavy bunches of grapes. The music wraps me in its ectoplasm of emotion. Really, if you forgive the precious litotes, I am an executant of no mean caliber. In my imagination the tears are running down my face, on to my fingers, on to the lush ivories. My bowels are running out of me like tap water. I am become a figure of sodden cardboard. The notes rap holes in me, smothering me in bullets of sound. Mozart claws my liver and nibbles my tongue like a woodpecker. . . .

It is the same when I sit down to write. The submarine profundities of my imagination are suggested by the florid sweep of my pen.

My intention is always to become the very paper on which I write. Alas! the rhythm is sadly uneven. My brain, like an engine, gives the first tug, which communicates a series of bangs to the carriages. Bang, bang, bang—all the way down the line. My teeth chatter, and my vertebrae clang together. Very slowly and stiffly we are off, puff, puff, puff. The nib squeaks at every level crossing. I am in mortal terror of a collision. All the signals are dead against me. . . . Pity me, etc.

However it is not for long now. The decision has been made. I sit here on this final Monday morning of the world, with my pen in my hand, and contemplate those infinities of feeling which I would like to express. There is nothing in the Lamentations of Jeremy to touch the terrible thin squealing which I would like to rise from this paper and stifle you. This thin, astringent script of mine—let it be poured into your ears, most delectable of corrosives, until your brains turn green, cancerous, nitric. . . .

Per fretum febris—by these straits to die! There is nothing here that is more than marginal. Here, take me, and rip me to pieces. Undress me, coat, waistcoat, vest, pants—stratum by stratum. I am again standing naked in front of the mirror, puzzled by the obstructing flesh. The great problem is how to get at the organic root of the trouble. How to locate and diagnose. There, I spread out my genealogical chart before you. The family tree must bear some traces of the ancestral pollution. The paper is black with little monkey-like gregories, climbing from the square loins of their parents. On top of one another like acrobats, the high ones crushing down the lower ones into history. On stepping-stones of our dead selves, etc. Does this bore you? Then join me in a bowl of sherry and some lascivious drawings. Put on some jazz. Let us embrace one another. Let us dice with my false teeth. . . . Tarquin has started a novel about the life of Jesus. He is excited by his own fertility. He comes down and reads me what he has written. "I've made him turn into a woman," he giggles. "You know the bit in the garden? She is there weeping on the ground. She is so delicate and trembling that John's bowels are moved. He goes up behind her, not quite knowing what he is doing. She is quite broken and limp, like a smashed bird. Eh? Is that a good touch? Like a smashed bird. Without knowing he puts his hand inside her robe and feels the great heavy lobes of breasts. Lobes, Gregory. *Lobes!* He turns her over and deflowers her as she lies there weeping and imploring him not to. Eh? Very softly and heavily he enters. Eh? Like Lady Chatterley. John mounting the spouse of Zion, while she weeps over the fallen cities? My God, don't you think there's passion in it? John entering the dead bird like a slow heavy battleship? Eh? And all the terrible and agonizing misery of her soul, her tears and all that, turn into the most excruciating, tortured, terrible, blasphemous, piercing delight?" He is trembling all over and biting his nails. Then we both begin to cackle; we are consumed; we lie there and howl until we are nearly sick. The tears are pouring down his face. . . .

Abstractedly, on the drawing-room carpet, I create the wilderness, the deserts, the stone crop, the thorn. Infinities away I see myself, bloody-footed, stumbling along under the sun. Tarquin is talking, whining, protesting. I could lift my glass and throw the sherry into his white, hairless face. "It is not sex," he is repeating over and over again, half to himself. "It's something to do with me. . . ." It is a monologue to which I am supposed to be attending. His eyes are full of tears. He coughs over the drink and swallows. The music suffocates me. The bow is fiddling across my very nerves. What a terrible ointment for the tears in my womb!

"It's not sex," he says, larghetto. The ache of the strings sends little shooting pains through my teeth. The clarinet. The delicate variation. O the bassoon as mellow as port, cherries, cigars, mahogany, black bile. "For a long time I thought it was. But it only disgusts me—even with him. Listen, we borrowed Durrell's car and went out of London. Imagine us locked in the back seat, O Christ, buggering each other like a couple of billy goats. I thought my heart was broken. I was sick and sick. That's what gave me the idea to write all this about Jesus."

A violin in an empty house, remote in its meditations as a ghost. Such a quiet solo voice speaking to creation. It could only come out of a madhouse. The quiet pouring of the selfless action. The scissors snipping away the threads of the brain, quietly, quietly, in secret. And then this music settling like white hot steel into the mold of my ears, stiffening, gleaming. The variations shuffled coldly out, like a pack of blue and silver cards. A pack of aces. Music to hear, why hearest thou music sadly? The responsive medulla quaking like a custard. O God, there are no tears for this madness, but dry eyes, dry tongue, dry throat, parched scrotum.

"I had a dream last night." Larghetto. The long curving planes of wormwood, gall, spikes in the liver. "I was in a butcher's shop. Quite naked, my dear. My scrotum was a yellow leather bag. The kind of moneybag the rich merchant wore in his belt. You know. You've seen the medieval pictures. Well, it was tied round the mouth with tape. I undid it and looked inside, and it was full of little parched brown seeds. Before I had time to do it up I was picked up and slapped on the counter, with a sickening thud. And all the seeds fell out and rained down on the floor. I got such a fright that when I woke up I thought for a moment I had wet the bed."

The family tree hangs on the wall beside the wrestlers. My poor aunt Jane owned a bloody nevus. Henry, the third cousin who had made a packet out of estate, was a little berry of a man, with peachdown chops, and patches of fluff behind his ears. His waistcoat would swing open like a door and show you that he was worked by a clock. Tick, tock, tick, tock . . . His face was a relic of the Sung dynasty. Such a delicate green patina! My mother wore him round her throat. Tick, tock, tick, tock, the white pulse that Henry had given her.

Old Fanny walking the streets of Bournemouth; and young Fanny who killed me on the Black Rock, above Brighton. God, the soft lips and hair and hands. So delicate were our first inexpert attempts at love. Gather her up in the palms of your hands, softly so the powder won't scale, and feel her flutter. Those queer green stone eyes, like a foal. And the warm loose mouth. The leaning body on the long fine legs, so elegant and insecure like a foal. The long pointed breasts that swung hard against you as the sea birds flew out of her hair, softly whewing, and the tide came licking up over loins. Whatsoever things are just, whatsoever things are pure, whatsoever things are lovely, whatsoever things are of good report: if there be any virtue and if there be any praise, think on these things. My face taken up softly between

205

mountains and the cold iceberg coming down upon it, melting in my mouth and nostrils. "Herbert, are you telling a lie?"

"No, Mother." Mother of God, Mother of Misery, Mother of Jesus, Mother of Man. Aphrodite on the rolling brown horse, triumphant, with the menstrual blood flowing in a wave to her ankles. Old Fanny, with the permanganate bowl, and the store of old soiled rags. "Herbert, will you serve God?" Softly with the white throat beating over the hymnbook, tick, tock, tick, tock, the white pulse Henry had given her. Can I have fallen in steam from between these loins? Cattle breathe on my face, and her breath is more delectable than the cattle, I will not betray her. Save me, seize me, open me, have me. I am a gift that nobody wants. Lesbia, let me be your sparrow.

Very well then, I give in. It is no good trying to conceal it. I am afraid of these simple things, the lusting, the crying out in the night, the blood and whipcracks, the ring of money, the seed vomiting, the child, the lamb, the eagle, the leper—I am afraid of them all. *I am afraid of the great, the terrible simple things.*

Old Fanny used to say in her hoarse crazy way: "What's to be ashamed of, young master? Blushing because of my blood? Bless you, we all have blood." And the too elegant and deadly Rachel: "You're undersexed, my dear. It interests most men." You could almost picture her sealed in a glass case in Tottenham Court Road, while the whole world watched her change them. I quiver like a struck ship when I face these things. Fanny, too, had blood. It was the rule. Newt's blood. I wouldn't be surprised if Tarquin did too. But the bowl of permanganate sails up and takes me by the throat. "Herbert, praise the Lord." "To Him be all honor and glory, Mother." Chip, chip, chip. My father at work in his apron, hewing out the cornices of the tombstones. Tock, tock, tock, and the fine stone slipping away under the steel. He has made three tombstones, the biggest for himself (In Memoriam), the next biggest for her (tick, tock, tick, tock, the white pulse Henry had given her), and the smallest (Hic Jacet). It never occurred to him that I might grow up. In the greenhouse, secretly as a leopard, he sits and plays Mozart, among the ferns, potted plants, arabesques, and fossils. I shall never meet him again. The terrible plangence of those chords reaches out at me, ten sentimental white carrots of my mother. O God, I am empty inside like the first chaos. My gestures are carried away over the gray sea by the gulls. Fanny and my mother and the ten sentimental carrots laid in my memory to desiccate and powder slowly, and give off this strange nostalgic aroma. My life is unwinding itself inside me like an empty spool. I have become a disc not played. The lid is closed, but I rotate forever in darkness. Fanny, I need nothing but your moth's face, your furry eyebrows, your devil's quivering like a pigeon held against the breast. You belong to the picture book, to the gibbous moon, to the tombs, to the pack of knaves. The bowl of your face became the bowl of the sky. There was a psalm due to you, but sitting at my mother's knee, pale domestic, regimental in my starched collar, I could not make it.

"It is all dead, do you realize?" Tarquin is standing up over me in the firelight, shouting. The light is twinkling on his palate, on his charred molars. "It has all been used up and dead. It's gone. We can't get back. Gregory, do you realize? It's the past now."

His head is cocked sideways to hear the drums again. Then he is shouting again, in that high voice of his. His nose sticks out like a bandaged thumb. "My God, how seldom we realize time. Do you hear me? Eh? And it's going through us the whole time. We are running through it without realizing it." Then once again, whining. "Gregory, where are you going to? Please tell me, eh? I must know. I can't stay here alone, without someone to confide in. Eh?"

We are sitting in the drawing room among the pile of boxes. All day I had been burning the more expensive of the books in the grate. There is still a stench of pigskin hanging in the air. So much for my buried talent. Let it stay buried. I shall clamp the lid down on it. Tarquin is talking again. Excuse me. I must transcribe what he says for posterity. "Is it something wrong? Couldn't you confide in me for once? Think of the intimate things I have told you before now. Intimate, intimate things I would not divulge to a soul. Gregory, where are you going? You can't just leave. Tell me."

What shall I answer? "I am going, my dear Torquatus, to marry Kate. I am going to become a barmaid's homely plunger. You would like Kate if you met her. She wears a thick rubber washer on her vagina." I am chuckling as I write this and read him it, syllable by syllable.

"Oh, do stop fooling now and be serious. You've been japing enough this evening. Tell me. Eh?"

"I've told you."

There is a long pause. Count twenty.

"Well if you won't tell me I'll sulk."

"I tell you what. I'll write it all down as a piece of homely fiction and give it to you to read when I leave. With my address on the bottom left-hand corner, by the impression of my ring. The one with the phallus on it. What do you say to that?"

He has begun playing his Wagner on the piano. A Teutonic wet dream. For a minute I feel I would like to drive this pen into his back as he sits there playing. His lifelessness is such a satire on my own. Then suddenly he moves into a hard glittering travesty of Mozart. An uncut furious diamond, which scratches the windowpanes. Fanny walks along the cliff like a ghost, dressed in gull-gray, from the gullet to the loins. Blown black against her body, the material lies on her, clings and blows about her breasts in relief. She lies there like a stone figure in a forgotten desert, doucely outlined by dunes. Such a tenderness in the loins, such a blindness, is required to recall this in music or green writing. My eyes are lead plummets. There is a glass bridge built all of a sudden in my brain. I tread softly for fear of breaking it. My knees are made of isinglass. I am afraid of her. My blood pours out into the soft sand as I kneel beside her. Hot, hot, like lava between the arches of the pelvis. Tarquin has begun playing the medulla obbligato. I remember the blue cracks in Gracie's rictus. The rigor mortis. Most delectable of laws. We shall all of us have the last laugh. When there is nothing to fill the hole between my burst heart and the nearest star I shall still have the divine gesture, the Epicurean pose.

"This barmaid, is she real?" says Tarquin casually. "Or is it another jape? You seem full of japes. All this book burning. Eh? Give me your books. I'll sell them and stand Lobo a woman. I'll buy myself a new hat and some music. Eh?"

"You misunderstand the gesture."

In the evenings we used to walk together. That means nothing to you? I don't wonder. It was my world. We used to walk together in holiness, damn your uncomprehending face. If there was any passion in the earth then we exhausted it all. Nothing has remained since then. Mrs. Vengeance used to sing "My soul is like a flow-er." And we used to sit rapt with our fingers linked, the eyes so frank and green, like the eyes of my rocking horse. Close the finely cut head, delicate as my beautiful rocking horse, with the soft cut-away lips, like twin dolphins.

Where are the snows of yesteryear? Thank you Mrs. Vengeance. That was lovely. But where is Fanny, Gracie, old Fanny . . . ? Grins I suppose. A trio of Cheshire Cats. Or all melted into the essential grin? The wizened rictus of Lao Tse gouged on the terrific face of death. I remember suddenly her running toward me in the music, offering her wrists. I was a quivering fiddle until she laid that cool pad of her hand on me and dumbed the strings.

Today I noticed the bald patch spreading. Signs of the times. The spreading baldness in my bloodless scalp like red ink on blotting paper. I have composed my last will and testament. In the mirror my eyes seem to incandesce, turn a cold steely blue. It is like looking down the oiled barrel of a gun.

To the green eyes I offer the nostalgic fit of weeping, a rocking

209

horse, a bundle of flowers, a hymnbook, my seal with dolphins on it, and any of the apocryphal testaments.

He who smiles firsts, laughs last. Fiat Voluntas. As it was in the beginning, is now and ever shall be, grin without end. Amen.

"You are unjust," says Chamberlain, his hair in his eyes, his teeth gleaming. "Passion doesn't flourish like a potted plant."

He has heard I am leaving, and in a fit of warmth he has come round to say good-by. I am furious now because I have told him all about Kate. The little secret over which I have been chuckling and hugging myself for the last few weeks. Under his infectious warmth I found the facts slipping from me. . . . It was so natural to admit the soft impeachment—for Kate is nothing if not a soft impeachment—that now I am furious. "It's not passion that interests me," I say.

"I'm sorry," he says, with a queer quiet humility, utterly unlike him. "I suppose we're not all alike." As he leaves he says, a little sentimental, "Drop me a line, will you, if you feel like it?"

I shake my head. The steep flight of stairs detains him for a moment. "You'll change your mind," he says, "I have a feeling you will. Good-by."

Very well, I return to my desk for the final audit. This diary must be finished before I leave.

I am tempted to write a little about my father, about him standing in a trance hour after hour in his workshop, absorbed and selfless as a bobbin in a loom, going through the motions of creation. But there is nothing alive about this retrospect. The illusion, perhaps. But in reality what a terrible galvanic twitching. It is the world's disease. The balance has been lost which alone makes action live, which alone creates formidable work. Now there is only the illusion of action. Faster, we cry, faster. After a time the illusion of action is lost, the sense is dulled, the last fearful stalemate of the soul sets in. This is the death I am participating in.

Well, everything is in order, or rather disorder. The hall is blocked with trunks. There is not a single artistic or aesthetic object in them, but they seem very full. The hearth is awash with ashes.

Morgan brings my dinner down with the face of a jailor, and then leaves silently, banging the door. I expect Tarquin to call but he does not. Very well. Stone walls do not a prison make, so I shall eat the cold pork, and crack a Pale Ale on the bows of the departing Viking. Yet, I protest, this place has the atmosphere of a slaughterhouse. This is my wedding breakfast. After it they will come in with their hands behind their backs, shamefaced, like butchers, in their uniforms and tell me to stand up and turn round. I shall feel my arms pinioned. Weeping with relief. I shall allow them to lead me out, a passive sheep, into the little adjacent shed, where IT stands. There I shall be washed in the blood of the Lamb, choked, and given the long clean drop, footfirst, into the absolute. Let them cut out my blackened tongue, and my charred liver, and pickle them for the Museum. Let me tell you a little about Kate, as soberly as fits a condemned man. Firstly, I am very happy. I have poured out my decisions like small change, and selected one clean new sixpence. Kate is the lousiest, tightest, dumb and most devaluated sixpence that ever came from the mint. Let me not affect this bitterness. It is not real.

When I think about Kate I am as dumb and passive as a bullock. It is the only solution really, the only way out. In Bournemouth, walking the streets, while the rain pronged the lights and houses, the whole shape of my future rose up and choked me. In the municipal library I found myself all of a sudden sitting with a book on oceanography open in front of me. I was looking for the Logos. The face of the squid attracted me. Later, in a cozy little bar-parlor the face of Kate was the face of the same squid I had seen on the title page of the tome.

We got into conversation in quite a classy way. She trod on my foot and said she was sorry. I knocked her glass against her teeth and said I was sorry. "We seem to be in a proper pickle tonight," she observed. When I agreed she went on to make sundry trite observations about the weather, etc. "Are you staying long?" she asked. "Down here for a spree?" I explained that I was down here with a dead wife, and was immediately taken in hand. I was mothered. It was tedious but pleasant. Being a widow she felt herself competent to deal with a strong man's grief. We went to cinemas together, flirted mildly too. This, she gave me to understand, was what all widowers did. They felt so lonely. She was a knowing little thing. "Don't you worry, chicken," she said, patting my thigh, "I won't snatch you."

"Don't call me chicken."

"Okay, chicken."

She knew all about men. Her husband had been one. But her honor would not stoop to mere bawdry out of wedlock. " 'er," she said modishly, knocking my hand away. "Lay off that mucking about. I'm not one of those."

"O, but you are, Katie. You are a proper one. I have never seen such a one in my life." She could never make out whether I was sneering at her or not. However, it seemed unlikely to her way of thinking. It was just my way, she used to titter. I liked to have her on. Dilating those hard eyes of hers she would put her face close to mine and titter. Immediately the humorous squid would come to life in her.

Do you find Kate a bit of a puzzle? Here, I put her photograph before you. A trim little craft with that predatory squid's jowls. Brass wouldn't melt in her mouth. You can see at a glance that here is someone who knows right from wrong. You are still puzzled? I will explain. I chose Gracie, because she was, as women go, extraordinary. With Kate, I employed the method so much in vogue with the writers of best sellers. I chose her because she was the most ordinary person I could find. If I had not met her I should have had to go into a bank. Kate is the sanctuary which I have been wanting for so long. When I saw the little house, with its cheap and hideous furniture, the linoleum floors, the garish cushions, I said to myself: I am home at last. Sitting in my slippers under a steel engraving of Holman Hunt, feeling the damp sprouts of flame from the gas fire warm my trouser legs, I said to

myself: This is my sanctuary. Hereafter I shall bury myself
beside the wireless, behind a paper. Kate shall minister to my
soul with a meat and two veg, and leave me to my private battle
with God. This is deadly true. Kate is the monastery in which I
am about to be interned. I have nothing to say to her, nothing in
common with her. I have given up all those childish nostrums and
charms with which I hoped to find salvation for so long. Hush, I
say to myself, from now I am going to lie in secrecy. A prediluvial secrecy. No demands will be made of me in this private
madhouse. Kate's husband gave her so little that she expects
nothing from me. An orgasm, for instance. She does not know
what that is, has never experienced it. I will take good care that
she never does. She has a deep-seated nervous grudge against men,
the dirty brutes. This will ensure the sacred void between our
stars. She lies under one with that white, painful, Christian face
of hers, and puts up with the more loathsome side of the business
with the air of a real stoic. It does my heart good to see it. I need
fear no intrusions, no wringing of hands or bowels.

Tomorrow I will go unto my father, by the four-fourteen. I will
be met at the station. I can see it all, I can taste the manna in my
mouth. The smoky little road with the hoops of iron round their
dreary hutches. Home! The segment of sopping grass outside the
green house. The one sick dwarf apple. We shall sit down in the
kitchen by the range and eat dinner together—she very wise and
skittish and hard as a bell. And with our knives shall we scrape
the rich brown dripping from the pudding basin, and smear it on
our bread.

"Everything fair and square," is her motto. She is a great be-
liever in the equality of the sexes. She shall pay for herself wherever she goes, even at the cinema.

There will never be any question of personalities, because she
is too much of a lady. I shall never be lonely because there will
be no relief from loneliness. Chamberlain used to say: "Let us have
more of the metaphysical beast, Gregory. Come on, gird up the
loins of anger." I am weary of the cult of bowel worship. Weary,

utterly weary and sick from my very soul. All these pious resolutions have bled themselves empty in me. If there were an organized religion which were strong enough to grip me I would welcome it. There is something in me, I know, that must be chipped away, like dead mastoid. But I shall not bother to fight for it. The struggle is too hideous, the inner extraction of dead selves, like giant festering molars, is too too painful. Let be, and suffer the disease to run its course. From now on my hands are folded across my breast. Let the grass grow under my tongue, between my teeth, let the scabs form on my eyeballs, let the buboes burst between my toes, I shall not lift a finger.

This is the going down toward the tomb. The weather has been, on the whole, very fair. There is a slight belt of pressure settled round the south coast of Ireland, but who cares about that? Fair to fine is the general forecast, with slight local showers, and sensational fluctuations of bullion. The pork trade is doing well. The ductless glands are in training earlier this year, under a new coach. Their time from Hammersmith to Putney is already doubled. It is hoped that they will carry off the Ashes this year without any difficulty. At a twelfth reading, the bill for the distribution of more milk to pregnant members of Parliament was carried by a majority of twelve. Mr. Baldwin concurred. Altogether the outlook is magnificent for the coming year, with a definite promise of worse to follow. Stocks are falling owing to a recent eruption of Mount Rothermere, but hopes are rising. Recent excavations in Fleet Street have been suspended owing to a discharge of speckled venom. However, business proceeds as usual, with slight tremors.

Lobo is having a terrible time, they tell me. He is in love, and is finding it painful. While he was abroad he met a German girl, a pneumatic Teuton frau, of the love me or leave me breed, who held him down with her thumb and gave him something to think about. He spends all night weeping for his sins. "I have not been an angel," he says, rolling his sore, swollen eyes. He is in two minds about cutting himself. He wants to marry her, but how can

214

he? Such a foul, leprous little whoremonger as he is—can he marry a fine pure seafaring blonde? If she found out about him she would go into a monastery. And then he would have to go into a monastery too to equalize things. And if he does marry her, how can he keep away from prostitutes and enthusiastic amateurs? They are in his blood. "I am a dirty leetle leecher," he says wildly, beating his thigh. "I was a pure Catholic once until that woman got me. Since then I have been thirsty . . . like thirst, you understand?" I understand. She taught him many peculiar refinements, did his friendly widow. She used to say, "Better to keep the shoes on when you do it. It is better shoes and long black stockings."

From my present sumptuous boredom I sit and laugh at Lobo through the bars. What a droll little ape. I can no longer even be amused by his antics. Tarquin can be funny when he squalls and whines, but Lobo—no, I have put away my microscope for good.

I can hear the train wheels beating their rhythmic revolutions in my head as I write. The four-fourteen carrying me homeward to the slippers, the gas fire, the paper, the dripping, the text on the wall. And Kate waiting for me, trim and cheaply scented in her Marks & Spencer knickers. Done up in colored crinkles for me like a cheap cake of aromatic soap. We shall stand together before the deputy of God, and partake of a manly little service for the connubial felicities to be legalized. Dear Kate, like a canvas doll in bed with a white stoic face, whetting the appetites of cruelty in her brand-new hubby. And all these acres of tragic struggles, of boredoms, despairs, delusions, will fall from me as I enter my prison. The ubiety of God. The fantastic zero to which I shall reduce the terms of living and so find happiness. The slow gradual ascent into silence, into dumbness. Why do we fear the modern world? Why are we afraid of becoming insects? I can imagine no lovelier goal. The streets of Paradise are not more lovely than the highways of the ant heap. I shall become a white ant, God willing. I shall have my swink to me reserved and

215

nothing else. Let the hive take my responsibilities. I am weary of them.

This is the meaning of the smashed etchings in the grate. The dislocated books. The large red discs. From the wreckage, however, I have saved certain things that have the death in them. These I will give to Tarquin to assist his disease to kill him. To sew the tares of a greater madness inside that great throbbing egg-like cranium of his. Anything with the real taint in it, the real green gangrene. Peace on earth and good will to men. But I speak after the manner of men. I am in the grip of this slow suppurative hate, which lingers in the provinces, planted in our nerve centers. Fiber by fiber it has eaten into us. Whether I shall yet escape its ultimates—rape, havoc, murder, lust—this remains to be seen. It seems to me at times that these narrow wrists moving here are the wrists of a murderer.

I, Death Gregory, by the Grace of God, being sound in mind and body, do make and ordain this my last will and testament, in the manner and form following, revoking all other wills heretofore made.

The bequests have been carefully weighed. To the literary man I leave my breath, to fertilize his discussions, and cool his porridge. To lady novelists and chambermaids my tongue. It still retains a little native salt. To poetry a new suit of clothes. To the priest the kiss of Judas, my cosmic self. To the pawnbroker my crucifix. To Tarquin my old tin cuff links, and to Lobo the worn-out contraceptive outfit, with all good wishes. To the English nation I leave a pair of old shoes, gone at the uppers, and a smell on the landing. If they want my heart to bury beside Ben Jonson in the Abbey, they can dive for it. To God I dedicate my clay pipe and copy of the *Daily Express,* and my expired season ticket. To my mother I offer my imperishable soul. It has never really left her keeping. To Fanny my new set of teeth, and a bottle of the hair restorer which didn't work. To my father a copy of the *Waste Land* and a kiss on his uncomprehending, puzzled face. To my charlady I leave all those books in which the soul of man is

216

evolved through misery and lamentation. She will find them incomprehensible. To the young poets I offer my sex, since they can make no better use of their own. To the journalists my voice to assist them in their devotions. To lap dogs my humanity. To best sellers and other livers off garbage, my laughter in the key of E flat, and the clippings of my toenails. To the government my excrement that it may try its sense of humor. To the critics what they deserve; and to the public their critics.

To Gracie the following items: a cross section of my liver, an embryo torn quivering from the womb, a book of sermons, a tea dance, a dark partner, love-in-the-mist, passion and mockery, the laughter of the gulls, eyelids, nettles, snuff, and a white sister to sponge her gaunt thighs when the night falls.

And now it is time to take the long leavetaking of ink and paper, and all the curious warm charities which have been corrupted by bile and ruined by men with the faces of cattle. Mantic, the dream-self projects this vast saturnine grin across the taut cosmos. I see men and women again, moving softly with expressive hands across the floor of the mind's sunken oceans. Softly and dreadfully in their voicelessness. The strange dumb movements of plants under water, among the blithe cuttlefish and wringing octopods, and the forests of gesturing trees. What I had to offer I gave gladly. It was not enough. What remains is my own property. To the darling of the gods I give the long warm gift of action. It was no use to me.

I shall be sitting here when they find me at midnight, watching the laughter stiffen and crumble with the ashes in the grate. It will not be difficult. A brush and pan will be all that's needed. I shall sift gently into fragments as I am offered to the plangent dustbins. The record and testament of a death within life: a life in death.

To these tedious pages, which I shall burn before I leave, I offer the gift of life and the reality of the imagination: the colors of charity and love without bitterness. A sop to kill the worm which fattens in them. A few grains of honesty. And a last phoenix act of revelation among greater beauties, in this iron grate.

And to myself? I offer only the crooked grin of the toad, and a colored cap to clothe my nakedness. I have need of them both. Amen.

Here ends Gregory.

*
**

There is no news—none whatsoever. The summer went down at last in a hush of bows, and now we are waiting for the first iron statements of winter, the first gruff breath from Tartary. The constellations are pinned out for us like specimens, sharp and malevolent. The Sickle and the Twins, the Pleiades and the Dog Star —Sirius. Now the night breathes authentic lungsful of arctic air on our bodies. In the hotel gardens the crazy declamation of statues is already frozen. The first chains are being drawn across the flesh of the traveler as the earth leans on her journey. The liners are going out into the night, warm and melodious with lights. And in the long blue spaces of night curious premonitions of death halt in the still air of the playing fields, linger and disperse. The avenger's hour when even the lovers' voices turn to vapor, cold bodies in cold beds arch up like bows and stiffen; when deserted on a deserted pier the husband scribbles a post card to his daughter, and the gloved talons of the blind man spell it out, painfully, in Braille. This is the doldrum, the icy limbo between seasons, between the new self and the old, between the death and the being born. The sky is lyrical with stars but there is no news.

Cross over to Bethlehem. They will be able to tell you for certain whether something will be born from this discord of the elements, or whether the fiat has gone forth; whether this is a pre-nativity or a post-mortem.

It is the particular moment when the pen hangs suspended over the paper, with the absolute phrase hanging in the nib. The phrase that will not be written.

But we have called an armistice for these few days of limbo. We have made a truce in the private and endless war which has been with us for so long. We are hardening our arteries for the last lap, the victory or defeat. Tarquin, of course, has scampered into his cell and locked the door behind him. "I have entrenched myself securely," he lisps, "against the inclemency of the season. I shall hibernate." But it seems to me that this winter is not something on which one can lock doors. It does not exist only on the painted tradesmen's cards, but in the individual himself, in the very bones of the protagonist. It is more than the bones of the fingers which have gone dead. What is this fanciful emanation which seems to have turned the blood to custard in our veins? I do not know. The very marrow of speculation has been turned to icy phlegm. The sonorous dewlap of the Brigadier has turned purple. A thirst has stiffened the hocks of the curate. And the sore wattles of the immortal Mrs. Juniper crackle as she walks backward and forward in the blazing lounge.

"If one were false," broods Tarquin, "how nice to put oneself away for the winter. Take out the glass eye, unscrew the legs, the arms. Remove the wig, the teeth, the silver plate in the skull, the tubes in the anus and abdomen, and just climb into bed and wait for summer. In the late spring you could have a good repaint and clean up, and sally forth in August like a late crocus. How lovely it would be." All day the sullen traffic passes outside the window. Tarquin gloats in darkness, behind drawn blinds. Lies in his winding sheets, fingering the nailholes in his feet and hands. On the table lies his latest effort in prose, fresh from the typewriter, and collecting the dust. It begins, startlingly enough, in the dislocated manner of the early Surrealists:

The pudendum of the maid winces as winces only the bowl of bubbled suds and the elfin hopscotch of the street boy. Never, I say, to myself, I say, never. Rising, I turn the tap on, and the soft gaslight ignites the spurious maidenhair. Here, fill your pipe. Shall we smoke blotting paper while our noses bleed?

He is making experiments in dissociation, he admits coldly, though nothing interests him these days. This is because he cannot get his feet warm. "Chafe my toes for me, will you?" he says, extending a luxurious foot out of the clothes. "But don't excite me, whatever you do."

In the apathy of the long evenings we leave Lobo's little room, where the ghost of guitar chords seems forever to hang, and let ourselves out of the big lighted doors, into the snow-lit landscape outside. It is like a cold dive into water, so numbing that one can hardly breathe or speak. Tarquin walking like a gaunt automaton beside us, exhaling long windy streamers of smoke, like a horse, and whining through his teeth. The Spaniard draws his scarf taut over his mouth, muffling his voice. He is quite hysterical about this German girl, and has lost all control over his hysteria. He can't eat, he can't sleep, he can't do a damned thing without bursting into tears. It makes me very miserable. Tarquin is delighted by these exhibitions. They strike him as immensely good entertainment. Nowadays, if I want to get him outside the front door, I have only to suggest a walk with Lobo.

We have covered the utmost confines of the map in darkness these nights, crossing the bare white roads, the long avenues of smoldering shops, the tram routes, the deserted parks. In my soul there has been such a misery as I have never known before. It is the real stratosphere of emotion, where there seems to be nothing left but the anodyne of cruelty or physical pain. In the darkness Lobo will suddenly begin talking about his German girl, the fearful oaths they swore, and the mixing of their bloods, and all that incomprehensible barbaric palaver which is settling on his memory like a leech. The minutest of gestures, the tilt of her body, the inflection of a word, will occupy him for an hour, while he describes it, broods on it, even acts on it in his queer dinky little way. Then, suddenly halting in his tracks, as if about to be sick, he will burst into a long throaty sob, and a recitative of broken Spanish. His eyes are hung with huge tears. Tarquin begins to laugh, and I am forced to repeat miserably: "Lobo, for Godsake now, come on, will you?" He leans against the fence and wraps his scarf over his face. He is shaken with huge juicy sobs. Tarquin watches curiously as I try to get him walking again. "Leave me alone," he croaks, like a child. As I take hold of his shoulders he turns and runs at me as if to strike me on the mouth. "You don't feel it," he says angrily, "what I feel it is the misery you don't know it." His cheeks are quivering. There is a trembling tear on the end of his nose. A little disgusted I begin to plead with him. His eyes light up with fury: "You say that you suffer with the girl you know, but I say SHIT. The word is no meaning you . . ." Tarquin lies against the fence silently shaking. I feel I could murder him. Snow is beginning to fall again. Lobo is standing there like a maniac expecting me to defend my capacity for suffering. He hates me for not being able to join him in a wild emotional outburst. Then he turns and begins to lurch down the road again. We follow him at a distance, giving him time to cool down. Tarquin is delighted. "Tally ho, what?" he pipes cheerfully, "tally ho. My feet are warm at last. Are yours?"

In the dimly lighted room, we sit on the floor and watch Perez lift the great living guitar into his hands, and make it sing. His great head is lifted as he sings in a beautiful canine hysteria at the ceiling. He is strangely beautiful. And catching sight of Lobo by the gas fire, his hands over his ears, he suddenly shouts in his perfect English: "Suffer, for heaven's sake, Azuarius, and be happy. If you can still suffer." And choking with delight he pulls open his jaws and sings with a terrific vengeance, his features curiously pure-looking, curiously fresh, somehow like a coin.

Tarquin is lying on the operating table. The frost has cobbled up his mouth. He feels nothing yet, is not thawed under the check quilt. "Give me some brandy," he says, and drops back like an opium addict, to dream of the Mediterranean and the dark boys with whom he should be gathering saffron above Knossos.

In the corner by the fireplace Chamberlain laughs himself almost hysterical over the new magazine. Crouching down with one hand spread sideways in the blaze of the fire he flicks the pages, marveling. Tarquin affects a huge detachment, lying there with his eyes shut. The little hoots of laughter electrocute him: "My dear old man," says Chamberlain at last, leaning out toward him in the darkness, "my dear old man. This couldn't have been written by men, but by plants. Plants, Tarquin!" Tarquin gobbles indistinctly. His chin dissolves and flows slowly down his dressing gown to the bed. The room is full of artificial yawns. "Come," says Chamberlain, rallying his shock troops, "Come. My dear fellow. *Come!*"

We are all sitting there frozen by apathy. Chamberlain fires glances around the room, looking for sympathies. No one gives a damn. Tarquin snuffles something about "palpable literary ability." "It's not their ability one questions for a moment," yells Chamberlain, "it's their existence." He pauses in midleap as if struck by an expanding bullet. We avert our eyes and lie back in our corners sleeping and muttering. Two days since the feast of Saint someone or other, and we are still groggy from the celebrations. The gramophone pours itself endlessly into the room, record after record slung on by the new changing device which Tarquin has just bought. Bach throws out a long rope of counterpoint, but I am too weary to rise to the lure. The room is full of rope. It goes in at your mouth and comes out of your anus in a single long thong. Muttering and shivering we doze in the damp room, like drug addicts.

I recall an infinity of smoky evenings shared with him and since forgotten, the fumes of the pipes hanging in the stiff air of the obsolete billiard room. And the white face preposing axioms, dogma, amputating its own words to lean low over a shot; and the inflated symbols of our abstraction, love, death, desire, etc., clicking and crossing in their meaningless impacts. Chamberlain's disease is the disease of the dog collar. Outside the accepted fence of ethics he finds himself face to face with his anonymity, and is unable to outstare it. His rhetoric, his stampeding, his fulminations represent an attempt to herd back into the enclosure again.

And his discovery of this state of things only produces greater and greater efforts, more steam, more energy. Gregory I admire, though I do not understand him so well. His choice was the trap, because he could not stand the stratosphere. Chamberlain would like to take his own cage with him, and pitch it in the deserted stratosphere of life. He is nothing but a spiritual colonizer, to whom the wilderness is intolerable until it is cultivated, pruned, transformed into a replica of home. He does not respect its own positive laws. He would transplant his own. To such a man there is no meaning in the word "exile." He will never be an inhabitant of that private pandemonium which Gregory peeped into once before closing the lid. The darkness which I myself am beginning to inhabit, to construct incongruously for myself on the rocky northern cliffs of this Ionian island (perhaps, who can tell, even interpret by the tapping of these metal pothooks on the paper you hold before your eyes).

In this theater it is all or nothing. Oneself is the hero, the clown, the chorus; there are no extras, and no doubles to accept the dangers. But more terrible still, in the incessant whine of the chorale, the words, words, words spraying from the stiff mouth of the masks, one becomes at last aware of the identity of the audience. It is my own face in its incessant reduplications which blazes back at me from the stone amphitheater. . . . In the mirror there is no symptom whatever: take me, I am to be accepted or denied; not to be understood, but experienced; not to be touched, but a funnel of virtue; not a Christian, but an admirer of God in men. Do not inquire of the ingenuous mask, I say, it can tell you nothing.

In these damp winter days the first germ is sown in me, as we lie against the wall, shivering like addicts; the germ I shall take away southward with me; which in this act of tuism I am learning to control. The struggle has been medieval almost. Long winter nights, lying there while the sea drove up night-long over one's dreams, washing, forever washing and breaking up into one's thoughts, purifying, healing, destroying. This writing, then, is the projection of my battle with the dragon who disputed my entry into the heraldic baronies. For me, at any rate, it has been cardinal, for I have suddenly grown up in it. I am falling westward steadily, entering the region of the pneumatic gift! A latitude where even a lifeline is no good and the diving bell of the philosopher crumples with laughter.

And yet, at the other end of the telescope through which I can see my own pygmy history projected, is always for me Chamberlain's white face, its utter incomprehension a mere mask for ideal certainties and delusions, hanging above an obsolete billiard table, hungry for news in a world which has no news to offer. The summer went down at last in a hush of bows. That much is history. The rest, the winter for instance, is so much a part of us that we are unable to dissociate—to distinguish it from our other diseases. The empty stage on which we clown brilliantly under the audience of stars. A ballet of human beings rigid on our hooks, gently swinging, like frozen meat.

Hilda is lying in Bethlehem, dead drunk. This winter is eventful for her, veteran sportsman that she is. She has lost both ovaries. The season therefore is no longer closed, but open. There is no more the great enamel bowl by the bed swimming in used condoms and carbolic acid. The bowl to which Perez once wrote an ode of fruitfulness. The bowl against which Lobo held his racked forehead as he vomited. The wilderness is paradise enow. And in the great stallion's face there are new markings, new "fields" of experience, which show that the struggle is beginning again. The verb "to fuck" has become synonymous with the verb "to be." It is as if this act were the one assurance of existence remaining to us still. Staring at the enlarged pupil of the old stallion's left eye, arriving in state in the plush corridor lined with stools, and going over the murderous details of a brilliant hysterectomy. All these things I go through blindfold. It is when the guitar begins to sing in Perez' fingers that it is all recalled to me. Lobo in the attitude of the billy goat. A medieval scribble in his underpants. Or Perez rising suddenly out of the bushes, blind drunk, and huge in the moonlight, with the great bell rolling under his shirt.

The penis of the whale for instance! Or the book-lined walls of Tarquin's room. Everywhere books on the pathology of madness. How is it that we can be mad, and yet so saintly quiet, with hands folded in our laps like empty gloves? It is the persistent miracle. Out of this drug addict shivering the face of Hilda forms, apocalyptically round as the bowl of the heavens, and scarlet as the dragon. Or Connie turning over on her side to let the tide sluice her out. The Indian Ocean propped open before Clare, and his delicate Levantine features hanging over her, pale and afraid. Turning over, for example, in a huge lather of foam, winnowing the poles with their great female flukes. Connie and Hilda. Dead blubber in a chaos of arctic lights, churning and moaning, until the pale Levantine face is broken up into its components and sent revolving down the gullet of the whirlpool. And to the question: "Who introduced you?" Tarquin now gives the answer, "My mother." This is extremely significant. The wall is lined with books which are hardly ever opened. "A book," says Chamberlain, "is a testimony of inefficient action. I shall live instead."

Or the world of El Greco, smoky, ill-lighted, glowing like radium. (Take your choice, take your choice, but leave me in peace. Geology has no terminology for these fissures, schists, bosses, snags. Take your choice.)

Or the bit from Gregory's diary which I did not dare to quote. ("What can I do? What can I do? There is no action in me. The very sperm that runs from my penis is null. It is not virtue going out from me, but a dead loss to the body, the psyche, the will. My vitality runs out of me like pus, and there is no figure of grief strong enough to express it. Shall I pour my hair through my fingers? Shall I tie the grin of the madman round my face like a scarf?")

In the deserted billiard room where the pockets hang like plundered scrotums Lobo dances the dance of the Incas, quite naked. He stops on tiptoe, whistles like a wren, and sneaks behind the curtains giggling. Chamberlain is talking about England, the Puritan Father of the world. His face is the face of a burnt-out duchess. The old Babylonian whore that is England, burnt out, gutted, with the disease melting her eyes in their sockets. Then Lobo appears again from behind the curtain with an erection almost twice as big as himself and we all stop in consternation. We are celebrating the second coming of Christ with a mammoth party. Rye whisky, rubber, and a colored argosy of fine slang whores from the West End. Poppy and Ethel have already fought with Connie. And Clare in trying to intervene received a blow on the side of the head with a loaded handbag that nearly took his ear off. Poppy is pure litmus. Dip her in urine and she turns poppy-colored, somnolent, drug-eyed, myopic, hayseed. Now the men's trade union has intervened. It is, after all, the second day of the debauch, and we want a bit of male privacy. So in the billiard room we rearrange the cosmos according to a new pattern, while the women squabble in the lavatories and tear each other's hair off. So much for the cosmos.

Incongruously Chamberlain and I construct the new idealism over the billiard table: an idealism more damning, more hysterical, more ruinous than any that has yet been known. Had I not written it out of my system already, I should be dead print today, instead of this macaronic poem which is designed to bore clean through the middle ear, and leaven the craniums of the wise. Enough. One should never write of accomplishment, because nothing is ever finally accomplished. That is the trauma of the ideal. It is the timeless action in its immediacy that I must concentrate on, here, now: this paper, this pen, this counterpoint along which the mimes carry, in a funeral measure, the corpse of the Theme. I have kept them rotating in me so long, like a prayer wheel. Like a great roaring merry-go-round of faces. The horse vermilion-nostriled, the peeling unicorn, the dragon breathing acetylene. I am continually forced to stop and marvel at the incongruity of peopling the Ionian with such a ballet; as if, in a clear watery moonlight one night, while the shepherds on the

226

lagoon piped their slow bubbling, curdling quarter tones, a fleet of heraldic fish were to swim up under the house, and deploy flashing across the paper, across the bookshelf, the painted peasant woman at the well, the ships on the carpet and my wife asleep in the armchair. . . . Lobo, with the beak of the swordfish performing watery acrobatics under the Albanian snows! It is very curious.

Perhaps it is our loneliness here, on the bare rocks of a rocky coast line that makes my connection with these subjects tenuous enough across the foam, the rock pools, the little lighthouse-shrine where St. Barbara on wood broods forever on a smashed lamp and a pool of oil—that makes this connection be love: even for Tarquin a love—*a humour*—which is all friendly. Diving from the lowest scrap into the green teatime water I recall suddenly that Tarquin, in his dressing gown, is writing a letter to his lover beginning, "Dear dear Dick"; or under water, painfully swimming with webbed feet and hands, see Chamberlain's body, bullet wounds and all, dragged up under the river lights, celebrating a suicide that he was too timid ever to commit. He is often with us: in the morning when the sails slip down toward Crete, red, yellow, green; in the afternoons dancing the old dances on the empty rocks with Theodore; at night when the apocalypse of moonrise shivers up into one's throat and the lone fishermen light their buds of flame and put out; when the man and his wife swim noiselessly under the house like dogs, quietly talking, toward the open sea.

Sitting here, on the prophetic black rock, where the Ionian comes in and touches, stealthy elastic, like a blue cat's-paw, I have seen Chamberlain lift that gun to his mouth a dozen times, always to drop it again. I have seen more than ever the modern disease looming in the world outside this sea, rock, water; the terrible disintegration of action under the hideous pressure of the ideal; the disease of a world every day more accurately portrayed by Hamlet; the disease which made Gregory label the remaining days of life left to him, his death. The disease which . . . I examine my own face carefully in the mirror, finger the battered skull, consult the sunken orbits. It is not the first time in history that the gulf has opened up between the people and their makers— the artists. But the chasm has never been so vast, so uncrossable. The creator, terribly mauled and disfigured, has become the audience instead of the prime actor. He can do nothing. In the subterranean Hades of the self, on the wet marsh flowering in great festering lilies and poppies, the delusions gather and hang, miasmic. The curative virtue is being turned to black bile, to poison, to corrosive. It is the Dark Ages opening again. We are going down, in a supreme Dance of Death to the terminus, among the extreme unctions of the violins. This is the going down into the tomb which Gregory experienced as a unit. "Ended. It is all ended. I realize that now, living here on the green carpet and living there in the mirror. So profound is the conviction that there is nothing I can do to reassure myself. I am a little aging man, gone bald on top, with not even a thumbed season ticket to salva- tion. What shall I do? I am falling apart, the delicate zygon of my brain is opened. I am rusting, my knees are rusting, the fillings in my teeth, the plate in my jaw is rusting. If I were only Roman enough to own a sword we should see some fine conclusions to this malady. Alas! Are there only the dead *left* to bury the dead? It is the question not of the moment, but of all time. This is my eternal topic, I, Gregory Stylites, destroyed by the problem of personal action."

In the falling night of my Tibetan memories I sit by the bed lamp and read these lines over and over again. Once I was moved by them. But in this fatal third act, this last masque for which paper and words are inadequate, I have hardly any room for feeling; not that so much, but it is as if I have gone dead in the vital centers. I have become a puppet, without any volition of my own. When I am with Tarquin, I share his death, with Lobo his prejudices, with Chamberlain his ideals. For my own part I am falling into an utter anonymity. I accept everything and examine nothing. Dead, in a queer way. Amputated at the taproots. And inside me the suffocating misery which I associate with her body, though it is unjust to do so. I sit over my books like an insect these long nights, or walk the long cold streets, shaken with the torment of indecision and mania, whose cause I cannot fathom. I wake at night and find tears on my face, from laughter or sorrow, I do not know which. Tibet hangs like a sphinx over the revisited childhood which my dreams offer me: the craters crammed with jewelry; the hills curving up into their vertiginous flowers of snow; the dawn opening like a coral umbrella on Lhasa; the yak and the black bear the only visitors of that immense vista in time; the monasteries as remote as stars on the hills; everything has fallen upon me in this stuffy English room with a pathos that is beyond ink. Well, I am one of the generation which I would like to murder. I cannot escape. That is what comes of being born with an erection, and thrown for dead in the basket; perhaps we must end on the gibbet, under the levers of the hired butchers, with the same erection in death that we knew in birth. There is much to be done—work worthy of a man; and if there were the least chance of my being understood I would begin. Here, I have the dithyramb, here, in this very room, on the second shelf from the left. It is only the *faith* of audience which seems to be lacking. I have traced the germ of action to the poem, and it is the poem which I would like to embed in the personality: an everlasting spatial heraldry to burn across personal action like the brand of Cain. Forgive the arrogance. I am not even a Master of Arts. Simply a bastard child of the humanities. There is no distinguishing label. I realize this when I talk to someone like Bazain (*Doctor* Bazain), that cockeyed idiot who has not the least idea of the meaning of the word "therapy." His universe consists of the frontal lobe, the temporal lobe, and the occipital lobe; not to mention the parietal lobe, or the medulla. Any phenomena which exist outside this domain puzzle him. Even simple phenomena like Morgan, for instance. This morning we met him in the lounge, dressed in a blue serge suit and huge creaking brown shoes. It was his day off, he explained to us, and he was taking Gwen up to the West End. "Going to marry her?" I suggest playfully, whereupon he becomes very expansive and confidential, something quite unusual for him. "Marriage?" he says, bending down to us where we sit on the sofa (he pronounces it "merritch"), "well, I always said it's not for me, sir, but if she wants it—well, I don't want to disappoint her." Then, leaning down, ever more confidentially, over us, he beams like a lighthouse and whispers, "She's that good, sir, I could eat 'er shit, sir." Whereupon Bazain nearly falls to the floor. When Morgan goes he begins to say angrily how outrageously disgusting the man is, and the idea of talking to *residents* in that way! Parading his sexual perversions like that . . . "But maybe it isn't a perversion," I say mildly. "Maybe it's just a figure of speech." Bazain coughs stiffly and says in his most Harley Street manner, "Well, it sounds like the frontal lobe to me!" In the beginning was the word; and the word was Bazain; and Bazain was an idiot. As for Morgan, any more honesty on his part and he will lose his job! The idea!

Well, all these incidents have the ring of immense triviality when I think of them, sitting here among the books at night, aware of the statues and the snow outside. Lobo complaining of his latest woman because she farts incessantly while they are in bed, and makes him "disgust"; Perez, talking in his perfect demented English about Anne who was so beautiful and who has no teeth in her mouth—just two soft rows of gums. The first shock of kissing her, and finding everything pulp. What an experience, he repeats, for an English Sunday afternoon!

Sunday afternoon! Blinds drawn, snow falling, shops shut. The terrible cadenzas of the late buses under an ice-bound moon. A million miles of boredom stretched tight across the earth by the seventh day of the week. Fornication and lockjaw locked fast in the chilly bedrooms of the poor by the wallpaper, the china washstands, the frames of the pictures. Deliver us from the blind men of Catford. We have meetings in these chilly rooms, but it is a meeting of specters, so withdrawn into his private pandemonium is each of us. The helmets hang stiff, as if frozen. The fires are lighted, go out, are relighted. The snow opens lethargy in us like so many razors. Nowadays even the final stages of Tarquin's disease seem significant of nothing. When he gambols or appears to gambol, when he tosses his head and makes a kittenish epigram there is nothing to do but to answer, "Tweet. Tweet." This infuriates him. I tell him about Morgan's conversation with Bazain and he is nearly sick. "Leave me," he says stiffly, "since you do not share any decent feelings on such a subject. Pugh! Gwen, that dirty little skivvy, smelling of stale piss and grease from the sink! What an idyl, my dear, how can you smile?"

I smile because I can feel nothing. I suspend judgment on everything because so little exists. I am strangled by the days that pass through me, by the human beings I am forced to meet. Nothing, nothing, across these acres of snow and ice, this arctic season, except occasional rages, occasional fits of weeping.

In the drab picture gallery I come upon Chamberlain suddenly. He is sitting under the faded Nat Field, disheveled, untidy, miserable. I recall that he has been missing for three whole days; no one knows where he vanished to, or why. There was some talk a few days ago in Lobo's room, but I did not pay much attention to it. The suburban mythology was beginning to bore me. Now it is a pure fluke I have run across him in this deserted gallery, dropping with fatigue and wild-footed. I go up silently to him, fearful that he might try to escape me. His face is very ancient and sleepy-looking; hair matted; his eyes are surrounded in huge developing marks. He does not attempt even to speak, when he first sees me, let alone run away. We sit side by side and stare at the snowy gardens, the loaded hedges, the icicles on the gutters. He says at last he has been walking all day and sleeping in the parks at night. In such weather! He must have lost his job too. The whole gamut of theater has been running through his mind like a strip of film: himself dying, himself being noble, himself weeping, himself lifting the revolver. All false, false, false. He admits it hoarsely. As for his wife, God knows what she's doing. "I loathe her," he says, "but the breakup is terribly painful. You can't understand that unless you've lived with a woman, old man. I adore her." And so on. Slowly it all comes out—their quarrels, her gradual settling apathy. He is almost composed as he talks, his fingers latch together firmly. "It's not theater entirely. I feel half mad. If I had the strength to go mad it would be wonderful, the responsibility, I mean. I would all be out of my hands. They could put me away. But here I am, answerable for my life, don't you see, damn it? I'm culpable, I'm responsible—I don't know what to do."

His curious fatigue-lined face chopping up the syllables. "There are no more theories for me from now. Fuck the illusions and the flourishes. From now on there are only people." He gets up and starts to walk away. Then he comes back. "Listen, you don't know where Gregory is by any chance?"

"I never met him," I say.

He turns and runs lightly down the steps, faunlike, graceful, into the snow, turning up his coat collar. At the gate he gives one furtive look back and begins to run. And all of a sudden it is as if I am bleeding into the snow myself when I face the breakup of that world. Across this sun-blind Adriatic landscape Chamberlain is running blind, cat-foot across the snow to his conclusions. A weird crooked light shines on the walls of Lobo's room, on the farmland, the frosty turrets, the land of lakes where you are lying. What is all this misery beside the misery of the hills, the immense agony of the rain, the thaw, the new fruit buried in the earth? There is a spirit outside us all which is affecting me, inciting me to join its poignance, its suffering. I do not know what to call it. I open a book at any place in any weather and begin reading, because I do not want to concern myself with this thing, this . . .

Death. Death of the bone, the tissue, the thigh, the femur. In the same deep snow a year later at Marble Arch I run upon a face like Chamberlain's mouthing from a wooden pulpit. A terrible strained shouting in the void of self, and outside—actually outside —a dancing gesticulating leader of the new masses. New styles in the soul's architecture, new change of heart. Yes, but ideal for ideal. Compensatory action for action. In that shabby arena, surrounded by the lousy, damp, bored, frozen people of Merrie

England the speaker offered them an England that was ideally Merrie. We hurried aside in the snow, too involved in each other to bother the blond beaky face: the satyr led captive in his red halter. "Shall the hammer and the sickle take note of a few tears and cherished bottles?"

From this to that other circus where Tarquin plies the fluted drinking glass and carves himself Pan pipes. Let us escape together, you and I, he is always saying. We need not move. Look, here is Knossos, under the blue craters of mountains. Here is de Mandeville's world. Here is a stone age of the spirit, taciturn as the mammoth. Here is the Egyptian with his palms turned outward, softly dancing and hymning. The Etruscan treading his delicate invisible rhythms into the earth. *Escape!* (In a small cardboard box on the mantelpiece, wrapped in cotton wool, he keeps a renal calculus and a bit of dry brown umbilical cord!)

"The physical world now," says Tarquin, weighing his scrotum gravely in his right hand. "Take the physical world for instance." He is gravely weighing the physical world in his right hand. Very well, then. Let us *take* the physical world. There is no charge. We confront that abject specimen, the modern physicist, and discover the shabby circus animal he owns, hidden away in the darker recesses of the metaphysical cage. A lousy, dejected, constipated American lion without so much as a healthy fart left in it. "The maternal instinct in mice can be aroused by subcutaneous injections of prolactin," says Tarquin, weighing anchor at last. "This pushes your set of values sideways. Now take the thalamus. They are just doing some wonderful tricks with that. Or Bacot filling the intestines of lice with Rickettsia-infected blood. My dear fellow, can you seriously tell me whether the breath of the Holy Ghost enters from the navel, the thenar, the colon, the hip, or the lobe of the ear?"

Here is Tarquin, very excited by the new heresy, as he calls it, weighing his scrotum gravely in his right hand. Come, I say, in my pert way, separate the yolk from the white. In the hall I have a fine new cedarwood cross for you. I offer it to you free of charge.

Exchange it for this dead preoccupation with the components of the physical world. We are dueling now all day over this theme, and frankly it gets tiresome after a time. Tarquin has deluded himself for so long about his "psychic superiority" over me, that he is sad to see me escaping his clutches. "You're a funny little bugger," he says, lying on the bed while I chafe his toes and pour out the hot coffee. "I suppose you don't understand me. You lack faith, that's what it is. Dicky was here last night and he was saying that too." Dicky, of course, has the brain of a newt and the dash of a sprat, so such an idea needs amplification. "He was saying that you were arrogant."

I am pained by this; after all, it is only my abject humility which has created this omnipotent attitude in Tarquin, which he glorifies as a superiority.

"No, but you don't understand me, really," insists the hero. "You only see the façade: underneath there are enormous reserves of strength, withstanding crisis after crisis. If there weren't I should be dead by now."

I close down and sit at the desk, reading some of the latest love lyrics that the new mode of life has been hatching out for him. "The springtide of desire, my dear," Tarquin said to me. "Positively a lyric vein running through me—a nerve of lyricism."

There is no news. Day by day we are breaking down, boring down, into the pulp chamber of matter, and day by day the world becomes less integral, less whole; and the unison with it less pure. This is the ice age of components.

At night I fuel the car and set off on immense journeys of discovery, plotting my path across the icefields, the land of polarized light where everything is lunacy and lanterns, and the Ganges of the spirit flows between the banks of black sand. On the eastern shores the boats snub quietly at anchor. The snow pelts them, and rimes their rigging. All sorts of new languages seem to be coming within my grasp: the formulae of the sciences, the runes, the surds; I am such a vatful of broken, chaotic material that it will be a miracle if anything can ever reassemble this crude magma, detritus, gabbro, into a single organic whole—even a book. But the hunger, the ravening at the bottom of all this, I recognize at last. It is not a thirst for love or money or sex, but a thirst for living. The pulp chamber is desire, the principle a sort of mania, a love—in which you play almost no part whatsoever. I refer to you now as I refer to the moon, anoia, or sordes. In my journeys I puzzle over our relationship, our mutual acts, our occasional miseries: and find them always outside the mainspring of this principle, this progressive dementia, in which I am reaching out, forever reaching out with crooked arms and an empty mind toward the inaccessible absolute. This is the theme of travel whether the towns whirl by me under the moon, or whether I am at my deal desk in the Commercial School. Thule, ultima Thule. There is a stepping-off place—a little Tibetan village, stuck like a springboard in the side of the mountains. There are no friends to see us off: our banners, our catchwords, our heroism—these things are not understood here. The natives have other criteria. Beyond us the passes open like flowers in the setting sun, the delicate gates of the unknown country's body, the Yoni of the world, luteous, luteous, unbearably lonely. Is the journey plural or am I alone? It is a question only to be answered at the outposts. I will turn perhaps and find a shadow beside me. No tears can scald the snow, or the malevolence of the white peaks. I can invoke no help except the idiotic squeaking of the prayer wheel. We move softly down the white slopes, irresistible as a gathering landslide, toward the last gaunt limit of flesh. Now we have nothing in common but our clothes and our language. The priests have stolen the rest as gifts for God. The ice under our hoofs aches and screeches, murderous as the squeegee. This is the great beginning I planned for so long. How will it end?

I am recalled from this excursion by a rap at the door. Chamberlain. "What do you think?" he says, throwing his hat on the rack with the air of a matador. "She's pregnant." We sit down on the sofa and he collapses with laughter, showing every tooth in his head. Then he sits a while sniffing hysterically, stroking my knee and talking about morning sickness, evening sickness and mid-night belly bumping. He is all unnerved, but filled with a kind of fanatical happiness. "So everything seems settled. God! what fools we make of ourselves. All the agony I've been through, over a damn ten-centimeter fetus. By the way, I've got a marvelous job, two hundred a year more. I'm through with the body mystical and all that stuff from now, I can tell you. . . ." He is planning a beautiful suburban existence, complete with lawnmower and greenhouse, I can see that. I have not the will to mutter anything but compliments to him. The child will be stillborn, I know, but I am not allowed to tell him that. I try to see him not as a person but as part of the active world—the world I am trying to create here: the snow, I mean, the blind crooked snow like soft immense drifts of needles, and the unresponsive hotel beds to which my other mimes go at night, expecting to draw comfort from them, but get none. Lobo and Tarquin facing each other over the fire, the muffins, the counterpoint of the third Brandenburg. Two separate continents. Spanish America like the crucifix over the bed, the thin gold chain round his hairy little wrist. The rows of colored shoes in their ballet. Perez, the most elegant loafer of five continents, in whom all languages blend and become accessible, all women become a single archetype. Morgan the comic fiend of the Inferno stoking the boilers of God. Bazain, Farnol, Peters petering out in saltpeter. Or Tarquin, his great grammarian's cranium spinning like a top in the candle shine; his great white feet frozen in their furred slippers: participant in a European death as yet incomprehensible to most Europeans. Or Perez, on his huge twinkling feet, sparring with Morgan in front of the boilers at midnight. "Pull your punches, now. Don't forget," he says; and this idea Morgan holds in his mind with great difficulty, ponderously, like a dog. But when there is blood soaking into the soft leather of the gloves; blood in a long wave flowing over Perez' mouth and chin; blood that marks his man wherever he hits him; then the control goes, and the butcher lights up in Morgan. An almost visible light, like candles shining under the skin. And the air is thick with their shuffling bodies, falling, chopped, panting.

Or even Miss Smith, if you like: carried on a pole before the tribe, yet sitting in the corner of the car, tittering at Lobo's gallantries. Diving into her handbag to produce more powder, which runs off her dry face into her lap. Talking to Eustace Adams in tones completely inaudible. Being afraid of Marney. And above all mugging up Chaucer's obscenities solemnly in the notes. Incomprehensible, incomprehensible.

There is a lot about death in this; too much perhaps, for I have subscribed very heavily to Tarquin's bucket-shop ideals. For him it is really the death—the Bastard Death, if you like, or the Death Under the Shield—really a death to the ultimate cinder; but for us, why, we are vividly alive as yet. That is why this cathedral absolute appals us. Your hands as they turn outward to take flight, for example; the action of the bee, the tree, the fistful of feathers my brother murdered last winter with his gun. All living in an exquisite tactuality by their action, ultimately living. Under the bone the living twigs of the cypress, the beak of the snipe, the foggy klaxons of the mallard coming up across the guns. Or asleep, and the fingers laid about your face, and hair washing up under the house in a long swish, a sea of hair breathing under the windows, over our dreams, into the night. If there is any passion in this writing, anywhere, it is because I am creating a death I almost shared. I mistook it for my own property. I know now, for the first time, where I stand. We are nothing if we cannot convert the dross of temporal death; if we cannot present our check at the bank, and receive for our daily death, a fee in good clean sovereigns—images, heat, water, the statues in the park, snow on the hills. The terrific action of the senses. The dead bullion of dying cashed in clean coin day by day, and every morsel of broken tissue redeemed for us; by this love, perhaps, this winter comet, a poem, the landlady, scholarship, Zarian or the shape of Mexico. My battle with the dragon has intoxicated me. Day by day now, increasingly day by day, I can feel the continents running in my veins, the rivers, the oceans balanced in a cone on my navel. I am no longer afraid of this heraldry. I have given myself to it utterly.

"Come," says old Tarquin, afraid to be left alone in the dimension he has begun to inhabit. "Come, share with me. We shall control the temporal world. We shall be monarchs of all we survey. Look. In this room I have the sum total of all human and esoteric knowledge, printed on paper. Need we ever stir outside to examine the apparent reality? The essential truth lies within us. Come."

But already I am too concerned with the details of the journey even to answer him. I try sometimes to explain to him what I am feeling, but it is no good. "Why move?" he demands indignantly. "What is wrong with my intellectual attitude, sitting still in the Lotus pose? It is airtight, my dear."

Well, incomprehensibly enough, I decide to go my own bloody way, whether he understands it or not. I have entered into the personality of the external things, and am sharing their influences. I skate along the borders of the daily trivialities like a ghost, observing but withholding myself from them. There are such things as the Banquet of the Sydenham Cycling Club, for example; which I would write about if I were less tired. There is Honeywoods and the vexed problem of the drainage. There is Marney talking about getting married; and a host of other data for which there is no room. There is Eustace, going down, as he says, "into the valley of shadow" as his wife has her fourth. There are also the incest ceremonies in the Spice Islands, the five-foot negrito with the everted lips, and races dying out in Iceland because of pelvic rickets. . . . Above all there is the journey. It has become so real to me that I have developed a sort of evasiveness when refusing invitations. "If I am *here*," I say, "on Tuesday I'd love to come." Or, "Tuesday? Well, I may not . . ." Etc., etc. Very soon I shall have to take at least a weekend return to Cherbourg in order to satisfy my friends. Everyone inquires solicitously: "Let me see, you're going away, aren't you?" Or, "By the way, when did you say you were leaving?" I shall begin on the first fine day in spring. May will find me scudding southward under the trades, in the direction of the quest—perhaps in the wrong direction. There is only trial and error on a journey like this, and no signposts. The end is somewhere beyond even Ethiopia or Tibet: the land where God is a yellow man, an old philosopher brooding over his swanpan.

In the light of Sunday afternoon this must be read quaintly. On Sundays we have a nice matey card party in Hilda's room, at the bamboo table with three legs. The wireless is turned on full, and occasionally we get the most beautifully incongruous things through it. The Ninth Symphony, for example, or an aria for the toothbrush. No one is worried, not even Peters, who feels compelled to acknowledge art even if he has no taste for it. "Ah!" he will say cleverly, "Bach." He is puzzled when we laugh at him. Imagine it. That stale room with the Ninth Symphony scratching away and Clare smoking his scented fags and polishing his fingernails; and the stuffed owls on the mantelpiece looking so damned critical and deprecating that one could weep with hysteria. Hilda in her scarlet flannel nightgown pouring weak tea for us and losing farthings at *vingt et un*. Or Lobo crossing himself over every natural he gets. I tell you it is a sort of picture for a Spanish almanac.

*
**

Upstairs, in the long room overlooking the Adriatic, where the tide blows up clean from Africa, you are lying. Your face is as clear as water. Softly posed in the moonlight like a forgotten desert you are lying, living and dying, lulled, systolic, diastolic motion, as the waves shiver their enormous spasms on the beach. What is poignant is this hour, this late waning moonlight, the Pleiades wheeling over your dramatic Sapphic, the enormous clouds, the surf, the monk shivering in his cell among the candles, the dolphins turning, and the face, the white face turned up blind to Africa like a pilgrim blind with dream. Nothing else. In this dead night under a dead Greek myth I tell you finally that it is not death. It is life in her wholeness from which one draws this terrible system of love, of creation, of loss. In Cyprus under the trees, Athens, Sicily, the same long purifying tides throw up their pure lotion across the statues, the robes, the eyes of the huddled philosophers who outfaced the truth. The churches are stiff with beards and candles, celebrating the dark mass of the spirit as it enters its absolute aloneness. In the cathedrals under the sea we tread the aisles of weeds, and listen for the long chime of bells, bubbled under water for centuries, among the cargoes of grain and millet, raisins and fruit: argosies which are reckoned on no merchant's sheets. Cross over to Bethlehem. They will be able to tell you for certain whether something has been born from this discord of the elements, or whether the fiat has gone forth; whether this is a pre-nativity or a post-mortem!

Out of that void in which the dream lies, coiled and fatal as the dragon, I conjure these few pieces of religion above a body lying silent as death, and as spacious. Hushed, in a new temperature, as if under glass the single dark candle of the torso ended in little blunt pebbles, toes. Or hair like a soft bed of breathing charcoal laid about the islands, twisting up its coils in soft explosions on the beaches. Outside on the beach the old women are sweeping up the seaweed in a heavy wind. Can you hear what is said in the screaming of the olives, in the dramatic archery of the cypresses? Verminous, the top-hatted monks huddle to mass in Athos, going through the familiar litanies, without comfort. What does it mean, this language, this voice raised to the roof like a thick stump of sound, these vulgar armed candles? In England there is an old man who feeds the swans, slowly burning down, damp, rheumy, sour, into the hollow socket of his breast. The poets hymn his simplicity. What does this mean? If he were an old bun-nosed Tibetan feeding the wild swans under the Greek Islands, they would deplore the incongruity of the world.

Then there is that other moment when I come into the room

just as the dawn is breaking. You are alive. There is a lot to say, but the morning is so reverent, the smoke on the bonfire lies about in parcels, the ice on the pond like an altar cloth, morning . . . The first long hush, like a breath drawn taut before the swimmer dives into the icy river. There are huge warm places in the field-grass where the cattle lay. Dew heavy. The black jersey still lying out over your left shoulder like a sofa on a green field. Dew heavy. The deep scent of the castle standing charred on the hill. There is much to be said, but no possible way of saying it. I can hear the ivy crawling on the walls. The sun is shining on the spoon, the toast, on your tongue. The chickens are going to market, very chilly and disgruntled. Someone is cutting wood for the fires. I am as nerveless as the morning sausages on the board. The knife slits the sun strides up over the hill and we are able to talk again, slowly and without emphasis. Italy is mentioned. There are four gutted candles in the room. Yes, and the first edition of Baudelaire. Your voice starts queer responses in one: a bone in the groin, mastoid, the nerves of the throat, the fibers of the tibia. I cannot tell for certain, but I am bound to get a letter within a day or two. Let us walk quietly in the declension of the season, smoke a pipe over the gate, take note of how the aspho-dels are doing. In the little house run over the accounts, select a book, doze over the fire, or at bedtime light the candles and start the piano hymning. It is all the same, for this is a piece out of another book. It is significant merely because Tarquin is men-tioned. Over the fire and the crusader's hearth, in the smoke of pipes, Tarquin is mentioned. It is a strange immortality to be consummated here, in this cottage, drowned in flowers, under the glimmering bottoms of the books. I record it now merely to re-assure myself that we are never forgotten. There is always the strange consummation of memory taking place, over the whole world, the whole of time even, until the vocabularies in which you are created fall away and are renewed.

Between that submarine cottage and this fanatic Adriatic land-scape, where the tides beat up carrying us away in the impetus of their struggle toward history, there is a gulf fixed. More vast, more unexplored than the Challenger Deep. In that gulf, dancing, as in a colored shadow show, are the figures I keep talking about. Their shadows lie across the paper. Yachts cross, and rolling caiques: occasionally a gray warship slides across the windows, but the shadows are constant. The dolphins idle all day in clumsy regiments, mixing into the picture, crowding it. Embassies from Minos and the litmus Cretan women, but we do not forget, we do not forget, we do not forget. In spite of the immense sea, steering up and down, attacking, feinting, wheeling its range of colors under the house which stands like a white ark on the black rock. Within the thirtieth parallels North and South of the Equator like a huge hummingbird ultramarine to the South of lat. 30. S. a deep swollen indigo. Under the terrible fires of the Antarctic Circle, a glib and fearful olive-green; always the old nurse, the Poseidon, cherishing her dead like a bear, washing through the imploded strongrooms of liners, breaking open the trunks of sailors, with a maniac love, cherishing. This is the element to which we shall be delivered up at the final moment, lulled, kneaded, softened and gushed. Smooth round shot, footfirst, parceled in linen, shrived. Then with a long cool drop to drift down, adamant, to the drowsy levels where the meadows grow invisible fish, and the planktonic organisms dither and skate, sprouting exotic eyes on floating stalks; where the sperm whales munch dredgefuls of cuttle fish and prowl like bardic Tennysons, muttering in their beards.

Come, I am always saying to Tarquin. There are still new universes to be inhabited, if you have the authentic disease and the courage. Come, drop down with me to the limits of the photic zone. Let us construct out of the sensitive bodies of this twilight race our new systems that we talk about all day long. Bathypelagic, myopic, optical, shall we dawdle away the aeons over this one problem, making a little personal propaganda as we go? At a hundred fathoms fish like silver bullets. Under the viscous scalp itself phenomena like Porpita and Ianthina, blue smoke in water.

At three hundred rufus, brick, claret. The violet flesh of ptero-
pods, wicked, wicked, wicked. Here is a philosophic reality whose
terminology is lying there, complete but unused. Come, you
white-livered tapeworm, let us get busy. The problem is how
to destroy the fatal passivity of the plankton, and give it the
nektonic virtues; the ability to move with the time, and against
tide. I am not concerned with the Benthos, the mud eaters, shit
gobblers, and their brood. We must concentrate only on those
who have a chance of being saved. (Hilda, the great sonsy whale,
for instance. I have seen her dragged out on the beach and hacked
open from chin to navel. Her belly so crammed with crustaceans
that they put spades to work on her.) Hilda, one realizes, has
fulfilled the primary law in her way. She has a baroque nobility
because her gift is total. She lives with her great swollen dugs
pressed out against time, in a perpetual delirium of service. And
now, in the winter of our discontent, she has given up all she
had to the poor. Watch her. She is sitting there calmly drinking
tea, with one shoe off. Her nostrils are cut like ancient anchor
ports of a ship. One expects at any moment that a length of
hawser will clatter out of them and—splash!—anchor her in her
own teacup. Indifferently Clare clips his frayed cuffs with her
scissors. And Peters sits lugubriously on the bed and wishes he
were dead. Peters? A nicely clothed dummy fresh from school.
The kind of waxwork that has given the English their reputation
abroad. He has read all that the well-dressed man should read.
His poise is superb with members of his own class. One has the
idea that he could pick his nose with a cigar in his mouth and
still look genteel, old cottage English, pure, bred on the bottle,
etc. In the drab vertigo of Sunday afternoon we perform our
motionless almanac together. We share with painted things the
loss of personality, sitting here in this exotic gas-lit hothouse,
among the owls and cosmetics. Hilda I know is not with us, but
already entering that third ocean which has been prepared for
her. Crossing the zodiac of the new universe alone, pioneer, adventurer, forerunner: from house to house, her great turbines

shaking her free of the muddy littorals. Nosing down with that predatory beak of hers deeper and deeper, across the fucoid belt, the laminarian, the zosteran belt toward the absyssal deep which is marked on no card. Yes, beyond the territory of those remote tribes we only live in illuminated names: the pycnogonids, the nudibranchs, the brittlestars, the chitons, the crinoids, and the penatulids—away beyond these into that region from which we are going to receive the new myth.

Attempt it, I am always saying to that sallow bastard, *attempt it*. There is nothing to lose. All the hope in the world is here, between my legs, between the joints of my fingers, in the eye, the liver, the reins. Attempt it and become the symbol of failure, but only make the attempt. It is useless. He has not even the courage of Gregory's death: that quaint suicide. Gregory who shot himself dead with the green pen. In this mythology, so fragmentary, with so many drops of feeling and expression, Gregory is almost a complete symbol. It was a gallant suicide. But Tarquin? He molders away visibly, nerveless, blanched, waxen, into a kind of pus-drunk senility of his own. The stench that goes up from that decomposing cranium these days! I am forced to stand near an open window to speak to him. He is the living symbol of Mr. Valdemar, galvanically twitching in a sort of creaky life of his own. What is he, what are we all? I cannot tell with any clarity. Sometimes I puzzle over these pages, trying to work out for them this riddle of personality, but I am always too much inside them to see clearly. I am afraid, also, to inquire too closely into my own symbol here, alongside all these, because it seems foreign to me. A little frightening. What am I doing with this noisy machine and these sheets of linen paper? It is a kind of trap from which I cannot escape, not even by shooting myself dead with words as Gregory did, or said he did. When I think this I am too afraid to continue writing. There is an iron bar pressing down behind my eyes. A sensation of some filament in the brain, some fiber, some internal fuse wire, strained to breaking point. I am afraid it will snap and blind me. It is then that I get up in a panic and go to where you are sitting, working, and knitting, and put my hands on your hands. Then in a moment or two my courage is restored and I return to the pages, turning them over, reading them slowly, wondering: I am back in that menagerie again, shouting at Tarquin or following Hilda in her immense voyages from crater to crater of the Atlantic, gorging crustaceans. With Lobo rolling in the ditch on top of the blond shopgirl, he squeaking in copulation like a frog. Or listening to Chamberlain reading me the sonnets, and sniffing like a schoolgirl. Or Perez cherishing his clubbed penis, and handing it casually to Hilda, as one might give up one's ticket at the terminus. Without a sigh or a word handing up his ticket and entering the cathedral on his knees. Or Connie impaled in her own dirty sheets, wriggling and pissing until the blood runs into her boots, and her eyes are as expressionless as handbags. It is all there, going round and round forever like a great Rabelaisian merry-go-round, faces flaring out at me.

And then there is you. You wait behind the faces and the signs which puzzle. A pale hieroglyph scribbled across these pages, across these faces, these whales, symbols, ideographs. You speak to me from the trees with the spirit of trees: the delicate human bark of the Eucalyptus, you are living among your green sickles. In bed it is a tree that grows upward from the scrotum, choking me, stuffing soft tentacles and flowers into my arms, into my throat, into my knees. I am a scarecrow filled by the trees which grow upward through me. When I speak of you my throat is lined like bark, and my tongue is soft rotten juniper-loam, cloying.

I cover you with my body and whole universes open silently for me, like a door into a sudden garden. Suddenly I am awake and standing in you like a turret, speaking to the elements, the dwarfs, the delicate nebulae, the circus which grows on you and stifles me in fleece. I am carried onward through you like angry water, like a plague, a ferment of agony for which there is no

245

cross, no nail holes, no last act, no broken veil of the temple, no agony in the garden.

In the belly, the hips, the huge cathedral of the vagina, you shadow me, moving from statue to statue, seeking your death mask. In the amniotic fluid, the marrow, in the dark cunt you live, in the fetus jammed at the neck of the womb. In the clavicles, the tarsus, the sour anus. It is not words which grow in me when I see the tendrils of muscle climbing your trunk; it is not words at the fingers laid about your face and still: these delicate cartridges of flesh and bone. Not words but a vocabulary which goes through us both like the sea, devouring. A nameless, paralyzed singing in the backbone. An interior mass, blacker than sacrilege. A dancing of fibers along the skin, a new action, a theme as fresh as seed, an agony, a revenge, *a universe!* God save the mark, it is I who am chosen to interpret these frantic syllables which rise up between us, apocalyptic, dazzling, clarion. Here are the pearls that were his eyes. I reach through you like a drunken man toward the million fathom universe, but it is difficult. I am entangled in your flesh. My footsteps are hampered by the rich mummy wrapping of flesh, by the delicate rupture of membranes, the quivering sockets from which the eyes have been torn. It is difficult to know my direction. I have no needle. Only this parcel of agonies which move in terrified recoil as the guts slide away from the surgeon's intruding fingers. Pity me, I was born old. Not dead, but old. Not dead, but old. Incredibly ancient and a martyr to the hereditary taint.

All that comes out of me is a landscape in which you are everything, tree, bee, flower, toast, salt; you are the hard bright stamen of the kingcup, the Greek asphodel, the nervous speaking calyx. This old Venetian fort dying, the flags, the soldiers like bluebells are your landscape, the hot gleet of summer, the fine mucous, or the brumal bear licking her culprits the baby dogfish. Sweet, it is not your decorations I am putting down here, your soft wagging cypresses, stoles, cathedrals, covenants, bones of dead saints. It is this new barony whose language I am taking at dictation, without even waiting to know whether we can decipher it with the help of a known hieroglyph!

In that last winter banquet, among the candles in the silences, the talk of Rome, of poetry, poor Johnny Keats spitting nightingales—that night with the whole safe aura of the English death around us, the ambiance of candles, masques, cottages, pewter, I saw that your face was utterly Judas. The piano was kicking in the Beethoven, and all of a sudden it was as if the ten ridiculous fingers were opening like umbrellas, pregnant with symphony. The room was a cathedral, massive, choked. And the review of faces was as expressive as the line of shadows on the roof. Connie so brazen, returning the stares of the newcomers like a mirror. Lobo, Perèz, Anselm, Gracie—a company as various as a packet of stamps. Tarquin with the kiss of Judas branded on his sagging cheekbones, smiling with the Egyptian smile. Tarquin sitting there like an empty tomb, hollow, hollow, even the microbes dead in him. It was then that I knew the cycle was complete for him. The wheel had spun full circle. From now he's just powdering down like a thrashed flower. He sits all day alone, wrapped in rugs, afraid to walk, his bones are so brittle; afraid to talk, his tongue is so dry; afraid to piss, he is so scalded by the stale urine. The gramophone plays from morning to night, but he does not hear it. If I go in to see how he is I find him there, abstractedly sitting in rugs with a sweet smile on his face. "Put on the laughing record," he says; "it's in the album with the third piano." This is terrifying. This insane disc is one that everyone must know. The crazy attempts to play a saxophone punctuated by a forest of terrible forced laughter. Female squeals, enormous tickling of the ovaries. And the terrifying male bellows. Only a world gone mad could issue a document like this. He plays it over perhaps forty times a day, sitting there in rugs, his vacant eyes on the black fent of the instrument, his skin held out on sparrow bones:

a queer taut smile, answering the terrible squealing and roaring. This is his *vale* in my memory, before they take him away. In the immense stale corridors of the hotel, among the broken statuary and the views of the Parthenon, Tarquin. It is so elaborate this symbol, the Tarquin of the new vocabulary, that I am almost tempted to try and make a short *précis* of him: à la novel. To make him comprehensible enough for the reviewers. But I can't. I just don't know what the hell he is all about. Any more than I can "explain" the new myth which I am undoubtedly on the point of creating, or the double eagle, or the symbol of the fish. I have simply gathered up the little pieces and offered them to you on a plate: it is for others to decide at what date the explosion took place. At that last insane banquet I was on the point of discovering, I think, but am not sure. You were in the way with the lotus mask and the bangles gnashing on your arms. I had only half an eye for the piano simmering; for Connie swallowing the penis in a series of thirsty gulps. There was precisely you and this fertile vocabulary running out of you, rich, sappy, evocative as musk.

Little pieces of the drama have come to me in different places, on the great liners nosing southward, in the trains, between the trim spars of the sailing boat: all merging and flowing upward in me through the bugles and sheep and dancing. I thought I understood. But beginning this act with paper I can only say for certain that I am not responsible. It is transcription purely.

Here, it is real enough the stage on which I re-create this chronicle of the English death. There is Bach playing in the roars of the wind, the piercing slatterns of the rain. There is you dancing, and the million yous who persist in matter, echo, weep, cry, exult, in flower powder, smaragd, Italy, moon, veins of rock. There is the cadenza of flesh here naked, and the you who run to the conclusion of autumn, selfless and melancholy, or smolder

on the beach savagely. In all particulars of the body you are
working, in the dark sump of the vagina, brewing vegetable
history, sewing continents in whom I am the reaper; in the dusty
sandals or the naked toes. It is forced upon me to write of you
always in the gnomic aorist. For this is the new vocabulary which
I am learning with ease. I am beginning my agony in the garden
and there are too many words, and too many things to put into
words. In the fantastic proscenium of the ego, when I begin my
soliloquy, I shall not choose as Gregory chose. To be or not to
be. It is in your capacity as Judas that you have chosen for me.
The question has been decided. Art must no longer exist to depict
man, but to invoke God. It is on the face of this chaos that I
brood. And on the same chaos printed, across the faces of these
hideous mimes of mine, your pale glyph. The white illusion of
bone and tissue, the firm cheekbones set in soft plates of flesh, the
pouting mouth, the soft jawless head of the snake, the lips as
delicate as the biscuit. Lubra in the dark, and when the swords
grow up from Constantinople, marmoreal, caryatid, pupa of flesh
growing upward among the bones, carrying them upward from
the hip, irresistible leaven. The hills snooze on with the liths of
your fingers laid over them: the sensitive calyx of the pelvis like
the dish of land which holds our sea, silent outside the house. All
that is dying in me in this fatal landscape, your mine among
active things, stone, shards, language, meteors, butter. Nothing
but the punic body, our essential traitor, which stifles me with
its pollens. Snore on, you winter sea, there is no more in here
than the seven hectic elements can offer me: more than the
fantasy of the third ocean, dipping its brush among the molten
colors, leaking down to the hot magma of things. More. More.

It is morning. Born in an empty house, no zodiac; spawned by
the fish, volatile, cunning, durable in passion. Boy in an ark on
a black rock. Greece lies dead among the oak leaves, the bare
mulch, the merdes, outside the window, littered in sails. There is
nothing in this enormous six-foot bed but the eyelashes of God

moving, delicate as talc; or the warm sticky gum, oozing from the lips of the trees. From between your legs leaking, the breathing yolk, the durable, the forever, the enormous Now.

This is how it ends.

This is how it begins.

THE END

The house of
Anastasius Athenaius Kotoura.
Corfu, 1937.

p. 196 - Writing as kenosis
an emptying of the internal death (p. 195)
hence a Black book - a book bearing
death away.

Death Gregory writes away
death at Regina, L. Lucifer - also
formerly D. Gregory feels the death
on Corfu + attempts to write it out
p. 197 - Drawing Phoenix on MS.
Cf. Use of green ink - rebirth thru
   writing.
   p. 202 - "My desire is to become the page
   on which I write."
p. 218 - "lost photing act of revelation
p. 224 - I have grown up in my writing
   244 Gregory's suicide - self murder

Lucifer will not merely depict
self but move outside of self -
project self → p. 24 4 - invoke Gods
man as larger than man, man as
myth.

Artist as artificer — p. 81, 95, 118✓
         + orderer 131, 166, 196,

Reader addresses — p. 99, p 118

Merging of past / present / myth — p. 105, 103, 1✗
   126, 147, 153 ✗, 154*, 155, 161, 180, 206
projection of self into world, p. 118, 125, 138
   199

Rebirth, 131, 140
Internal death, 195
Divided Self, 201

, 35